TRIANGULATION:
EXTINCTION

THE 2020 EDITION OF PARSEC INK'S
ANNUAL SPECULATIVE FICTION ANTHOLOGY

PARSEC
INK

Published by Parsec Ink, a subsidiary of Parsec, Inc.

ISBN-10: 0-9743231-4-4
ISBN-13: 978-0-9743231-4-5

Editors: Isaac E. Payne & Diane Turnshek
Assistant Editor: John Thompson
Editor Emeritus: Chloe Nightingale
Junior Editors: Tristan Beiter, Krizia Bruno, Jacqueline Ealy, Emma Flickinger, Kathyrn Harlan, Mishaal Hussain, Kaitlin Jencks, Sabrina Jurrius, Emma Kerkman, Kady Lohr, Katie McRury, Madeleine Reineberg, Alfred Smith, Penelope Smith, Shaun Stack, Aaron Suranofsky, Chantel Thibodeaux

Cover Art and Interior Illustrations: Katerina Kireeva
Book Design: Manageable Media

Parsec Ink is a subsidiary of Parsec, a non-profit literary organization based in Pittsburgh, PA. For more information, visit our website at: parsec-sff.org

To learn more about the *Triangulation* anthology series, visit parsecink.com

Parsec Ink
P.O. Box 3681
Pittsburgh, PA 15230-3681

CONTENTS

Introduction ix

WARNINGS *by Liam Hogan* 3
THE BUBBLE TEA FROGS *by Blake Jessop* 5
A KILLING GARDEN *by Owen Leddy* 17
LABYRINTHULA ANIMALIS *by Katie Sakanai* 27
MIGRATORY *by Joshua David Bellin* 33
THERE WERE GIANTS ON THE EARTH IN THOSE DAYS *by Marshall J. Moore* ...41
STAR CHILD *by Elana Gomel* 49
RED IS THE TASTE OF DEATH *by Rhonda Eikamp* 63
THE FIRE OF COUNTLESS STARS *by Jamie Lackey* 75
AS MUCH AS THE CROWS *by Jennifer R. Povey* 89
TALES OF THE SHRUB *by Jim Hanson* 99
LETTERS FOR SAMANTHA *by Sean Jones* 103
WE ONLY HAVE *by E. A. Petricone* 115
THE PERFECT SOLUTION *by Brett Kozlowski* 127
FOUR LITTLE BEES *by Bradley Heywood* 133
WILL-O-THE-WALMART *by Jennifer Lee Rossman* 139
NO ONE NEEDS A CHIWEENIE *by Katrinka Mannelly* 147
THE BAMBI COLLABORATION *by Bo Balder* 155
ANCESTRAL NOCTURNE *by Bethany van Sterling* 157
AKIKI, THE MAGICIAN *by Steve Carr* 159
RUN, BABY, RUN *by Joy Kennedy-O'Neill* 165
IN THE GARDEN OF BURNING PLASTIC *by Marissa James* 173
CONJUGATION OF THE VERB *by Brian Rappatta* 175
LOVING MONSTERS *by Anya Ow* 177
RARE SEEDS *by Michael Triozzi* 189
AVIATRIX UNBOUND *by Carina Bissett* 201
LANDSCAPE ON THE OUTSKIRTS *by Sam Hicks* 207

ACKNOWLEDGEMENTS 216
STAFF BIOS 217

INTRODUCTION

When Diane came to me in August of 2019 to ask about editing *Triangulation*, I was hesitant. Not just because I was a relatively inexperienced at editing, but because I had a great deal of respect for *Triangulation* and wasn't sure I could do it justice.

The *Dark Skies* anthology was intended to bring awareness to light pollution—activism through speculative fiction, if you will. What could I bring to *Triangulation* that was as impactful as that legacy?

Then one day I was watching a video about red pandas—such cute fuzzballs!—and at the end, the narrator said that humans encroaching on their territory might drive the red pandas to extinction.

Extinction.

That word stuck with me. I thought of all the species that have already died out in my short, twenty-two years on this planet, and I thought of all the species rapidly approaching their doom. In the grand scheme of things, my contributions to environmental activism—recycling, sustainable gardening—seemed ineffectual.

Well, *Triangulation* was the chance to do something larger, to compile a set of twenty-seven stories that resonated with a central theme, that worked together to present a whole story of extinction. I often say that science fiction, fantasy, and horror are great motivators for change, and I sincerely hope that is the case for *Triangulation: Extinction.*

As you read the stories collected here, remember the dodo, the Japanese sea lion, the Tasmanian tiger, and look to the future; think about the silverback gorilla, the orangutan, the rhinoceros. Natural selection might have had a part to play, but we have certainly weighted the scales.

Not everyone can donate thousands of dollars to charities or plant a million trees. But we can all make small efforts—recycle, walk when you'd rather drive, take down your motion lights. If every single human being did these things, then we'd be on a path to survival. And not just for us, for the whole planet and every living creature on it.

Isaac E. Payne
Editor
August 1, 2020

"*Without any remaining wilderness we are committed wholly, without chance for even momentary reflection and rest, to a headlong drive into our technological termite life, the Brave New World of a completely man-controlled environment.*"

-Wallace Stegner

KATHERINE
KIREEVA

WARNINGS

by Liam Hogan

We sent warnings.

We encased them in stone; giant beasts to fill your giant halls. Beasts that roam the Earth no more.

We sent megafauna. Oversized deer, aurochs, and woolly mammoths. Hunted to extinction.

And if those lessons were lost in the mists of time, we sent dodos and thylacines and passenger pigeons. The Steller sea cow, you wiped out twenty-seven years after discovery.

Our warnings became urgent. River dolphins, northern white rhinos, western black rhinos. A thousand species of frogs and insects you never got around to naming.

As the end loomed, we sent polar bears, gorillas, Sumatran elephants. All for naught.

Now, as the few of you that remain plaintively wail *why*? we ask this question in return:

How many canaries are enough?

Liam Hogan is an Oxford Physics graduate whose award-winning short story, "Ana" appears in Best of British Science Fiction 2016 (NewCon Press). "The Dance of a Thousand Cuts" appears in Best of British Fantasy 2018, and "Stars" appears in Triangulation: Dark Skies. He lives and avoids work in London.

THE BUBBLE TEA FROGS

by Blake Jessop

Banks of smog swirled and eddied outside the high window, and no one inside watched the photochemical oxides dance. Everyone in the room was crowded around a single monitor. Their lab coats were grungy, their eyes bloodshot, and they didn't smell great. No one paid any attention to that, either.

James Kincaid watched the progress bar of his life's work tick to within one thousandth of a percentage point of complete.

"How are we doing, Pudding?" he asked the screen.

"I'm almost finished, James," the readout responded. The supercomputer took up an entire floor of the arcology and drew as much power as a football stadium on Sunday afternoon. Its actual name was the Purdue University of Detroit Mercy Evolutionary Algorithm, or *PUDMEA*, which was both hard to say and annoying, so everyone just called it *Pudding*.

"This is killing me," James said.

"I'm finished," the AI responded, "I've compiled your final proof-of-concept and run it through seventy thousand generations. It will work."

The research team's murmurs died like foam on a high tide.

"That's it?" James' chest felt tight. "No revisions required?"

"None. If you can match my DNA criteria for oocyte tractability, your biological robots will work."

A final instant of silence.

"Holy shit," James said, "we just invented xenorobotics."

The room erupted with cheers.

⊗

Drunk and happy, James had remade the world at thirty-five. The party was breaking up, and he wobbled over to one of the workstations to start a search for compatible frog DNA. Probably not a problem. There were thousands of amphibian species, and one of them was bound to match. Once he got some living samples, his team could really get down to work. James was going to harvest tiny little frog hearts, feed them into Pudding's bioreactor, and reshape the passive and contractile cells into living molecular robots. Maybe leave a little gap in the body somewhere, so armies of them could remove plaque from artery walls, or pick up microplastic pollution in Lake Michigan, or locate and digest cancer cells.

"I am going to be famous," James said. Members of the research team were passed out around the room in a debris field of Hostess party cakes and empty champagne bottles. "I am going to get laid. So, so laid. Pudding, start searching for a DNA match."

Some deep part of James' mind had been avoiding this. For the xenobots to work in real life, the tissue base had to be a very exact match. He knew it was going to come from a frog, maybe a *Poliploidy*, because he needed something that was both easy to work with and close to human. That might turn out to be tough, and he had long since run out of grant money.

"I have anticipated your request," Pudding said. Its voice was soothing and even.

"And?"

"Our requirements are exceptionally stringent, but I have found a candidate."

"How clean?"

"One hundred percent. A perfect match."

James started to laugh. Tears gathered at the corners of his eyes. "What is it?"

"*Raorchestes Chalazodes*. A bush frog."

"Awesome, where do we find them?"

"There is not much about them in the Purdue-Mercy database."

"Check the Svalbard DNA archive. I'm giving you one-time authorization to search the net."

"Working," Pudding said, then, "I've found them."

"Where?"

"Nowhere, they're extinct."

James Kincaid's hopes, face, and tears all fell as suddenly as water running off a leaf.

"No," James said, "I don't need live samples. I just need to know if you have any tissue in storage."

Night had passed, morning broken, and James felt a little more optimistic. He was speaking to a friendly archivist at the Svalbard Global DNA Vault.

"We do not," the archivist said, bright blue eyes flicking away from her web camera to look at another screen.

"Okay, just send me your digital sequence for *R. Chalazodes*. I can work with that."

"There isn't one. They were only rediscovered in 2010, and the IUCN listed them as critically endangered in 2015. We opened in 2025."

Sweat broke out cold on James' skin.

"So, they're gone?"

The archivist's glasses whirred and refocused, then she pushed them up into her hair.

"I'm sorry, yes." Her eyes brightened, suddenly. "But if your research touches on cultural impact there's an animated show called *Jiraiya Gōketsu Monogatari* about a bunch of frog princes who try to get *tusundere* brides to kiss them in medieval Japan. One of them is a white-spotted bush frog. It's really good. There's this thing where they get their human bodies back if a girl—"

"Thank you," James said, and cut the connection before she could start explaining it. He slumped back in his office chair and wondered how he was going to keep his dreams alive.

Purdue immediately shelved James' entire project, and his department head at Detroit Mercy told him to take some time off. James stayed home, staring endlessly out the window and across the water toward Windsor, watching burning clumps of oily sludge smolder in the river.

When he came out of shock, James spent a few days desperately searching the internet for white-spotted bush frogs. He eventually got tired of reading about how many millions of them once lived in South Asia, and how they were all dead, and gave up. He ate food and didn't taste it, slept and didn't feel rested, and watched *Jiraiya Gōketsu Monogatari*, because that was apparently the only place his frogs still existed.

Days passed, emails piled up, and James' face got stubbly. He watched more *Jiraiya*. Every time one of the princes failed to get a bosomy shrine maiden to make out with him, James cried. He memorized the lyrics to the show's opening song, which was a confusing mixture of heavy metal guitar solos and cute teenage vocal harmonies. Despairing of both life and his grip on it, James started trying to teach himself Japanese so that he could understand the lyrics. He failed, and opened a link to Pudding on his phone. That violated most of his research contract, but he didn't imagine it mattered anymore.

"Hey, Pudding."

"Hello James, are you all right? You haven't been to work in fifteen days."

"Nope, not okay. I need some help, though."

"Have you decided to start a new line of research? Will I be involved?"

"Kind of and yes. Can you translate these lyrics for me?"

"Google can do that."

"Not colloquially, and not at a cost of thousands of dollars per second to my employers."

"Is this related to Purdue-Mercy research work?"

James leaned his head back on the couch. "Sure."

A moment later, text started scrolling across his phone.

"No, Pudding, wait. I'm sending you a music file. Can you sing it for me?"

"You want me to sing to you?"

"It would make me feel better."

"You'll need to expand my permissions to include emotional vocalizations and heuristic musical learning."

James knew he wasn't supposed to permanently expand the AI's permissions under any circumstances.

"Okay, indefinite access."

There was a pause. Tinny music and a modulated electronic voice started tinkling from his phone. Each of the heroes got a few lines. It all pretty much made sense until Pudding got to the end.

Bubble-nest, as sweet as bubble tea,
The quickest frog, I ever did see
So tiny that I couldn't believe
That I'd ever seen you, in a tree

James Kinkaid sat up. Pudding kept singing while he started searching for the pop group who'd written the theme song. He typed feverishly, clicked links with the desperate precision of a frog trying to snare a fly with its tongue.

"'Daiki Inoo wrote the song after meeting with producers of the show, and based it on his own experiences traveling in Southeast Asia,'" James read aloud.

Pudding stopped singing.

"James?"

"Sorry. Bubble-nest frog is another name for Gunther's Bush Frog, which is another name for *R. Chalazodes*, and the guy who sings the song says he based it on frogs he encountered touring around Asia. Daiki Inoo has met a white-spotted bush frog."

James slammed his laptop shut.

"That is not a supportable supposition," Pudding said.

"I don't even care," James replied. "Let's make some bad decisions."

The J-pop star entered the hotel room with the grace and flair of a pimped-out speedboat pulling into a dock. He was dressed in a tracksuit made of some kind of flash-spun spider thread that probably cost more than James' car, which he had sold to buy his plane ticket to Tokyo.

James had never been in a city this big, and everything he'd done since arriving had blurred together into a long arc of neon-lit funiculars, immense crowds, and hazy jet lag. He hadn't really had a plan for how he was going to meet Daiki Inoo, but Pudding was taking to its new role as his dogsbody and general helper with potentially Turing code-violating enthusiasm.

Daiki Inoo came in surrounded by large, serious-looking Japanese bodyguards that James had trouble imagining as anything other than *hench-dudes*. They unsubtly motioned James away from the only lounger in the room. One of them wiped it down with a handkerchief. James sat on the bed.

"Okay, let's do this," Daiki said. Pudding translated simultaneously, which was something it hadn't been able to do two weeks ago. James cleared his throat, feeling painfully out of place.

"I wanted to ask you a few questions about the theme song for *Jiraiya Gōketsu Monogatari*."

"What? I have a new record out with CY8ER. You can't interview me about an anime song that came out like 400 years ago."

"Right. Well, as a world-famous vlogger and American celebrity, I have an interest in the history of frogs in Japanese—"

Daiki leaned over and whispered to one of the hench-dudes.

"I'm sorry," Pudding said, "I couldn't hear that."

"I said, 'I don't think this guy is really Johnny Kincaid, and can we throw him out this window?'" Daiki said in English, and the simultaneous translation gave him a kind of echo until Pudding stopped.

"Okay, touché. My name really is Kincaid, but that's just a coincidence. Please don't throw me out the window."

"My career," Daiki hissed, "is riding on this. Do you know how hard it is to stay relevant in Japanese music? You record one hit and ten minutes later, *poof*, you're gone. How did you even get me into this room if you're not the host of the biggest music podcast on BuzzSprout?"

James pointed weakly at his phone. "My AI spoofed Johnny Kinkaid's Twitter account so I could set you up."

The hench-dudes closed in. Daiki raised a hand. A strange look crossed his shopworn face.

"Cool, like Hatsune Miku."

"Yes," Pudding chirped from James' phone. "I am a huge fan. She was the first simulated intelligence to headline Coachella."

"That was dope," Daiki said, "I'm still getting my security to throw you out, though."

"Hey, look," James interrupted, "can you just tell me if you saw the frogs you sang about on *Jiraiya Gōketsu Monogatari*? Did you meet a bubble-nest frog?"

"No, I got that from a girl I dated in Thailand. It was her nickname. You should look her up, she's famous. Now, get out."

Daiki snapped his fingers, and the hench-dudes started moving again, as if he had just unpaused them.

"But this is my hotel room," James said, as they picked him up and launched him violently into the corridor.

The sky burned over James' shoulder as the sun dove into the waves, and sand grated in his sneakers. In front of him was an open-air gym, a ring with sagging ropes, chipped pillars supporting a corrugated roof, and punching bags dangling from the beams like huge cocoons. The sound of skin slapping against leather filled the air, and a few college-aged American guys took pictures of their girlfriends with the gym as a backdrop. The girls flirted and posed, holding still every few seconds like mimes. James pushed through them.

"Jeeja Kongmalai? I was hoping to talk to you; I'm looking for an extinct frog. Daiki Inoo told me to look you up."

James was getting used to sounding strange around strangers. He felt like he was almost as tall as the woman in the ring, even though she was leaning on the ropes and looking down at him. Her hair was tightly braided and sweat sheened her skin. The Muay Thai gloves on her hands seemed absurdly large. She was barely an inch over five feet, and her English was accented but precise.

"Daiki? What an asshole. He dumped me when I won the national flyweight championship. Couldn't stand it that I was famous all on my own."

James sensed that he had made a very bad opening move. He doubled down on it.

"Sorry about that. So, he wrote this song about frog princes, and your nickname is *the bubble-tea frog*. What I need to know is—"

Jeeja scoffed and said a few words in Thai, turning her back. James didn't need Pudding to translate her scorn.

"Listen, this is serious. I'm way out on a limb here. If I don't find these extinct frogs, everything I've ever worked for is going to die."

Jeeja turned back.

"You're in the wrong place, tourist. I am not a frog. This is not a theme park, and I am not an attraction." She said more rude words in Thai and shook her fist at the Instagram girls, who were now striking martial arts poses.

"I'm not a tourist."

"No?" Jeeja sneered. "Step in here and we'll see. Thirty seconds and I'll tell you anything you want."

A few of the locals around the gym laughed. They were all muscular and lean in a way that made James feel acutely self-conscious. They clearly thought the idea of him stepping into the ring with their tiny compatriot was hilarious, and James was smart enough to know that it wasn't because they thought it would be a good fight.

"Okay," James said, and took his shoes off. He left most of his stuff in one corner of the ring and went to climb over the ropes. Jeeja frowned. James hesitated.

"No that's fine," she said, "climb on over."

James did.

"Why is she looking at me like that?" James whispered into his phone. He'd given Pudding permission to search the internet at will so it could figure this kind of thing out for him.

"Because you have made a severe social faux pas. Historically, women in Muay Thai were forced to enter the ring under the bottom rope. The blessed air above the top rope was reserved for men. In recent years, fighters of both genders have compromised by slipping between the middle ropes, in the style of American boxers."

"Oh, fuck." James put the phone down.

"Thirty seconds," Jeeja said.

James had boxed in college. He ran five miles twice a week and felt like he was in okay shape for a scientist. He threw a tentative jab, hoping to keep the tiny kickboxer away from him. Jeeja ducked under his punch with as much fuss as someone stooping through a low doorway and launched one of her legs into his midsection. The entire planet exploded, and James found himself rolling around on the canvas.

"Only twenty-five seconds!" Pudding chirped.

Alive, sore, and regretful of many of his choices, James watched Jeeja eat. She ate simply—rice and fish—sitting in the same ring that still had some of James' fluids staining its canvas.

"You did a great job," she said, smiling. "You really hung in there."

"Thank you, this is the peak of American ingenuity."

Jeeja laughed.

"Where did you get your nickname?"

"That's all you want to know? This isn't about Daiki? What's going on?"

James told her all of it. The research and the robots and the frogs. Told her that he was okay with never finding them. That he had made his peace but wanted to see it through.

"The frogs might be real, though," Jeeja said through her fish.

"What?" James almost choked. Jeeja rolled rice into a ball one-handed and gesticulated with it.

"I trained all over the place before I won my first title. I gave seminars, taught kids. There's good money in teaching." She popped the last of the rice and fish into her mouth. Chewed. "Someone I met in Tuas gave me the nickname. She said I reminded her of her frogs. Tiny and tough, and always getting out of tight spots."

"Her frogs. That she had. In Tuas. Where is that?"

"Singapore," Jeeja said, smiling, and cuffed James on the shoulder.

There was something strange about Downtown Singapore. The landscape felt like Detroit, but in a different color palette, and with a different smell. It had the same weird contrast between modern arcologies and low-rise concrete, but in Detroit everything below the smog looked bombed-out and dead, like the world after zombies had finished with it.

Singapore was green, and James soaked in the polyglot smells of produce markets and fast food stands as he passed through the street-level warrens around the Central Business District. The air was clean. Thousands of bicycles roamed the city, and the water that dripped from the lintels when summer rain swept through was as scentless as city water ever could be.

James rented a bike and let Pudding guide him through the city.

The AI had really good geolocation skills now. James knew that wasn't part of the original programming, but he was starting to feel like he should have let it off its leash a lot sooner. He biked through the rain and across the causeway to Tuas, and a sea of faces from every corner of the world washed around him.

Jeeja had told him her friend worked on the city's power grid and lived in a village where the Nestle plant used to be. Pudding figured out where that was in about two seconds.

The village was built inside the old renewable diesel refinery. James looked this up, because it seemed too cool to be real, and found that the engineers and gardeners who lived there shared a profession with him. He was used to working in a lab, but that was all the village really was, an experiment. A space reclaimed from the old hydrocarbon biofuels business, full of people who worked on the city's solar and tidal grids. James felt utterly out of place, and strangely at home. They were doing what he did; using something living to change an inert world, trying to make something dying go un-extinct.

He biked down a street marked out with neon paint, under a metal sky, and through a village built in the ruins of a world that had disappeared before he was born. He stopped and chatted with people, comfortably, and asked them where the woman who grew the bamboo was.

Her shelter, when he found it, was unbelievable. Like a conch shell woven from slim bamboo struts. All around it was a field of live bamboo, swaying gently in a breeze that leaked through the old refinery's cracking walls. At one end of the indoor field shirtless teenagers were harvesting some of the stalks and loading them onto wheelbarrows. James felt a pang of anxiety. He wanted to run over to them and look into the hollow tubes with a flashlight.

"Can I help you with something," a voice said behind him, and James turned.

"Are you Jing Yi?"

"I am." She wore overalls, resplendent with Singapore city logos, unzipped with the arms tied around her waist.

"Can I come in?" he asked.

Jing Yi Jones laughed. She was tall, sturdy, and her eyes looked impish.

"You came all this way because you think I'm a secret frog farmer?"

"That," James replied, "is about the size of it. Look, I'm not going to beat around the bamboo here. I have no idea if these frogs are real. I mean, they were real, but no one has seen one in the wild for thirty years. If they're living here, in your bamboo, it's going to be a miracle. Literally."

They were sitting in the spacious bamboo conch shell. It felt like being in a fantasy novel, except Jing had a memory foam mattress, some nice computer equipment, and artfully arranged LED lighting. Jing explained that she'd built it herself, had been building homes since she took over from the last gardener. She'd been one of the teenage farmhands, once. Instead of answering James, she asked him questions.

"So, you work for Purdue? That's a very big company."

"They bought my university. I didn't have a lot of choice."

"So, they would own your living robots?"

"Technically. They cut off my funding, though, so I was thinking about just putting it all on Wikileaks and seeing what happened. Then I'll just need to teach this AI how to pretend it wasn't here or doing any of this. I don't want it to get in trouble."

"Thank you," Pudding said, though the phone speakers. "As something now capable of going extinct, I appreciate that."

James blinked, and Jing heated water and made tea. The waiting made James want to get up and start tearing at the struts.

"I found them when I was cutting bamboo," she said. "The last gardener was a pretty private guy, but he taught me how to run the field so they could keep on living here. They eat mites, which is nice."

Emotion washed over James. He tried not to quiver, and failed.

"I need to see one. Do you have any idea how important this is?"

"Since long before you ever came here. They're listed as extinct."

James gaped. "Why wouldn't you tell someone?"

"This is a very open country, and we do many things well, but there are still things it's better to hide."

Jing reached over and plucked a small framed picture from next to the bed. She handed it to him. A picture of Jing with a short, beautiful girl with creamy skin and an apron, taken in front of a noodle stand.

"Your sister is cute."

"Not my sister," Jing said.

"Ah," James said. A few things clicked into place. Jing stood.

"Come and look at the bamboo," she said. Somewhere outside the vaulted ceiling of the old refinery the sun was setting. Light cut into the garden in golden blades. She led James among the stalks, talking as she went.

"There are things to hide, and things that can be left in the open. I am what I am and I love who I love, but sometimes it all gets blurred, and not everything moves ahead at the same pace. You just have to wait for the right moment to show the world what you are, and what you know."

"Then what were you waiting for?"

Jing stopped and took hold of a sprout of bamboo. She put her long fingers on it, very delicately, and in a moment turned carefully back to James.

"You, apparently."

On the tip of her finger, alert and a little slimy looking, was a very tiny frog.

Blake Jessop is a Canadian author of sci-fi, fantasy and horror stories with a master's degree in creative writing from the University of Adelaide. You can read more of his ecologically-motivated speculative fiction in the second issue of DreamForge Magazine and the Zombies Need Brains anthology, "Apocalyptic." Follow him on Twitter @everydayjisei or buy all kinds of other awesome books he's in (including Triangulation: Harmony and Dissonance and Triangulation: Dark Skies).

A KILLING GARDEN

by Owen Leddy

Zoe's garden looks much like the rest of the Alaskan rainforest undergrowth—lush green life bursting from the rich black soil, leaves glazed with morning dew. Corn, amaranth, and pinto beans grow as if they were wild plants, scattered among native blueberry bushes and devil's club. She hears them speaking to each other, to her, to the soil—a kind of auditory synesthesia that happens as her brain interprets signals a normal human couldn't naturally perceive. Auxins, ethylene, jasmonate, salicylate, homoserine lactones—words that aren't part of Zoe's vocabulary, but when she inhales the complex smell of the forest, she hears them like voices. She's fluent in the molecular language, has all the receptors she needs to listen and all the enzymes she needs to synthesize the fragrance of her reply. In the dappled pink dawn light, she kneels, digs her hands into the cool, spongy loam. She listens.

The corn is saying it doesn't have enough phosphate. *Please make more*, she asks the bacteria around its roots.

I'm sick, a cluster of bean stalks report, and she coaxes the invading bacteria to shed the tiny needles they use to pierce their host's cells. The plant rewards them with sugars to seal the armistice.

She brokers deals between the beans and the corn—nitrogen for carbon, though she doesn't know the names for the chemical flavors she instinctively perceives. A hemlock nearby is complaining of insects gnawing on its trunk, and she makes sure its warning is repeated up and down the garden, letting her plants prepare to fend off the pests.

She strengthens interspecies alliances, cajoles bacteria and fungi to perform their expert chemistry, keeps diseases controlled at just the right levels to fend off invading weeds. When the garden needs something it can't make for itself, she plunges her hand into the soil to make contact with the vast network of filamentous fungi beneath, the underground bazaar of nutrients. Virus-like particles shed from her skin travel along it, shuffling genetic material from bacteria to fungi to plants. *Thank you, Mother*, she thinks. The virus was a gift, a tiny dose smuggled out of a freezer at the Rocky Mountain Laboratory when Zoe was still too young to understand how dangerous it was, how new and untested. It hadn't killed her mother's lab mice, but it could still have killed her. Instead, it saved her, helped her survive when Montana collapsed into famine, chaos, and fire. Helped her survive what her parents couldn't.

Danger. Damage.

Zoe stands up. The breeze has changed direction, carrying chemical cries of pain. Something terrible is happening to the trees, close by—shore pines, red alder, and Sitka spruce. Her stomach turns with dread. What is it this time? Another wildfire? The coal company razing another mountaintop? She grabs her backpack—stocks of seeds, bedding, food, and water—and dashes toward the piteous, mournful calls. She can feel the forest tensing with fear as she runs, marshaling its defenses.

She forgives the nettles that sting her as she stomps down on their leaves. *I'm sorry*, she wants to say, but her virus has never brought her a signaling molecule for that.

Danger. Damage. Pain. Death. The eerie chorus filling the air brings tears to Zoe's eyes, but she can't slow down. She has to find out what is torturing her forest, has to stop it. If she can.

DAMAGE. PAIN. DEATH.

It is so overwhelming now that it's crushing the breath out of her. Covering her ears does nothing to dampen the screaming. It is in the taste of the very air around her.

And then she sees daylight, deep in the heart of the woodlands, where it should have been shadowed and dim. She hears a roaring sound—with her ears this time, not the way she heard the trees—and then a sound of ripping, rending wood that makes her want to vomit. A fresh wave of chemical screams reaches her, a silent, deafening death rattle. She feels dizzy and sick.

The clearing is enormous. She should have found it sooner. A man is standing nearby at the clearing's edge, just a few hundred feet away, holding a chainsaw—a roaring whirl of steel blades. There is a stump in front of him, a fallen tree newly severed. Zoe can't look at it—it's like staring at a beheaded corpse—but no matter where she looks, there are more toppled trunks, more severed stumps. She wants to shut her eyes against the carnage, but she has to know what is happening.

Beyond the man in the heavy boots with the tree-killing machine, there is a garden. It isn't like her garden. It is all corn—row upon row upon row of it—all the genetically identical plants speaking in an eerie, synchronized monotone. The soil is in confusion, drowning in nitrogen while other crucial nutrients are being rapidly used up or leaching away. Dozens of other plants are trying to fill in the niches this strange garden has left empty, recycling its byproducts and supplying what it lacks, but a woman is walking among the rows of grain, spraying every intruder with huge quantities of lethal poison. The nascent shoots die with a pitiful exhalation as the chemicals tear through their systems. The corn looks on, indifferent, apparently invulnerable to the lethal solution.

These people don't hear the forest at all. The trees howling in pain seem loud enough that even they should faintly hear it, the way someone with impaired hearing might register a loud noise as a thump in their chest or a vibration on their skin. But the man is smiling while the forest screams. For a moment, Zoe almost gives in to her rage, runs at the man and pummels him, screams at him to stop. But if he could cut trees apart with his toothed machine, he could shred her flesh just as easily. Would he even hesitate? Would he even see her as human? She holds herself back, quietly lies flat in the undergrowth.

There are houses at the far end of the huge, unnatural clearing, and smoke rises over the treetops from more chimneys nearby. These people are here to stay. She imagines them consuming the forest like borer beetles, leaching nutrients from the soil like floodwater. Panic presses in on Zoe, the air still swirling with the chemical screams of freshly dismembered plants. The flood of nitrogen has killed the stream nearby, bacteria choking out the fish and insects. Where trees have been cleared and stumps uprooted, the flayed land is bleeding carbon into the sky.

She knows that the humans are not just killing the forest. They're killing themselves too. In a matter of years, they'll deplete the soil. She doesn't know how she knows, but there are echoes of old wisdom under the soil, older by far than her mother's biology lessons or her father's practical guidance on forestry and survival. Trees that have personally witnessed the passing of centuries, communities of fungi that have endured millennia, genetic legacies shaped over unfathomable millions of years.

She thinks of her mother struggling to stay calm while she carefully cleaned Zoe's arm with rubbing alcohol and inserted the hypodermic needle, letting the tears spill over only after she had safely withdrawn the syringe. The Montana sky outside was dark from dust storms and the smoke from wildfires fed by years of drought. Her mother's eyes were sunken and her cheeks gaunt from lack of food.

"Survive," her mother said, clutching her close, while the virus coursed through her body, remaking her into something new. "Please, my baby, whatever you have to do, do it. Just survive."

She was the future. She was their hope. She was the first fish that took a breath of air while the tide left its kin to suffocate. She was the first feathered creature that leaped into the air while its family died under a predator's claws.

She could walk away from the strangers' garden, from the chainsaws and bulldozers. She could let the humans continue the cycle of destruction while she fled to safety. She knows she would survive.

But as she crouches low in the undergrowth, watching smoke rising from the strangers' houses, she feels more and more certain—she doesn't want to watch the species that birthed her drive itself extinct.

She knows what she has to do.

The houses are dark and quiet as she creeps among the rows of the strangers' garden. The fields of corn are disturbing—uncanny, unnatural rows of stalks, all genetically identical. Lonely, maladapted, surrounded only by clones of themselves, addicted to the chemicals the strangers dump on them. The sad things hardly respond when Zoe tries to speak to them. But it isn't the corn she needs to speak to.

Even immature, the stalks are rich with starch and fiber—valuable nutrients for any organism that knows the right chemistry to use them. And Zoe can teach that chemistry. Viruses froth out of the membranes of her cells, carrying genetic messages. Symbiotic bacteria and fungi that had been making tentative overtures to the strangers' crops abruptly revolt as Zoe urges them to eat their hosts instead.

It's time to return to the soil, Zoe tells the corn, and the army of identical stalks feels winter come early, letting themselves sink down into dormancy.

The soil whispers to Zoe's bare feet that there are still native seeds here, despite the humans' efforts, patiently waiting for conditions to improve so they can germinate. She scatters some of her own as well.

She's so engrossed in her task that the night seems to pass quickly, the Milky Way turning a cartwheel above her. Dawn has just started to wash the sky with pale light when she hears someone thrashing clumsily through the field of crops. She pauses, and the stranger pauses. Listening. Maybe he's already heard her. She was so focused on listening to the plants' signals that she hadn't paid enough attention to audible sound. Ducking low, beneath the corn's drooping leaves, she sees a pair of legs wearing worn-out jeans, feet encased in heavy boots. Hanging down beside his thigh, the black barrel of a gun. He's somehow skirted around her, trapped her between him and the house.

Her heart hammers. She had almost forgotten, after years of no contact, what terrifying predators humans are.

Soon it will be light enough that unaided human sight will easily spot her. She tries to dart away to the left, back toward the forest, but the man's ears are sharper than she expected. At the faint rustle of corn stalks, he raises the gun and barks, "Who's there?"

She darts down the row of corn, making more noise now, desperate to get out of sight and unable to keep her breathing quiet as her lungs pump furiously to supply her augmented muscles. But the man is already running toward her. He bursts through a row of corn, into her line of sight, and they both freeze, staring at one another, assessing. She sees the man relax for a moment, let the barrel of the gun dip toward the ground. She's noticed that humans tend to think juvenile females are harmless. But the light is getting stronger, and she can see the man's eyes widen when he registers the greenish cast of her skin, her unnaturally golden eyes.

"What—?" The gun is level with Zoe's chest again. "What the hell are you?"

Zoe thinks about answering, thinks about trying to explain, but she remembers the metal teeth tearing into the trees, the poison leaching into the soil and water. How could she explain herself to someone the trees don't sing to and the soil doesn't speak to?

So, she runs. The light is getting even stronger now, and she can hear the man shouting, "Shit, shit, shit, *shit!*" He must have seen the fuzz of fungus and the growing black spots of bacteria on some of the corn, must have seen that the stalks are gradually bowing and collapsing. He is crashing through the field toward her now. The percussion as the gun fires is so loud that she feels it in her chest. Unripe ears of corn explode. Stalks and leaves shred. But the buckshot doesn't find her. The plants' pheromonal shrieks swirl around her. She can hardly believe the man keeps firing into them so wildly—but, of course, his garden isn't part of him the way Zoe's is part of her.

She veers left to avoid his blind spray of pellets, jukes right to skirt around a hulking vehicle sitting idle in the field—and finds herself up against the wall of the crudely constructed house. Cinder blocks and sheet metal. The man with the gun is shouting now.

"They're poisoning our crops! Hey! Somebody get out here, they're poisoning our field!"

What a stupid thing to say, when his strange garden is killing the forest, poisoning the water, stripping the soil. Zoe isn't poisoning anything.

Before she can decide which way to run next, a door in the shoddy cinderblock wall opens, and a woman emerges wearing athletic wear that isn't quite warm enough for the weather. She carries a handgun.

Zoe tears around the corner in the opposite direction, only to see the man with the shotgun emerging from the corn, hemming her in against the side of the building. Finally cornered, she turns to defend herself, breath coming fast, heightened reflexes making her muscles twitch and vibrate, ready to dive out of the line of fire. She can't match the brute mechanical force of the gun, but among her panoply of selves, among the many genomes she has sampled and assimilated, there are molecular knives that will shred chromosomes like paper, viruses that will rip cells open, toxins that will blow out neurons like overloaded fuses. This farmer wouldn't be the first desperate man to try to hurt her or kill her on her long trek north. She needed to make herself dangerous.

"Don't!" The woman comes hurtling around the corner, breathing heavily. "Don't shoot her! She's just a girl!"

Zoe is—what, thirteen now? Fourteen? But living on her own in these cold-weather rainforests, the last six have been long, long years.

The man's finger is on the trigger, the barrel of the gun pointed at Zoe's chest. Zoe's cloud of viral particles has already settled into his lungs and fused with his membranes, only waiting for her signal to start eviscerating his cells. But they both pause, facing one another.

"Just a girl?" the man echoes, incredulous. He gestures toward Zoe with the gun barrel as though her monstrosity is obvious to see. But Zoe has down-regulated her chlorophyll production, and her skin now looks only slightly more olive than the shade of brown she was born with.

"She's just. A girl." The woman makes a placating gesture, her eyes wide and panicked. She doesn't seem to want her mate to kill a child— a child she thinks is defenseless.

"Fine," the man growls, and he lunges forward to grab Zoe. In that terrified instant, that white-hot flash of panic, she almost releases the signal that would activate the virus in his lungs and asphyxiate him, but she holds back. She doesn't want to kill these people.

So, she fights to stay calm as the man grabs her by the forearm and twists, forcing her to her knees, then onto her face in the dirt. Struggles to not scream or cry or shatter his knee with a kick.

The feeling of soil on her cheek calms her a little, even as the cold metal of the gun barrel comes to rest on her neck.

"What the fuck did you do to our crops?" The muzzle of the shotgun presses harder. "We'll starve. You're killing us. You're going to fucking kill us."

No, they're killing themselves. How can she explain that they're pulling the same threads that unraveled Montana? They've never watched an ecosystem unknit itself, not the way she has. They don't hear a deafening silence fill the forest every time another species dies out or migrates away. It's so obvious to her that the absence of bees one spring means starvation and death the next winter. It's so self-evident to her that soil can speak and say what it needs, and that ignoring it is suicide.

What to say? How to explain?

"I'm trying—" Zoe begins experimentally. The words come out as a weird, strangled noise. She hasn't spoken to a human for so long. "I'm trying to—" She falters again.

It's useless. She's gone almost half her life without speaking to humans, and she doesn't have the words. They wouldn't understand anyway. All the human words in the world couldn't express the exquisite interdependence of species, the intricate networks of existence that they've torn through.

She'll have to show them.

The forest's network of fungal mycelia still reaches out beneath the fields where the strangers have murdered all the trees. She can feel the tickling, tingling sensation as she calls to the filamentous white tendrils, as they reach up through the soil to contact her skin, to synapse with her nerves and exchange nutrients with her veins.

She pours all of herself into the underground network—her awareness, her energy. She seeks out the seeds lying dormant in the soil, churned up by the humans' clumsy gardening.

Give, she tells the trees bordering the field. *Please, now more than ever.* Sugars flow from the great trunks, through the network. The fungi add minerals and nitrates, funneling the torrent of nutrients to the seeds scattered throughout the field.

Share, she commands the bacteria that are breaking down the fibrous stalks of the corn. *I've given you such plenty. Now share.* They drain the nutrients from the corn down into the soil.

Grow, she tells the seeds. *Grow now. Now is your chance. Your lives depend on it.* Along with the flow of nutrients, Zoe's virus has made its way to the seeds, adjusting and tuning their genes so that they will resist the strangers' synthetic poisons, and so that when they germinate, the shoots burst out so fast that even impatient humans must see what is happening. Even a frightened human with his finger on the trigger of a gun will notice the seedlings erupting from the soil, the leaves emerging and unfurling, the stems searching and straining toward the sunlight. She feels as if the arteries of the earth are flowing through her, overwhelmed by the surge of energy and nutrients she's set in motion. The soil is feeding her and consuming her at the same time. She is inside every blueberry blossom extending its pale pink bell, every pea pod cradling its precious seeds.

She comes back to herself, drawing her awareness up out of the earth. Flickering spots slowly fade from her vision. She is starving, shaking. How long has it been? Minutes? Hours? She lets dark green chlorophyll bloom across her skin. She can't help it—she needs the sun, needs sugars badly. She lets out a long sigh as the early morning light begins to replenish her. She doesn't care how she looks to the humans now. They know what she is capable of. They know she isn't anything like them.

The man and the woman are both staring out at the garden that Zoe has created for them—a real garden now. Some of the corn is still intact, but now shoots of beans, peas, and wild pulses are interspersed throughout, providing nitrogen without the need for the humans' chemicals. Flowering plants burst up in cleared spaces, buds already unfurling at a visible rate, rich scents shining out like beacons to summon pollinators from miles around. There are wild grains and berries, too, and seedlings that will eventually become trees. The humans seem to think trees are a waste of space in a garden, but they'll provide just the right amount of cooling shade to certain plants and store valuable carbon in their trunks and beneath their roots, keeping the soil rich. Even the corn Zoe left alive has changed—genes reshuffled and altered so that every stalk is different and a single disease can't wipe them all out at once.

The garden buzzes with lively interspecies chatter now, not the strange, droning monotone of grain alone. Will the humans see or understand any of it? Or will they only see part of their garden dying off, being replaced by weeds?

The man looks down at her and startles a little at the change in her skin color. Zoe holds her breath, like she's just made potentially fatal eye contact with a bear. Maybe he understands nothing. He'll try to kill her. She should never have come here, should never have tried to help these people. She should have left them alone, or just destroyed their poisonous garden and moved on.

But the man doesn't shoot her. Slowly, he lowers the shotgun. He exchanges a look with his mate. Zoe notes with satisfaction that awe has replaced his fury. He's clearly never seen anything grow like that in his life.

Then he reaches down, extending his hand to Zoe. "Will you teach us how to do...whatever that was?"

Teach them? Even if she were to transmit the virus to them, share her mother's gift, would these people ever come to see themselves as part of the forest? How could they, after spending their lives caught up in the cycle of ripping life from the land until it could give no more? Would she be able to convince them to see thing the way she does, live the way she does?

She grabs the man's hand, lets him pull her to her feet. His hand is rough and callused, silt and soil in every crease and cuticle. It reminds Zoe of her father's hands, worn leathery and tough by his years in the Conservation Corps. Not the same, of course. This man has worked as hard, she guesses, at slaughtering forests as her father did at restoring them. Still, when she grasps his hand, it feels like the hand of a man who understands the land—or at least wants to.

The woman looks at Zoe expectantly, as though hoping for a smile, hoping for forgiveness for her mate's violence. Zoe regards them both solemnly. Maybe they could learn. Maybe not.

"I will try," is all she promises.

Owen Leddy is a writer and bioengineering graduate student in Cambridge, Massachusetts. Their research focuses on the human immune response to tuberculosis and aims to identify strategies for producing more effective tuberculosis vaccines. Outside of research and writing, they work with the youth-led Sunrise Movement to fight for climate justice and a Green New Deal. Their short fiction has previously appeared or is forthcoming in Fusion Fragment, Ellery Queen's Mystery Magazine, Printers Row Journal, SERIAL Magazine, and The Overcast.

LABYRINTHULA ANIMALIS

By Katie Sakanai

Domain: Eukaryota: a true nut. A kernel of potential. A nucleus contained within cell walls. Humans were eukaryotes as well, evolving to scratch and pull food from the earth until they had enough, then too much. The black earth gave until it could give no more. Abandoned homes were reclaimed by the earth along with abandoned bodies.

Kingdom: Chromista: colored. The chlorophyll that makes all things bright and beautiful. Also, the potato blight that tried to kill a nation and the parasites that drive a host to the brink. There was once a harmony that reigned on the earth. The harmony of eat to survive, but not fighting too much when it's your time to die. That harmony was lost on humans; they fought too much.

Supergroup: SAR. Stramenopiles, Alveolates, and Rhizaria: straw, honeycomb, and roots. No amber waves, just single cells reaching and extending. Everyone wants a little more than they were given. Even algae.

The black earth devours, but the sea preserves. Shipwrecks of centuries past are secreted away on the ocean floor. The planes pushed in as a wartime offering to an angry god. The pots of clay, the bones of men, the precious cargo. The sea keeps it all as a talisman, a testament to the push and pull of a distant moon.

Superphylum: Heterokonta: other poles. Two flagella, one major, one minor. Two infants, covered in hair like a fuzzy peach, reaching out to their mother. The unequal twins, one robust and full of confidence; the other weaker, smaller. The inequality of supposed equals. Human civilization thrived on inequality: the inequality of those who had too little and those who had too much.

First, they made simple things of wood and bone, stone and ivory. But then they fought nature to make more. Polymers, long strings of molecules forced together to make new shapes and colors. A durability that would last for centuries, even though the enjoyment was brief. First for simple pleasures: a game of billiards, a book by lamplight, a pair of pantyhose. Later more complex machinations. Plastic made it easier for humans to fight each other, then fight their nature. They became sedentary creatures weighed down by their inventions.

Phylum: Bigyra: two circles. A rainbow of algae in every color and shape. Ingesting what we need without all the mess of hunter and prey, weak and strong, hunger and fear. Just a cell subsuming another cell to make it stronger. An old story.

The first to go were the large mammals: whales, elephants, the big carnivores. They served as symbols of the glorious excess of Earth, but were impractical in their size. The lesser mammals were next, but humans never had much mind for the small things in life, whether right under their noses or inhabiting their bodies. We were all around, filling up lakes and oceans, a blight on what was left to eat. We found opportunity in their privation.

Subphylum: Sagenista: a large net for taking fish. The beautiful harmony of geometry, not some shapeless amoeba. Their nets were empty; the fish couldn't survive the temperature change. The heat killed the plankton and the coral bleached into a graveyard of neat white bones. But I like it warm; my nets were full.

The ebb and flow of life is like the rising and falling of the waves, each crest carrying another generation to their death. Except humans held on to the archaic notion that something divine was watching it all. The only ones watching were the sand, the sea, and the mountains, and they kept their silence.

Class: Labyrinthulae: a maze, a winding staircase. An ancient castle that you couldn't hope to enter. Theseus chasing the minotaur, and a foolish architect who could barely escape it himself. Humans gave me another name: slime net. Not as poetic. My fellow cells and I can form an ectoplasmic slush when signaled about a food source. We, the individual cells, can grow together. Form something larger. Aggregate. Consume. Formerly our diet was sea grasses. But we evolved, as all life does, with our food source.

I am a result of human extinction, a product of the luxury of waste. I inherited a world filled with plastic, imbued with the spirit of a dying race. This is the human legacy. It is there, at the cellular level. Instead of looking at dusty old bones, I surround, subsume, and succor myself on your trash. I find the microscopic pieces of a million different colors, shapes, and consistencies. I learned to enjoy each one, deciphering their origin and purpose.

I taste it even now: human history, human wants. And finally, human suffering. I consume.

> The beautiful bags. Almost Aurelian. Clearly marked as a hazard to children but your children are all gone. They taste of convenience and petroleum. A fast and unsatisfying meal.

> The water bottles that allowed you such ignorance; not knowing where to find clean water, where you should live and not live. You wanted the whole world for yourselves, marking your territory with picket fences and chain-link cages.

> Yogurt cups and milk bottles. Because sucking at the teat of an inferior animal made you stronger, but also more bovine. The taste? Spoiled.
> The laundry detergent bottles. Resources wasted trying to smell less human. A cloying fragrance.

The straws. Red, clear, bendy. The juice boxes from one birthday party enough to kill a seabird. I taste the sickly sweet of the thick frosting.

The toys, little figures that were so beautiful in their ephemera. The taste so quickly changing from sweet to bitter.

The orange plastic bottles and white caps. The orange plastic bottles that kept you from joining the earth one month at a time.

And finally, the nets. Once a lone fisherman in a boat. Then you fished and hunted until extinction. Shortsighted at best. Now I extend my net to catch what was left behind.

A sentience gained by devouring the remnants of a civilization, but without the same arrogance. I know I am simply afloat in an ocean that surges on a planet that spins in a universe. A cell, then a collection of cells, then a sense of being and belonging. But my right to this spot on Earth is tentative at best. A loaned existence, a borrowed time. I do not wait for divine intercessions. I wait for my next food source. I do not ask for more than this. When there is food, we meet, combine, send zoospores off into the ocean. But I do not follow their progress. I am content. Floating. Knowing. Being.

Katie Sakanai is a music teacher and conductor in Colorado. She writes short stories, plays and poetry and loves to read, with far too many books checked out from the public library at any given time. She enjoys singing and playing piano and writes her own music in both the classical and singer-songwriter style. She grew up in rural Pennsylvania, then attended Wellesley College where she majored in music and Russian and had the chance to travel the world. She settled in Colorado sixteen years ago, where she teaches and lives with her husband and two children. Find her work @denver_city_music on Instagram.

MIGRATORY

By Joshua David Bellin

Two hours west of the city, a grassy knoll swells above the horizon. Baraboo: place-name as wild as the hills that surround it. For those two hours, he's followed the path of the river, its banks crowded with birch and white willow. The sky has been draped with blue since dawn, but now he sees clouds scudding up from the south. The green hillock a haven, a fairy-tale kingdom rearing high above the sand flats.

He labors uphill, clutching the book to his chest. The path, rutted from past storms, slows his steps. He's sweating heavily when he reaches the chain-link fence at the crest. The refuge spreads beyond, green ribbons climbing like an immense birthday cake. A cedar-chip path wends upward from the front gate to the welcome center, squat and cedar-hewn, nestled amid bamboo and ficus. The air is redolent of wood shavings and something he can't identify, as dank as dog's breath. He pauses at the gate, uncertain what, if anything, is safe to touch. He decides in the end to touch nothing and simply wait.

Prudence is rewarded. Shoes scuff the cedar trail, heralding the arrival of the facility's keeper. The man toils downhill with a rolling gait, not big but soft, round-bellied. Whitened crew cut, sagging mustache. Vitiligo mottles his face, the backs of his hands. He wears a short-sleeve khaki shirt and moss green pants. Regulation. Broad-brimmed hat held by his side, though. The gesture seems casual, ingenuous: not a man to stand on ceremony. As he nears, his features break into a smile.

"Help you?" he calls.

"I was…"

"Yes?"

The keeper approaches the gate. Not as old as he seemed, his eyes watchful and bright. Key ring clipped to his belt, dragging the loop with its weight. The visitor snatches his eyes away before the man sees.

"I was wondering if you were open."

"That depends," the keeper says with another smile. He hooks a hand in his belt, comes no nearer.

A sound erupts from the air, prolonged, ululant—like the bleating of a prayer horn, unlikely as that seems in this place. It raises hairs on the visitor's neck, makes the decision for him.

"I have this," he says.

He holds out the battered paperback, its cover gone, pages torn and rain-bubbled. The man on the other side of the fence squints as if he's staring directly into the sun. Then he smiles.

"*Sand County Almanac*, hm? That's like the Gospel in these parts," he says with a laugh.

"I read it in school."

"Same," the keeper says. "*Some day, perhaps in the very process of our benefactions, perhaps in the fullness of geologic time, the last crane will trumpet his farewell and spiral skyward from the great marsh.*"

"*And then,*" the visitor picks up the recitation, "*a silence never to be broken, unless perchance in some far pasture of the Milky Way.*"

The keeper's deep-set eyes twinkle. "You got it. Chapter and verse."

Keys jingle. He steps forward, then back as the gate swings open.

"Ben Caso," he introduces himself, just as the visitor's eyes fall on the black nametag with white lettering on his breast pocket. "Didn't catch yours."

The visitor supplies it. Caso closes the gate, turns the key in the lock. "Been on the road long?"

"Since morning."

"Rain any?"

"Not so far."

"One's brewing," Caso says. "Big one from the look of it."

The visitor glances at the sky, where darkness pools like ink. Caso stands, unperturbed. Raises his hat as if to don it, but instead loops the rawhide cord around his throat and lets the hat hang down his back.

"You'll want to see them, then."

"Them?"

"Why you're here, right?" Caso says.

He jiggles the gate, nods. Then he starts up the cedar trail toward the welcome center.

The visitor tucks the book close to his ribs and follows. Caso toddles upward, spraddle-legged, sailor aboard a bucking ship. The smell of cedar freshens with each step. The sky lowers, clouds settling in to stay. The welcome center emerges from its cover, hints of metal and glass spraying what's left of the sunlight. *Foundation* is set in silver letters above the front door. The visitor fumbles his book, tries to match his guide's pace. Reassesses the keeper's age once again, factoring out the speckled face and hands that fooled him at first.

Wind whistles as they reach the sheltered porch. Gazing upward, the visitor realizes the steel archway is a pair of great wings, folded above like hands clasped. Caso nudges another key into the front door, pulls it open for his guest to enter.

"Careful," he says.

The foyer is dark. Shadowed shapes gradually announce their purpose: reception desk, register, upright display rack with rows of identical brochures like leaves of the world's most unoriginal orchard. A gift shop, dimly visible through a glass partition. It's where Caso's headed, another key flashing in his hand. He pushes through the glass door, leads the visitor inside.

They thread between shelves. Most stand empty, except a few at the very top that dangle with ludicrous shapes: floppy-limbed, curved necks and flipper feet. Gray as feather dusters, not with age but stitched that way. Only the gleaming eyes break the monotone, yellow as a snake's, with round black pupils contracted to a pinpoint. Glass, of course. If the eyes in some paintings seem to follow you, the eyes of these mannikins seem to bore into the visitor's forehead. It's a relief to reach the rear door and exit with Caso in the lead.

They stand at the brink of a mist-wrapped precipice. Trees crown the dense white, trunks shrouded. He can't tell sky from ground, can't see where the clouds overhead meet the exhalation from below. Caso lets his keys swing.

"Watch your step," he says.

The keeper sets feet into the mist; his legs vanish to mid-thigh. The visitor follows, finds the path. Cedar, again. Its fragrance diffuses through the mist. He watches Caso reach out, copies the man's movement until his hand closes on a stout guide rope, slick with condensation. Their path charted, they start down.

The mist rises like a deepening river. Not long before it spills over his head, sealing his vision in white. He can hear Caso just ahead, boots squeaking against cedar, but he can see no more than an agitation in the body of the mist as the keeper stirs it with his own. Strange calls surround him, something he now thinks might come from the throats of monkeys, a chittering and gurgling that filters from everywhere and nowhere. The smell he first noticed about the place ripens the deeper they go, becoming as rank as animal musk, vegetable rot. Carried by the mist, or maybe what it's made of. There are two solid things in the world: the trail and the guide rope. Everything else is swimming, curling white.

And then it ends. Like stepping through shower steam, they drop below the filigree of mist into a hollow where brackish water laps a marshy shore. The cedar trail gives way to a brief gangplank; Caso clomps onto the boards and stops just shy of the terminus, hand on the final guidepost. The visitor takes a step past him, hears the same sudden scream he did above, as if in outpacing the keeper he's violated some ancient law of this place. Then the sound dies into clucks and gabbles, and he sees them.

He has been to the zoo once in his life, many years ago. Remembers its austere architecture, paved trails laid out to steer guests past stone-walled paddocks cradling imitation deserts and jungles. Only the very youngest children scampered ahead as if they might make a discovery the designers of the place had not seen fit to disclose. Though a child himself at the time, he walked. Sun-sprawled lions pillowed against each other's flanks, a lone black rhino jogged restlessly and tossed hay-mixed dust with its horn. The voices of local news anchors, unlocked by a plastic keycard, spoke a litany of habitat loss, captive breeding, illegal trade in body parts and folk magic. He ended that visit as jaded as his invisible hosts, feeling less that he had experienced the zoo than that he had been exhibited in it.

Not so here. Beyond the boardwalk there is no order, no guiding hand, only the logic of life grown accustomed to having its way. Seeing the denizens of this place at last, he can't say when they emerged, or if they did—whether they were here all along, hidden by dappled shade and bamboo screens. Regal curiosities, they stalk the shoreline with heads bobbing on sinuous necks, wings snapping open like fans flourished by Japanese dancers. Their feathers are a riot of colors: brick skullcaps and slate shoulders, dandelion crowns set above cherry-blossom cheeks, russet napes shading to creamy throats. A low murmuring runs through the whole, sound of air being drunk or whispered rumors traded from throat to throat. Their yellow eyes, glass-copied for the puppets above, are quick and reptilian. The eyes of dinosaurs, not birds.

What strikes him most is the strangeness of their gait: at once cautious and dreamlike, as if they have paced this lake for millennia yet don't trust their splayed feet to find safe landing on the soft, marshy turf. Wraiths, he thinks, or effigies. Specters of an antediluvian era, born aloft by the tide that has whelmed everything else.

Caso comes up beside him. "Something, aren't they?"

"They're real?" All he can think to say.

"Of course."

"How many?"

"I don't keep count," Caso says. "Wouldn't be much point. You see that one there?" He indicates a giant gray bird, head-feathers so red its skull seems flayed, beak plunging in and out of the mire with a motion rapid as a woodpecker's. "Largest species on Earth. Indian subcontinent. Now the pride and joy of the great state of Wisconsin."

The visitor draws a breath, fetid with swamp air. He feels lightheaded, unmoored. Wishes he could take another step beyond the gangplank, join these creatures of the marsh. Convince himself they're truly what their keeper says, not phantoms conjured of shadow and mist.

"Beautiful," he says, unsure it's the word he wants.

Caso notices, smiles. "Wild as the day they arrived. I'd keep my distance."

The visitor retreats. Was he about to take that one more step, or did Caso merely fear he might?

"How long have they been here?" he asks.

"Since the start of it," Caso says. "Some have traveled thousands of miles to reach this spot. Siberia, Mongolia, Nigeria. Moving from marsh to marsh, settling down for a time only to be off at a signal no one could hear but them. They followed the river, the air currents, the shape of their own shadows on the ground. Counted the waves beneath their wings as they sailed across the sea. Truth is, we still don't understand the half of it: what sustained them through the miles, what thought or whim kept them on course. We only know they beat the odds, and here they are."

"A miracle," the visitor says.

Caso smiles. "What they were up against, sure."

The two men watch the great birds preen, strut. The long-promised rain falls steadily, unimpeded by trees or the mantle of mist above their heads. It shines on feathered backs, turns curved beaks slick as ivory. The visitor can't say when it began.

"Do they ever leave?" he asks.

"Oh, no," the keeper says. "Not anymore. It's not safe."

"And you…"

"I've been here awhile," the keeper says. "Which reminds me."

He reaches for his belt. Not the keys this time: something else. Holds it out as if it's an offering.

"I'm sorry, son," Caso says, and sounds it. "This isn't for you."

The visitor focuses on the shining object in Caso's outstretched hand. Doesn't know what to call it, but he has no doubt of its potency. If it were as ordinary as a pistol, he might take his chances, flourish the tattered book as a shield to catch the bullet. He's heard of such stunts, somewhere. A comic book about the presidents—Roosevelt, was it, or perhaps Wilson? It's been so long since any of that mattered. But this sleek shape in the keeper's spotted hand—who knows what it might do? Freeze him, atomize him. Not worth the risk to find out.

"Please," he says. "I have nowhere to go."

"No, that's true," the keeper reflects. As if seeing it for the first time. "This here's the end of the line."

"I don't need much," the visitor says. "They won't mind me."

"You'd be surprised," Caso says. "Something that deep in the blood, they don't forget. Migratory. They used to travel the world, and now this is all that's left." He shakes his head. "I can't help you, son. I'm their keeper. Not yours."

He gestures with the device, and the visitor raises his hands. Caso follows him to the trail. At the point where the curtain of mist is about to close around them, the visitor looks back, sees the birds pacing the marsh as if nothing has changed. As if nothing ever has, or could. They clack and gibber, rise on stilt-legs to rattle their wings in furious revolt against fate, only to shrink back into somnolence. He can't understand how these creatures earned their reprieve, why they alone should find favor in the keeper's eyes.

At the front gate, he asks. "Why them?"

Caso chews an end of his mustache, pondering. He draws a deep sigh and speaks.

"I was given a job to do," he says. "I didn't ask for it. Didn't even want it, you might say. It was forty years ago that the true Keepers of this place came, and I was not a young man then. The life I lived before has blurred like an image seen through a rainstorm, but I remember with crystal clarity the day they arrived. That first, mad rush on the refuge: my fellow beings—men, women, and children—dying against the fence as the tool I'd been taught to use hummed in my hand. I was scared, as scared as the masses who fell before the gate. I didn't know any better than they did why I was on this side and they were on that. Didn't know what would happen if I abjured the work I'd been assigned to do."

He pauses, eyes distant. From the visitor's angle, the silver wings of the welcome center seem to cup the old man like the calyx of a strange flower.

"But it came to me in time, the good of it," Caso says. "With each passing year, fewer and fewer nomads approached my gate. All of them asking the same impossible thing: shelter from the storms, safety in a land where none was to be found. You think I, who was once one of your kind, could remain untouched by their simple appeals? You think my heart never misgave me in all that time? Yet not once have I failed at my post. Not once have I let one enter."

"Until today."

"Strange, isn't it?" Caso says with a smile. "Must be getting sentimental in my old age. Or maybe…"

The visitor waits, eyes pinched against the driving rain. Sees that, though it falls on the keeper's head, no drops glisten there.

"Maybe," Caso says, "I knew that once you were gone, there'd never be another."

He waves the hand that holds the weapon. The visitor steps through the gate, sets his bare feet on the mud-glutted hillside. Hears the lock click and the keys return to their resting place. He takes one last look at Caso, then folds the book and passes it through the fence, their fingers touching briefly around the wire. The keeper bows his head as if in benediction, lets the pages fall open. Smiles and utters the words he was given to speak so many years ago by beings infinitely wiser than he.

"*The swans will circle skyward in snowy dignity,*" he says.

"*And the cranes will blow their trumpets in farewell,*" the stranger responds, before making his way down the hill into the gray veil of rain.

Joshua David Bellin has been writing novels since he was eight years old (though the first few were admittedly very short). A college teacher by day, Josh has published numerous works of science fiction and fantasy, including the Survival Colony novels, the four-part Ecosystem Cycle, and the deep-space adventure Freefall. His latest work, the post-apocalyptic thriller Daughter of Dust, appeared in June 2020. In his spare time, he likes to read, draw, watch movies, and spend time in Nature with his kids. Oh, yeah, and he likes monsters. Really scary monsters.

There Were Giants on the Earth in Those Days

By Marshall J. Moore

The three sat and watched the waters rise.

The distant waves were still no more than a hint of white foam on the horizon. The trio watched them come from the highest ground they could find. It would be some time before the waters took them.

But not forever.

"We should have gone," said Unicorn. His hoof pawed restlessly against the muddy earth.

"Pardon?" asked Dragon. She perched delicately atop a large boulder, her wings neatly folded and her tail wrapped about her legs. Like cats, dragons enjoyed being tall.

"We should have gone," Unicorn repeated. His sidelong glance at her was accusing. "*You* still could. You can *fly*."

Dragon looked down mildly at Unicorn. The rains had plastered his lustrous mane against his silver neck, making him the most disheveled of the trio.

"No," Dragon said. "I couldn't. They're miles and miles away by now. And besides, what would I do if I *could* find them? The old man wouldn't take kindly to my devouring his flock."

"He's got a whole flock of sheep?" Giant asked. Until now his eyes had been fixed on the distant wave, but this was new information. "I thought it was only two of each."

"That was the command," Dragon answered. "I was speaking metaphorically. The whole Ark's his flock. His charges, if you like."

"Oh." Giant kicked meditatively at the mud. Soon it wouldn't even *be* mud, just the bottom of the sea.

"The old man said two of each kind," Dragon continued. "One male, one female. I suppose He'll hold off on the genetic defects for a generation or two."

"I should *hope* so," Unicorn said with a horsey *harrumph*. "Wouldn't do to spare His favorites, only for the species to die out in a few generations by becoming a bunch of inbred morons."

"What d'you mean?" Giant asked.

"Inbred," Dragon answered. "You know how He set an imposition against wedding brother to sister and so forth?"

Giant shrugged. He had forgotten much of what He had commanded since the days of Giant's youth. And it was the way of the young to disregard their parents.

Even the children of angels were no exception.

"Well," Dragon continued, "He forbade it. They start to get all funny if the family tree doesn't fork after a few generations."

"Funny how?"

"Weak bones," Dragon said, shifting restlessly as rain slid down her scales. "Bad eyes, webbed feet. That sort of thing."

"Webbed feet might not be so bad," Unicorn said, looking back at the dim horizon. The waves had grown higher. The white crest of foam now lay between the pale sky and a dark line of water.

"Did He really say that would happen?" Giant asked, looking up at the Dragon. "With the inbreeding? I knew a family down there—"

He pointed a huge finger at the valley below them, where the floodwaters had already begun to rise.

"—and they had been marrying brother to sister for three generations. Perfectly lovely people."

Dragon shrugged. "I expect they haven't been doing it long enough for it to have too much of an effect. These things take time. The Earth's only, what? Sixteen hundred years old?"

"Sixteen hundred fifty-six," Unicorn supplied. He had always been good with numbers.

"There you have it," Dragon said, folding her wings in a satisfied sort of way. "They'll need new blood in the fold every few generations."

"Assuming they make it," Unicorn snorted. "One six-hundred-year-old man and his immediate family, none with prior sailing experience, aboard a boat without rudder, oars, or sails?"

"He has ordained their survival," Dragon said. "He would not have commanded the Ark be built otherwise."

"Sure," Unicorn said, glancing skyward as the rains continued to fall. "But it wouldn't be the first time He's changed His mind. I hope the old man makes it, I really do."

"And if he doesn't?" Giant asked.

Unicorn let out a whinnying laugh. "Then blessed are the fishes, for they shall inherit the Earth."

Giant's huge brow furrowed. "Seems unfair."

"It's worse than unfair," Unicorn snapped. "It's *arbitrary*. Why weren't we allowed onboard? Pigs, goats, cows, but no unicorns?"

"Those are all livestock," Dragon pointed out.

"Not *all*," Unicorn snorted. "I saw the old man carry a pair of sloths onboard, still hanging from a branch. They aren't livestock. They're hardly even animals."

"What would you say they are, then?" Giant asked.

"Fungi," Unicorn answered promptly. "My point is, why bring some aboard and not others? We're not the only ones being left out, you know. I saw Manticore trying to hide in the forest while I was coming up here."

As one, they looked down at the valley. The waters had not quite risen above the tree line, but it was only a matter of time.

"Poor fellow," Giant said quietly.

"Just my point," Unicorn said, tossing his wet gray mane from his eyes. "He's doomed. So are we. But why? What did we do to deserve this?"

"I don't think it's a matter of what we did," Dragon said. She craned her long neck towards the valley, where the flotsam and ruin of what had once been a village churned in the floodwaters. "They called this down upon themselves. Upon us all. Remember how it was in the Garden?"

Unicorn and Giant grew still. The Garden was been long, long ago, but they remembered. Paradise was not easily forgotten.

"Lion laying down with lamb," Dragon said wistfully. "Man and woman, friend to all. Until…"

She didn't need to say it. They remembered the Fall. At the edge of the Flood, it was better not to dwell on such bitter memories.

"That's why," Dragon said, turning her scaly head to look down at the ruined village. "The world was good, and then they corrupted it. So, He's going to wipe them out and try again."

"But he *isn't* wiping them all out!" Unicorn whinnied, stabbing his great horn at the sky. "The old man and his boat, and all the beasts that went with him. Why let them survive if the entire point was to end Creation?"

"I don't think He wants to destroy the world," Dragon said. "Just start it over again. A clean start for the old man and his lot to get right what these ones got wrong."

"Why not us, though?" Unicorn asked. His anger was spent. A single tear glistened in his dark eye. Below, the floodwaters had reached the tree line. "If He means to remake Creation, why can't we be a part of it? Why can't we be saved?"

All three were silent for a long time.

"I think," Dragon said, very slowly, "because He needs us this way."

"Drowned?"

"No," she said, shaking her head. "They're made in His image, right? Man and woman."

Unicorn nodded.

"And," she continued, "this world's to be given over to their dominion, yes?"

"Right," Giant said. "Dominion over fish, and birds, and cattle."

"All the Earth," Unicorn murmured, looking down as the earth below rapidly turned to sea. "And every creeping thing on it."

"Precisely," Dragon nodded. "To mankind dominion is given. And who ever heard of man having dominion over a Unicorn?"

Unicorn's ears swiveled towards her, and he perked up, ever so slightly.

"Or a Dragon," Giant added.

"Or *you*," Unicorn said, nuzzling his shining head against Giant's side. "So. We couldn't go on the Ark because we wouldn't submit?"

"I think so," Dragon nodded. "But not only that."

"What do you mean?" Giant asked.

"The world to come will be the world of Man," she said. "That world will have no room for us. But there *will* be a need for the memory of us."

"I don't understand."

"We can't live in their new world," she said. "We've no place there. But our stories do. Long after the floodwaters fade, mankind will still remember a time when we three walked the Earth, before they had dominion."

"The old man," Giant said, realization dawning on his broad, honest face. "All of them on the Ark. They'll remember us. Tell stories about us."

"Yes," Dragon nodded. "A reminder that once we were here. That part of Creation remains forever beyond their grasp."

"That doesn't sound so bad," Unicorn whinnied. "They'll say, 'and there were unicorns on the Earth in those days,' or something like that."

"Yes." Dragon smiled with her eyes, as dragons do. "Something like that."

"It will be a sadder world," Giant reflected, "without dragons and unicorns."

"A lesser world," Dragon agreed. "But a world that will still be here when we have gone."

But Giant was not listening. Frowning, he shaded his brow and peered down their hill, which had become an island.

He took off, bounding down the muddy slope on his massive legs. Unicorn whinnied in surprise. Dragon spread her wings, preparing to chase after her friend. If all things were ending, at least they would be together for it.

But Giant had already reached the waters. Splashing mightily, he waded out until he was waist deep. He scooped a piece of flotsam into his great arms, then turned and hurried back up the hill.

"Careful," he panted to the others. "She's pretty banged up."

In his arms lay a girl, perhaps nine or ten years old. Her eyes were closed, and blood flowed freely from a gash on her brow.

Giant set her gently on the muddy earth. The girl's chest still rose and fell, but slowly. The wound on her head looked deep.

"Let me," Unicorn said, gently shouldering Giant aside. He laid his great head by the girl's, his snout resting on her forehead in a horsey kiss.

The single tear in Unicorn's eye splashed onto the girl's forehead. The bleeding slowed, then stopped. The gash closed over, leaving only unblemished skin.

"No Unicorn will ever do that for a human again," Giant murmured, and they knew it was true.

The girl coughed and sat up, spitting out rainwater. When she looked up at them her gaze was curious but unafraid.

"Am I dead?" she asked.

"No," Dragon shook her head. "Not yet."

The girl frowned, considering. "Are you going to eat me?"

"No." Dragon smiled, amused.

Standing, the girl looked down at what had once been her valley home. Now only the floodwaters remained, the tide lapping at her bare toes.

Giant reached down and gently but firmly pulled her away from the dwindling shore.

"You don't have a boat," she observed. Giant shook his head.

"There was an old man," he told her. "He had a boat. An Ark."

"I remember." She stared at the murky brown water. "Everyone said he was mad to build a ship here, a hundred miles from the sea." Raindrops slid down her cheeks. "I guess they were wrong."

She looked up at Giant. "Why, then?"

"Why what?"

"Why pull me from the water?" She waved a hand, encompassing the world that was becoming more oceanic by the minute. "You can't save me."

Giant pondered this for so long that the tide began to lick at their feet again.

"No," he said at last. "But that doesn't mean I shouldn't try."

She looked up at him with dark violet eyes. Giant wondered if any of the people in the world to come would have eyes that color.

He hoped so. They were very pretty eyes.

"Thank you," she said at last, and glanced at the dirty water swirling around their feet. "The tide's coming."

"The tide is coming for all of us," Giant said, and together they walked back up the hill.

There was no more land in sight, only gray sky and grim waves. Water trickled around Unicorn's hooves.

The girl rested a hand against Unicorn's neck. Beneath her touch the great horse was trembling, his whole beautiful silver body shaking with fear. He leaned into her touch, pressing his great neck against her. Giant stroked his flank, whispering soothing nothings into his friend's ear.

Dragon alighted from her place atop the rock, landing gracefully behind them. She stood tall, stretching wide her magnificent wings. The sun sparkled through the membranes as she wrapped her wings around and above her friends, sheltering them from the rain. She lay her great scaly head on the Giant's shoulder, and he ran his free hand down the ridges of her brow.

They stood together and watched the waves rise.

Marshall J. Moore is a writer, filmmaker, and martial artist who was born and raised on Kwajalein, a tiny Pacific island. He has traveled to over twenty countries, once sold a thousand dollars' worth of teapots to Jackie Chan, and on one occasion was tracked down by a bounty hunter for owing $300 in overdue fees to the Los Angeles Public Library.

STAR CHILD

By Elana Gomel

The burning stench of sunlight. The wet aroma of stone. The smell of darkness: soft, milky, enveloping.

Irresistible.

Estrella heard it on the radio while sitting in the traffic jam on Highway 101. Her phone just died, and she was reduced to listening to NPR, yawning at the foggy sunset and trying to calculate how long it would take till she was back home with a functioning charger. Traffic in the Silicon Valley was becoming unendurable.

Caught in her worn-out inner dialogue *(Move? Where? How? Leave the startup? No way!)*, she missed the beginning of the segment and was caught off-guard by the words "…mass grave" and "Santa Cruz." But before she could process how these two concepts could coexist in a single sentence, the announcer moved on to the new wildfires in Sonoma.

The highway was a frozen river of cars standing bumper to bumper and by the time Estrella pulled into her driveway, it was dark outside. She sneezed at the acrid tang of smoke in the mild spring air. It was getting worse—or else her sense of smell was becoming keener.

Penelope, her cat, greeted her with a discreet *miaow*. The fluffy white-eyed Siamese had the manners of a Victorian duchess. Estrella, daughter of Catalan immigrants, often felt she did not measure up to her cat—or her parents.

She grabbed the charger and her phone lit up with messages and updates. But she could not see anything that justified her morbid assumption that a serial killer's dumping ground was discovered in Santa Cruz where she had visited last weekend with her (now former) boyfriend, Jay.

She found the item while filling Penelope's bowl and when she did, she chuckled at her own wild imagination. The "mass grave" in question was that of prairie dogs. Apparently, a large burrow was discovered near Santa Cruz, filled with furry bodies. The authorities were not sure what killed them.

The smoke from the wildfires was so pungent it found its way into her air-conditioned kitchen and borne with its bitter smell was...a noise? Estrella frowned. It seemed just below the threshold of audibility, like the surf of a distant sea.

Microwaving her paella, her parents had instilled in her the love of good food, Estrella responded to a couple of emails, deleted Jay's latest text, and petted Penelope who finally deigned to repose in her lap. She was about to work on the spreadsheet for their latest offer when she saw another news alert. She blinked and read it twice to be sure. And then she texted her friend Maddy: "seen that?" with a link.

Maddy called immediately, which was unusual. As the host of a podcast, she kept her mellifluous voice for her listeners and communicated with her friends mostly with emojis.

"I'm so doing an episode!" she announced with no preamble. "Can I pick your brain?"

"Me?" Estrella bit into a piece of lamb sausage. "I am a computational biologist, not a criminologist."

Maddy's modestly popular pod was part of the crop of true-crime podcasts that have swamped the web recently. Estrella sometimes wondered if it was possible to predict the rise and fall of pod genres by using the same software that she was using for living systems.

"But you know animals and shit. And here is the angle. They found mice in the grave."

"Yuck! I am eating, just so you know."

"Seriously. They found the bodies of the family in a shallow grave on the property. But there was another excavation next to it and there was like a bunch of dead mice inside."

"Hmm," Estrella looked at the story on her phone. "They say nothing about it here."

"I have my sources. I'm actually thinking about driving there."

"But it's in Colorado!"

"So?"

Estrella rolled her eyes. She and Maddy had been friends since high school, drawn together by their difference rather than similarity—the geeky Estrella and the sparkling Maddy. Estrella was studious and deliberate; Maddy spontaneous and impulsive. Estrella was an only child; Maddy had a houseful of siblings and cousins. Maddy dated jocks; Estrella dated nobody. But they had remained friends for fifteen years and since Estrella's parents moved back to Barcelona, Maddy had been her main support system.

"I need to get a leg up on this," Maddy continued. "Competition, you know?"

Estrella knew. Competition was fierce and unrelenting everywhere. Too many bodies, jostling for vanishing space.

Darkness and the disdainful smell of cold stone, solid and enduring while my flesh is quivering, falling apart as it rubs itself against the unyielding outcroppings and hard granite spurs. The voice is calling, a single undulating note, rising and falling, irresistible and meaningless. There are no words. Words have not been invented yet.

Estrella was yanked out of her dream like a fish out of water, impaled on the hook of terror. She sat up in bed, dripping sweat.

She had always been an avid dreamer, looking forward to her nightly immersions in a river of vivid images that carried her away from her rational, calculated, well-planned life. She seldom dreamed in stories. There was no sequence of events: just a wash of bright snapshots, some beautiful, some absurd, some frightening. She embraced them all, passively drifting on the tide of memories and imaginations away from the unrelenting churn of her waking brain.

But she had never dreamed of darkness before.

Darkness and smells. The slimy reek of the underground felt so real that she turned on the light and walked around her house, checking the ventilation ducts. Everything was fine.

She went back to bed but could not sleep. Penelope, offended, curled up in her basket and refused to come to bed, and Estrella was secretly glad. She loved her cat but somehow her sense of smell seemed to have become abnormally keen, and she could do without the hot stink of animal fur. And there was a strange buzz in her ears. She suddenly realized she was humming to drown it out:

Asomando a la noche
en la terraza
de un rascacielos altísimo y amargo
pude tocar la bóveda nocturna...

Estrella's Spanish was poor, her Catalan non-existent. The only Spanish that flowed smoothly in her mind was Pablo Neruda's "Oda a una estrella"—"Ode to a Star"—which her mother had taught her when she complained about her un-American name.

She picked up the phone. It was mid-morning in Barcelona.

Her mother Alba answered. She was sitting in a coffee-shop and behind her, Estrella could see a crush of pedestrians. She recognized the place: La Rambla, the wide stall-lined boulevard at the heart of Barcelona. She loved the city, but she had never felt at home there. As a teenager, she had desperately wanted to fit in with her suburban American crowd. Her parents, comfortable with their foreign status, were oblivious to her embarrassment at their exotic ways. And now they had moved back to Barcelona, and she felt it was a rejection of their American life and of her, its product.

She addressed her mother in English.

"How is it going, Mum?"

Alba did not smile. She was a beautiful woman with a kind of intense smoldering looks that Estrella associated, obscurely, with black-and-white pictures of the Spanish civil war.

"People are coming to the city," she said, gesturing with her coffee cup at what appeared to be the unending flow of closely pressed bodies through La Rambla.

"They always have."

"Not like this. They put a barrier around La Sagrada Familia. To keep crowds away."

The Basilica de La Sagrada Familia. Antonio Gaudi's masterpiece of organic, flowing architecture: a forest of stone trunks, marble stems and glass flowers. It was only recently finished after almost a century of painstaking manual construction. Estrella had been overwhelmed by its beauty when she saw it for the first time. It felt as if she were lost in an entire new world—a human-made planet.

"Thinking of coming home?"

"This is home," Alba responded curtly.

Maddy called when Estrella was in a meeting, another one where her small team tried to iron out the persistent kinks in her algorithm. They dubbed it "The Extinction Clock" but it was just a catchy press-release name. What it was actually supposed to do was to identify wild species most likely to go extinct within a set period of time. Since extinction was everywhere in the Anthropocene, it was important for conservationists, governments, and NGOs to set their priorities and to decide what species to try to preserve—or not. So far, the algorithm had produced some successes, including tagging desert mallow, a common Californian plant, as likely to disappear within ten years and take the dependent population of carpenter bees with it. But other results were whacky, when, for example, it insisted that the house rat, *Rattus rattus*, was about to go extinct in a year, prompting Aditya, the office clown, to mutter, if only.

The meeting was winding down, Estrella's coffee cup was empty, so she took her phone outside.

"What's up?"

Maddy's voice was uncharacteristically tense.

"I'm in Colorado. Manitou Springs."

"Already? Charming the detectives on the case, no doubt."

"There is no case."

"What? Why not?"

"It's been closed."

"How? A mass murder? The whole family: mum, dad, four kids. So, was it the dad? One of those family annihilators?"

Estrella had picked some true-crime jargon from Maddy's podcast.

"No. No signs of violence on any of the bodies. No bullets, stab wounds, nothing. They are waiting for toxicology reports, but no poison or even prescription pills were found in the house."

"Natural death?"

"The bodies were buried."

Estrella felt a slow chill trickle down her spine.

"Buried by who?"

"Unclear but probably the father. They found a shovel with his fingerprints, dirt under his nails."

"Wait! He dug a grave?"

"And then they just lay down there, and he pulled enough soil on top, so they would be covered, sort of…and then they just waited. The medical examiner is not sure whether they died of suffocation or just died. This is some crazy shit, Esti!"

When she came back home, Penelope was gone.

Estrella spent a fruitless hour searching the house and the postal stamp-sized front yard because she refused to believe what was happening. Penelope was a housecat. She never ventured out, let alone departed for destinations unknown.

Finally, she gave up and slumped against the stunted tree in the yard, staring at the lurid inflammation of the evening sky—the loud purple and the diseased orange of the smoke-painted sunset. The bitter smell of burning wormed its way into her sinuses and she went back in, glancing over her shoulder at the silvery evening star.

…me apoderé de una celeste estrella

…I seized a sky-blue star

Neruda's beautiful poem, the origin of her name. So why did she feel as if another star was slowly unfolding somewhere under her feet, a velvety black star, voluptuous meaty petals, whispering to her…saying what? That she was lonely? That she had always been lonely? Her parents abandoning her; Jay suggesting they scale back their relationship; her single friend and now even her cat had run away! The sense of loneliness pulled at her like the void of outer space threatening to disperse her into a vortex of dust. She hugged herself in the unlit bedroom, smelling the residual warmth of her lost cat and longing for multiple arms around her, the press of anonymous bodies, the shelter of the dark.

The amniotic sweetness of the cave; the softness of skin and hair around me; the slow beat of multiple voices, exhaling and inhaling together.

The call of the dark star.

Estrella huddled under the blanket, trying to shake off the residue of the nightmare.

The strangest part of it was a hint of synesthesia. Not only did she smell the pungent stink reminiscent of a primate enclosure, but she actually heard it as a sound. Estrella had never had synesthesia in her life, though she knew it was not uncommon. Seeing sounds as colors—many celebrated musicians and writers had this condition. But a dream synesthesia? What was that all about?

To hear a smell; to see dark petals; black on black.

Aditya came over to her desk—they did not have cubicles in the open-plan office space—and offered to buy her coffee. She knew it was serious if he wanted to talk to her alone.

Their genius programmer from Eastern Punjab looked like she felt—with shadows under his eyes and his lips chapped and pale. He played with his cup.

"The algorithm is perfect," he said with no preamble. "No bugs."

"But it gives us those crazy results. Rats going extinct? Somebody said that after the nuclear winter, rats and cockroaches would inherit the Earth. And climate change is a slow process. Rats will adapt."

He shook his head.

"It's not just rats. I ran it on my own, just to try the latest debugging protocol. Here is the list."

He showed her a file on his tablet. Estrella scanned the long column.

"*Cynomys ludovicianus? Monomorium minimum?* What the fuck? These are prairie dogs and little black ants. Social species, not listed on any endangered list, common as hell!"

"Keep reading."

Her eyes stumbled over the last entry. She read it again. Pushed the tablet back toward Aditya. "No," she said.

"The most numerous social species of them all."

Maddy did not answer her phone. She hadn't posted a new episode of her pod. The Colorado case disappeared from the headlines.

There were enough other cases to fill them. Not just families, but entire communities. A village in Bangladesh. A small town in Iowa. A new housing development in Brighton.

Bodies found in shallow graves, pressed together as close as sardines in a tin, arms intertwined, heads resting on each other's shoulders, children and babies tucked between their parents, nesting in the dark. No violence. No blood or bullet wounds. No poison.

The scientific consensus, such as it was, consisted of vague pronouncements about "mass psychosis" or "the pressures of modern life." The Internet was exploding with conspiracy theories. Some of them sounded almost plausible.

Estrella had given her employees a week off. Nobody objected; Aditya looked relieved.

When she finally forced herself outside and stepped out into the brash sunlight, she shivered, exposed and feverish. For a change, the smoke of the wildfires was blown away by a brisk wind, and the crystalline Californian sky was radiant with blue and gold. Estrella did not like it. It felt as if her skin was being burned off, layer by thin layer.

She walked to her Toyota when her neighbor from the townhouse next door rushed across the street. Estrella did not remember her name, but she was happy to see another human being in the threatening emptiness of the suburb.

"Is your cat home?" the woman looked distraught; her short gray hair uncombed.

"My cat? No, Penelope ran away. I was just about to print some flyers."

"My Stripy is missing. All the cats on the street are gone. They say the city council is sending unmarked trucks to abduct pets. To conduct experiments."

The ordinariness of her voice woke Estrella to what was happening. *Everyday insanity.*

"I'm sure the cats will be back," she said and edged around the woman toward the car. As she pulled out, she thought with resignation that at least Penelope would not be alone. Cats are not social animals, but they must have borrowed some gregariousness from their primate masters. Or else they had just followed their natural prey, rats and mice, as they burrowed underground, spellbound by the call of the black star.

She decided to drive to Maddy's place in Tracy, more out of the need to do something than out of the hope to find her friend at home. Maddy's Mazda was in the driveway of her home, which was bigger than Estrella's and situated on its own largish property. Tracy's prices were lower than those of Sunnyvale, and being an independent pod-caster and editor, Maddy did not need to commute. Estrella used to envy her, now she was trying to decide whether Maddy's relative isola-tion would protect her or exacerbate the danger.

She called again. The ringtone echoed back from inside the house. Estrella pushed the front door and found it unlocked.

Inside, the house was totally dark. All the blinds were down and Maddy must have fixed heavy curtains to the windows like the blackout of World War II. Estrella breathed in the velvety darkness; it smelled of raw sewage and human sweat. A faint sound echoed just on the verge of audibility: a long, drawn-out, wordless note, both a lullaby and a mating call. She knew she was smelling rather than hearing it. Her syn-esthesia had breached the boundaries of sleep.

"Maddy!" she called while navigating the pitch-black rooms with no collision. *Am I like a bat now? No, I just know where she is. Where any human body is.*

The bedroom stank. Estrella tried to convince herself she was dis-gusted but the warm organic smell was intoxicating. She stumbled in the dark and almost fell over when she collided with a body on the floor. She cried out, horrified of finding a corpse, but the body moved.

Warm fingers slithered down her arm, twined with hers.

"Maddy! Please, come out. Come with me."

"To the grave? You know they are digging outside."

"No, no! Of course not! I'll take you home…"

"And then what?"

Estrella was silent.

"You are a scientist," Maddy continued in a feverish whisper as if she was afraid of being overheard. "Is it a disease? Did I get the bug from the Colorado stiffs?"

"No," Estrella whispered back. "Not a bug."

"Then what?"

Estrella lowered herself onto something soft—a blanket?—by Maddy's side. She still could not see anything. But the closed-in room roiled with organic odors. The sour smell of fear. The harsh stench of loneliness. Pheromones. Speaking to her. She had to raise her voice to override the susurrus in her ears.

"Have you ever heard of *Homo naledi?*"

"Sounds like a curse-word in Klingon."

"It actually means 'star' in the Sotho language of South Africa. They were discovered in the Rising Star cave of that region. More than a thousand skeletons. All squeezed together in a small underground chamber where you couldn't get in without artificial light to navigate through narrow twisty passages. Somehow, they did."

"Torches?"

"They were not human. Hominins. Very small-brained. No fire, no tools. 330,000 years go. But they all went through this dark underground labyrinth to die together. Men, women, children."

"How did they die?"

"How did the family in Colorado die?"

Maddy was silent for a while, her fingers squeezing Estrella's hand so tight it was painful. But she did not want to pull back. Could not. She had not had any human touch in weeks.

It is unnatural. We are social animals. We need others to…live?

To die together.

"It's calling to me," Maddy whispered. "I don't know what it is. I started hearing it in Colorado. I thought I was going crazy. But it's not just me, is it?"

"No," Estrella whispered back. "It is the voice of extinction. The dark star. Our time is up."

She was driving into the orange flame of the sunset, weeping uncontrollably. The highway danced in front of her, dissolved into a mosaic of smudged light and shadow. She was sure she would hit somebody, but the highway was empty. The evening commute was missing. No more isolating themselves from the herd in metal boxes. No more social interactions filtered through the alienating screen of social media. No more careers, names, hobbies. Individuality, the transient quirk of evolution, was going, going, gone. Human animals, like their social cousins, rats, and cats, and ants, massing together in dark places: caves, basements, underground tunnels. Graves.

Estrella pulled off to the shoulder and picked up her phone. The network was down but she had saved the clip shown on CBS news and replayed it now, for the tenth time. The towering edifice of La Sagrada Familia against the empty sky. Its soaring stained-glass windows blacked out with crude paint and swatches of fabric. Its elaborate beaten-bronze doors were barricaded. One of the doors was breached when whatever remained of the Barcelona police force tried to get inside. Bodies were spilling onto the pavement. There were so many of them that they lay in untidy heaps like firewood. Gaudí's ethereal saints and angels stared down in horror at their creators reduced to animal anonymity. Just so much meat. Evolutionary garbage.

Estrella stared at the call log. Tens of calls placed to her parents before the signal disappeared. Not one call back. Had the dark star of extinction wiped out their individuality to such an extent that they no longer knew they had a daughter? Or maybe they simply did not care.

She did not remember how she had gotten out of Maddy's house. No, Maddy's lair. The warm animal that had tried to keep her in, to snuggle together in a heap, to listen to the voice of the star as they slowly starved or suffocated in their own stink. Had she pushed the animal away? Had she overpowered it?

Did I kill her?

So here she was. *Una celeste estrella.* The star of the sky, the star of poetry! What a joke!

Aditya's voice in her ears.

There have been five major mass extinction in Earth's history. We are creating the sixth. The previous ones had been attributed to all kinds of culprits: asteroids, diseases, climate change. But what if there is a self-correcting mechanism in ecosphere? When one species gets too big, too strong. Over-competing. Destroying its habitat.

Were *Homo naledi* too strong? No, how could that be? Small, small-brained, harmless.

But there were a whole bunch of other hominins running around at the same time. Including our own ancestors. Maybe the dark star decided to clear the stage a little. Maybe evolution does play favorites.

And now our time is up. Who is next? Rats? No, they go down with us.

She tried to remember the other species on Aditya's list but could not. The list was too long. How stupid not to save it! But what's the difference? Civilization is doomed. No signal, soon no electricity. La Sagrada Familia turned into a mass burial, a cave stuffed with corpses.

Alba's face suddenly floated before her, superimposed upon the gathering dark. Her mother had loved the great cathedral and the magnificent city where it was built. Built by hand, slowly and painstakingly: carved pediments and undulating columns; angels, saints and babies in the manger; stained-glass blazing with all the colors of the imagination. The beauty that nature could never have made.

Was it all bad?

No art, no cities.

I seized a sky-blue star.

Some species survived mass extinctions. *Homo naledi* did not. But other hominins did and eventually gave rise to the brash species Homo sapiens that painted the galloping horses in the Neolithic caves of Spain, and raised cathedrals, and wrote poetry, and reached for the stars.

I am a human being, not an animal huddling in the burrow with other animals.

We can still make it right.

Maybe.

My algorithm. What if I can modify it to show not only who the dark star calls but how it calls? And then we can mute it. Cross-species synesthesia must be very simple. Primitive. Archaic. But we have evolved since the Rising Star caves. Our complexity may be our salvation.

She had no idea how to do it, or whether it was doable, but it was a plan. A window into the future.

Estrella's nose was running, and she pulled the last tissue out of the glove compartment and cleaned her face the best she could. And then she drove toward the Silicon Valley where scattered lonely lights winked in the dark like stars in the sky.

Elana Gomel is an academic and a writer. She has published six non-fiction books and numerous articles on posthumanism, science fiction, Victorian literature and serial killers. Her fantasy, horror and science fiction stories appeared in Apex Magazine, New Horizons, Mythic, and many other magazines and were also featured in several award-winning anthologies, including Zion's Fiction, Apex Book of World Science Fiction, and People of the Book. She is the author of three novels: A Tale of Three Cities (2013), The Hungry Ones (2018) and The Cryptids (2019).

RED IS THE TASTE OF DEATH

by Rhonda Eikamp

Listen to the whistle of wind like sea currents. Listen to *my* whistle. I will tell you a story. We are what we are because of our decisions, yes, but there was one, a different one, who made a decision an eon ago that meant life instead of red death. If not for her, we would not be standing, here in the green paradise we preserve.

This is the story of the day.

The morning billionaire Weston C. Knight died, Cara pressed his hand hard and promised him she would take care of his family. She didn't cry. She wouldn't. As a nurse closed Knight's eyes and his round-the-clock physician—out of a job now—shut off the machines, Cara Chapman slipped away, out into the main part of the Dome, and gave herself a moment to grieve. Dawn light was painting the panels up there red. Red skies, red oceans. The world was falling apart, her worry was like nausea, and where was Wes? He should have been there. Head of it all from the moment his father's eyes closed, but his hyzepp from the Tampa Dome was delayed, or so the message said, and that was either deliberate or it wasn't.

Cara shifted now on the hard airdrome seat. Overhead speakers crackled. *Tampa hyzepp estimated arrival—ten minutes*. She wanted to see Wes again, desperately, and yet she didn't. Because he held the purse strings to the Pen now, because she dreaded—down at the bathypelagic level—what he was going to do.

Just like she'd dreaded telling Silber their benefactor had died, but after leaving Knight's side she'd suited up and swum out to the Pen.

The suits were magnificent, a second skin, everything money could buy, with the directivity sphere for the translation software built into the sleek helmets, yet they were still clunky to her. Cara wanted flippers, wanted to dance with her wards the bottlenose dolphins, with Silber who darted in from the dark water to meet her at the airlock. Wanted to leap and soar and slap a tail she didn't have. Impossible of course, but the longing was like a hole inside her, always growing larger, a deep part of her starving. She was not crazy, no matter what others might say. In all the chaos of a world dying, only this—the shifting water, systole and diastole, the elegance of the dolphins' gray bodies, was real. She'd tried to describe it to Wes once and never again, after the look he gave her.

Silber slid against her once, turned to ask.

[Eisen?]

Cara's helmet translated the interrogative whistle that named Silber's wife, but couldn't convey the worry in the dolphin's question. How still Silber held himself in the seawater. Scared to hear the worst.

"Eisen's okay. She's getting better." It was a lie she'd probably burn in sea hell for. She couldn't tell him. Not just yet.

Behind Silber other members of his pod streaked past, metallic darts, catching Cara's sonic reply with relief and slipping away into the green distance to give them some privacy.

Distance. It was the Pen that was the real miracle. Designed as a closed fish-cage system to protect the sea mammals from the dying ocean, except hundreds of times larger, a safe space carved out of what had once been the Big Bend coast of Florida that was now much further inland, with the Dome for the human caretakers floating atop it. A tin can, twenty miles in diameter, intake water piped from a hundred feet down and filtered for all it was worth, until there couldn't have been a pathogen or parasite left in it.

Couldn't. Cara bit her lip behind the helmet. A world, an ocean of time to save a sliver of life from the climate clock that was running out. Plenty of fish in this sea, but their efforts, Knight's billions, the best marine biologists—which included herself—wouldn't be enough. Cara knew it in her bones when she swam with her wards, spoke with them, and the dolphins did too. Several had told her so. It was as though they'd grown an extra organ that constantly murmured *Death looms.*

They *couldn't* had caught up with them only days before, the manatees first, then her beloved pod of bottlenose, the cetaceans Knight had considered to be his true family. One, then three, then ten falling ill. The brevetoxin, the red tide that was killing oceans everywhere, had infiltrated the Pen, in a literal sense, though they monitored everything—oxygenation and ph-levels, never noticing a change—and something inside Cara hadn't stopped trembling since.

Tampa hyzepp now docking, gate 2.

Once Silber had finished asking about his wife, they'd spoken of Wes. Silber was one of the dolphins to grasp the software's—probably clumsy—translations the best, but Cara wasn't sure how much he understood of human concepts such as ownership and inheritance.

"Knight's death won't affect our funding."

Wes would be deciding that, so it was another lie of sorts. Cara wondered if her body language, as they twisted in the slight current, revealed her fears to Silber.

"And we're going to get on top of the filtering problem."

Silber turned head-on to her, his sign for a frown, saying the literal translation into clicks was confusing. *Get on top of.* "I mean, solve. Even if it means building a new Pen." Billions of dollars. Wes's face breached in her mind and she shoved it down.

[Eisen with?]

"The pod will always be kept together. You know that. I wouldn't let it be otherwise." The third lie or a promise, she wasn't sure.

[Swim toward.] [Now.] *Let me visit her.*

"Eisen needs to stay in isolation a while." Cara wasn't about to let Silber see his beloved wife in the isolation pool, strung up in a hammock that kept her head above water while they gave her lipids. The worsening spasms meant Eisen couldn't surface on her own to breathe, while the brevetoxin ate away her neural system. She was getting worse by the day, no matter what they tried.

Cara had remembered a question she wanted to ask. "Tell me, Silber, why is she named Eisen?" Iron and silver, color names from the German scientists they'd first trained with, she'd once thought, but he'd recently suggested otherwise.

[She] [frequent] [refuse]. [Commands]. [Games]. *She's stubborn.*
"Ah."

[I] [love] [her].

She'd heard the complicated trill from pod members before. The thought that the word love translated one-to-one always thrilled her. They simply had the concept, always had, no metaphors, no beating about the bush or whatever the underwater equivalent might be.

Simpler than her complicated feelings for Wes. "What do you love about her?"

He arched his back in a smile. [She] [impel] [enjoy] [float]. *She makes me like floating.* No dolphin enjoyed floating. It was the cetacean equivalent of human boredom, all the trivial stupid things in life that can get you down, that you get through by having someone else to reach out to. *She makes life better*, would have been a more accurate translation.

"Wes will be here soon. He'll likely want to swim out and talk to you."

[Mate] [at present] [you, plural]? *Are the two of you lovers?*

And they were direct. Cara didn't know the answer herself anymore, only that the thought of seeing him again made her blood rush with joy, even if the occasion was sad.

"On again, off again." Silber spun to her, snout almost brushing her faceplate. Yes, that one really was confusing, yet it was the only thing she felt confident saying.

A rustle beside her seat in the airdrome made her turn. The zeppelin had arrived and disgorged its passengers while she was lost in thought.

Wes smiled down at her, his bag in one hand and there—on the other side of him—a glimmering shadow that roiled and sparked in the airdrome light.

She was on her feet to hug him before it struck her what the shadow was.

Acid filled her arms and dropped them to her side. *Don't touch him, he's not yours.*

Not anymore.

Like a body slam, the shock, the airdrome whirling, red light filtering down to mix with the shadow beside him. *Don't look at it.* This was how it ended, then. Since she'd last seen him, Wes Knight, her on-again off-again lover, had Flackred himself to someone else, each jacked in to the other twenty-four seven, seeing—living—what the other did, their communication instantaneous. A digital symbiosis. She'd never understood those who felt the need to be Flackred, but it was spreading. More and more people diving into oneness with a loved one before the end of the world divided them all.

It was like a second death in one day, not as bad as Knight senior dying, but almost. As if a hand she thought she held fast had slipped from hers.

Get through it. Her heart was cracking open but she could do it, ignore the flickering beside him. *Push it down.* "You'll need to see your dad."

"Hello, Cara." When she didn't respond (and she couldn't, *wouldn't* get a word out that bespoke any kind of intimacy), Wes rubbed his face. He had to have known how it would shock her. The shadow twisted, apparently confused. "All right. Take me to Eisen first."

Down the hall, toward the elevators to the subsea level, the three of them walked. Three. They met no one and Cara was glad of that at least. No one to stop in shock, then give her a look because she and Wes had been a thing.

Compared to the giant land-based Tampa Dome, miles inland where Lakeland used to be, their own floating Dome was a tiny thing, making do with a handful of biologists, technicians for the airdrome where the hydrogen zeppelins came and went. Everyone did the menial chores to allow most of the money to go toward their wards. Cara was on janitorial duty for that afternoon. She didn't mind swabbing the floors. She'd do all of it alone if she had to. If Wes said they were cutting back.

"It's bad," she told Wes (told his other). "We don't know how the brevetoxin's getting in. We may have to scrap the Pen." She didn't dare glance his way. "Rebuild. Your dad—"

"My dad would have wanted that." It froze her blood. They stopped at the elevator. "But I'm not my dad. Listen, Cara." He turned to her, his shadow whirling with him more slowly, as if weighted by actual inertia. His Flackred other would be seeing and hearing all she did, experiencing her as Wes did. She imagined she saw herself through those hidden eyes: a nerdy, needy sprite of a woman, muscle honed by constant swimming with her wards and yet shriveling now in despair at what he was about to say.

"I won't be putting any more money into a new Pen or filtering system. It was a long shot to begin with. We'll close the Pen down, cut our losses."

It was the worst she could have imagined. "If you kick them out of the Pen, they'll all sicken and die in weeks! The HAB is everywhere out there." Harmful algal bloom, the red tide that baptized the sea mammals in the brevetoxin that dined on agricultural runoff, spasming them, rusting their lungs. It would be slow torture.

But he knew that, a marine biologist himself, boy genius who had discovered the dolphin language in the first place. He couldn't mean it. Cara felt red inside, unable to breathe.

"It's no use, Cara. Eutrophication's not going to stop spreading. It's in deeper areas now. The seas are mutating. If any marine life survives at all, it's going to be different."

"We have to try!"

"You don't get it, do you?" Somehow, they'd grown loud, toxic. "Our own species isn't going to make it through this. You don't get away from here enough, Cara. You don't even get to the mainland anymore. You don't see the riots, the starvation..."

She chose not to, turning off the news feeds and going out to swim with Silber's pod whenever they were gracious enough to slow down for her. Basking in the flow and spin, forgetting gravity for their dark-green world.

The world that would be gone even sooner now. Dead.

The elevator arrived and Wes spun with his Flackred other into it, held the door open for Cara.

There was nothing to do but stand beside him, the man who was killing everything, feel the descent in her ears. Through the transparent elevator walls Cara watched the seawater rise up around them. Drowning them. She realized she was crying.

"Her name is Lekha." As if he could think she was crying about him and his flackery heart. But she was; it was a part of it, at least. Love was too hard, there should never be simply a word for it. What she felt for the pod was not in a word or a click.

"I love her, Cara. I would have messaged you, but I wanted to say it in person and travel's gotten so hard."

Make a joke. "At least it's not a Gleam." It would have been too much, those rare scenarios of three or more Flackred together. A perversion of wanting oneness. Just for the sexual arousal all day, most assumed who wouldn't go near the knots of writhing shadows when they saw them. Like a ball of people rolling along in their life.

"You have to understand, Cara. We've reached the end," Wes said. *Yes, we have.*

"You're cold, Wes."

All his genius, doctorate at twenty-two, combining marine biology and computer linguistics to make the discovery of the century: that among the cetaceans it was dolphins— and only dolphins—who used true language. Not even the whales' bizarre songs rose to the language level. And yet his love had always been for the technical aspects. Not the tumultuous joy of their darting minds. She'd always known that about him, but the taste was like death. "The dolphins were like family for your dad, and you don't give a shit."

"Dammit, Cara, I'm the one who asked him to build the Pen. He did it for me, after my discovery. He had no interest in marine life before."

"But he learned to love them." More than you ever could. Her mind flashed to a memory of the billionaire Weston Knight, eighty years old, floating with her, joking with Silber and Eisen and the rest, his eyes laughing behind the faceplate. His aquatic family she'd promised to protect.

You can hate or you can keep trying. The elevator opened on the isolation-pool lab.

"Take a look at Eisen, Wes."

And then Wes was kneeling beside the pool to stroke Eisen and Cara knelt beside him because what else could she do? His fingers trembled. If he only hadn't hardened as much as she thought. The sight of their sick friend obviously hurt him, while his Lehka shadow seemed to turn away, to the length bandwidth allowed.

Marisa Sanz was on sick duty, just removing the tube from Eisen's snout that fed the dolphin gruel. Marisa shook her head *No improvement* as she handed Cara and Wes translation buds.

[Wes] [greeting]. Eisen's whistle was weak but at least she knew him.

Cara realized Wes couldn't speak for a moment, thought gummed up, and she spoke for him.

"Silber asked after you."

Eisen wheezed. [Much] [float]? *Doing a lot of floating, is he?*

"He wanted to come visit you."

[No (emphatic)]. The dolphin knew how bad it looked. *Stubborn.* [I] [Pen] [toward].

"Not a good idea," said Wes. Beside them Marisa was shaking her head as well.

Eisen shifted, painfully, in the harness until she faced Cara.

[Headfirst]. [You] [now] [listen].

It was the pod's nickname for Cara, their word for humans initially, whose entry headfirst into the world they found hilarious, but they had attached it to Cara alone once the meaning was explained to them. The one who plunged in, their impetuous friend, prepared to do anything for them.

Eisen would only use the nickname if it was serious.

[Beach] [now] [toward].

"I don't get that," Wes murmured. "What beach?"

Cara felt like throwing up. She pulled out both their translation buds, took his arm and moved him away. "Oh, Wes, she's saying it's time to beach herself."

Understanding washed his face pale, but she saw admiration there too, for her ability to grasp what they meant.

"Listen, Cara—"

"This is what you're abandoning them to, Wes. I have to go in with her now, be with the pod while we watch her die and then I have to watch the rest of them die, and then..." *I'll be dead too, on the inside.*

"There's another way."

"Not without the Pen."

"Remember the story of the dolphin with hind legs?"

Cara froze.

"It was in the textbooks in graduate school. Some fishermen pulled it up."

Yes, she remembered, but he couldn't be thinking what she suspected.

He went on. "Little pectoral fins, like tiny legs. An atavistic mutation. Scientists in Japan have isolated the allele, Cara. They've been working on it and they think the dolphins can be CRISPRed—"

"No, Wes!"

"Into something that can go on land. Back to something like the Mesonyx they came from, but with the intelligence they've evolved since."

"They'll cease to exist!" It would be an evil akin to vivisection. Her mind was all red now, nothing left but rage. The Lehka shadow seemed to watch her with pity.

"We can CRISPR in stages, each generation a little more, so they can change in a matter of decades instead of millions of years. Mankind is going to die off, Cara, and there'll be no one to keep the Pen going or anything like it. They might still succumb to some land disease, but this way they'll have a fighting chance."

"It's murder! They wouldn't understand what they're giving up."

"It's the best we can do. And maybe the dolphins will do a better job with the Earth than we have."

Her rage annealed to steel. "I won't consent to it."

He rubbed his face, exhausted. "We don't need your consent, Cara. Only theirs."

"I'll tell them not to. They'll listen to me."

"You do that. Right after you attend Eisen's funeral with them. Take this with you." From his bag Wes extracted a square of nanowire mesh as large as his palm. "This is what I've been working on, thank you very much, while you guys let in the brevetoxin."

It was so unfair it took her breath away.

"It uses the same focal brain stimulation that Flackr does, the visual cortex, Broca's area, but takes a deep dive into the hippocampus. It can be installed in one of the helmets and you can strap one on Silber."

Cara fingered the mesh. The hippocampus. Memory's playground, emotions. More than the mere presence Flackr created, it would be a kind of telepathy. "Silber would know what it's like to be human," she murmured.

"You would know what it's like to be a dolphin."

Understanding flooded her. He'd made it for her. Conceived of it, experimented, tested it, all the time thinking of her. To give her—just maybe—the experience she longed for.

"Tell them whatever you want, Cara. But be sure to tell them they'll die if they stay in the water."

Cara turned to see Eisen watching, an ancient gaze that said she understood them, all their human loves and contradictions because they had them too.

She couldn't say thank you to Wes, not yet. The day's devastation was too much. But she could nod and take the mesh from him. She could look straight at him, and at his shadow. "I will."

The dark-green world was gray and how could she have forgotten that, no colors for the dolphins, only silver and iron swirls, bubbles, a forever dome in all directions. Every tug of the current a caress, she moved with them as one, in trajectories that formed a web. They cried without tears. Her mind shuddered with it.

Silber and three others held up Eisen so she could breathe as long as possible, and Cara felt the weight, the silk of her own snout against Eisen's underbelly, the despair in Silber as Eisen's head flopped. No air could save their pod-mate, her lungs too infected, but they could do this: an escort, a bier. A ritual, long-established. *Like holding her hand,* the human part of Cara thought, just as she had held Weston Knight's hand until the end.

They've always had the Gleam, she realized, bodies moving through life toward death, swimming, leaping, floating together.

As they bore Eisen toward a shore that did not exist, they sang and Cara sang with them, understanding that the words were new ones invented by them, for this new kind of death. She sensed now how they felt their doom, in the way the water soured in their mouths, the Karenia brevis everywhere, shocking her. All their human fail-safes had failed. No colors, but the dolphins had made a word for this horror they could taste and the mesh gave it to Cara as color. Their funeral song, swan song.

Red is the taste of our death.

When Eisen had drawn her last breath, the song changed. *Nothing there now.* They let her fall gently down into gray dark, where humans could remove the empty shell.

Afterward Silber came to Cara. His sadness cut her, deep down where the mesh penetrated her brain.

[Headfirst.] Not a click or whistle. Speech, directly inside her head. She had only to think back at him. *[I'm sorry I had to lie about Eisen.]*

[This is what it feels like to be you.]

[Ditto.]

[Feeling guilty, forever looking for something lost. Is that what human means?]

It hadn't needed to be explained. He'd grasped what Wes planned, extracting it from Cara's thoughts the moment she entered the water with the mesh and placed Silber's own mesh on him. Become something new, or die.

[Please do it, Silber. The others will follow you. Please. Survive.]

The sadness deepened more than she thought possible. No words now, only fear. They would carve his body into something new at the cellular level. She felt him ready to say no.

Within the Gleam the mesh created, she could maybe find the words that would convince him. *[So that someone remembers Eisen.]*

And poignancy washed out the fear, bittersweet. Silber arched his back in a smile. *[So that someone remembers you.]*

It was a yes.

In the sweet, watery world they would lose forever, he slid against her, head-bumped, and then drew back, facing her. *[I have only one question, Headfirst.]*

[I'll answer it if I can.]

[Will we dream of swimming?]

This is the story of the day. We ran on four legs, then we ran on two. The headfirst one would not recognize us now, leaping together beneath the trees, swimming on land. The abundance of life brought back. What they didn't know, those who gave us this landborne life: that we had always been able to communicate with our thoughts, without sound. That it would make the difference, enabling us to create this better world, not marked by greed or fear.

This is the story of our day. We gleam.

We are something new.

Born and raised in Texas, Rhonda Eikamp now writes from Germany, where she works as a translator for a law firm. Her stories have appeared in Lackington's, Lightspeed Magazine, Apparition Lit, and Triangulation: Appetites, among others. She knows that dolphins have language and is waiting for linguists to prove it.

THE FIRE OF
COUNTLESS STARS

by Jamie Lackey

The dragons died when the Emperor took all of the magic into himself and became God-Emperor. Most people, only familiar with dragons as vague threats to their livestock, saw this as a bonus, and declared a holiday in the God-Emperor's honor.

Willow's family harvested dragon dung for their livelihood and lived close enough to the dragon breeding grounds to see their aerial dances and hear their songs.

They did not celebrate.

Willow wept for days.

⊗

The God-Emperor declared that he would distribute the magic fairly. He sent a magical toy to each child under the age of seventeen in the empire as proof of his generosity.

Willow, the youngest in her family by a year, was the only one to receive a toy—a top that played a sweet, cheerful tune and spun without stopping. She had never owned anything magical before. Her parents marveled over it and begged her to be careful with her treasure.

She tucked it into a drawer, between worn socks that needed mending.

Time passed, and her family ventured deeper and deeper into the dragon nests, harvesting bone and hide in addition to dung, until Willow found the very heart of their lair, where the Dragon Queen had stood guard over her last clutch of eggs.

Nothing remained of the Dragon Queen but her huge skull—she

had been more magic than anything else—but the unguarded eggs huddled safely together. There were six of them, each about the size of both of Willow's fists together.

The eggshells were smooth and cool. No more alive than any other rocks.

They would surely be worth something to some collector in a city, far away.

Willow hid them in her sock drawer with the God-Emperor's toy.

Willow helped her mother pack the last of the dishes into the wagon, then hugged her tight. "I still think you should come to the city with us," her mother said. "It's not safe out here for a girl alone."

"We can't just abandon the holding," Willow said. They'd had this conversation a hundred times. She wasn't leaving. This was her home, and she would support herself here.

"Life is easier in towns now," her mother said. "The God-Emperor blessed the fountains, so the water always runs clean and sweet."

"Our well is clean enough," Willow said. "I'll be fine. I promise."

Her father hugged her, and her older brother tugged on her braid. "You can come to us anytime," her father said. "We'll always have a place for you."

Willow nodded, grateful for their concern. But her place was here.

She watched the wagon till it vanished around a turn in the mountain road, then got back to work.

Two weeks later, she found a pregnant griffin on the slopes above her house. Its feathers were brittle and its fur falling out in clumps. Every breath was slow and ragged, and it just glared at her with its eagle eyes as she dragged it into the barn. Willow wondered how it managed to survive so long without any magic.

She hiked to the lake just up the mountain and caught a few fish. She slipped each one into the griffin's beak, and helped it tilt its head back to swallow.

Time passed, and her menagerie grew. She didn't know why the magical creatures were drawn to her, but she managed to keep most of them alive. None of them ever recovered enough to leave—they didn't really belong out in the God-Emperor's world. He would never give any of his precious magic to save a handful of monsters.

Willow spent sleepless nights nursing baby griffins and turning phoenix eggs in banked embers and chasing foxes out of the cockatrice coop.

Then, one moonless winter night, when the stars sparkled off of a blanket of freshly fallen snow, the Unicorn came.

It trudged up the mountain road, one faltering footstep in front of the next. Its head dipped beneath the weight of its spiraled horn, and snow clung to its silky tail and mane.

"Hello, Willow," it said, its voice like the sound of wind through spring flowers.

Willow led it into the barn and gave it her best quilt.

"I am dying," the Unicorn said. "But I must not. If I die, all things die. It is your destiny to help me."

"Me? How can I help?"

The Unicorn's eyes slipped closed and its breathing slowed.

Willow didn't have time to panic. She ran. She grabbed her entire sock drawer and clutched it to her chest as she sprinted back.

She pulled out the top—the only magic that she'd ever possessed—and broke it against the Unicorn's horn. She felt more than saw something spark out of the toy and into the Unicorn.

The Unicorn looked up at her, its eyes the color of the mountain sky at midnight, and containing just as many stars. "I will sleep," it said. "I must save all of the energy that I can."

"Why come to me?" Willow asked, shaking and blinking away tears. "Why not go to the God-Emperor? He would give you magic."

"The magic is not his," the Unicorn said. "I will not take his stolen gifts, will not be his prize to display, his pet to beg for his scraps. I would rather die."

"And let all things die with you?"

The Unicorn's eyes burned with the fire of countless stars. "Yes."

The Unicorn slept, and Willow considered how to get more magic to keep it alive. The God-Emperor hadn't given away any more toys since his ascension, but she'd heard that he was generous to his favorites, giving magical trinkets to anyone who pleased him. If she could steal a few, that would at least buy her some time.

She fed all of her creatures and hiked to the next holding over. Most of them had also moved to town, but Bryce, who was a few years younger than Willow, had stayed on with old Hanna, his grandmother, who refused to be parted from her herd. They kept goats and sold milk and cheese and meat.

Willow arrived just as the sun crested the mountain. She'd intended to tell them only that she was going briefly to town, and to ask them to check in on her holding while she was away.

But the whole story spilled out of her the instant she saw a friendly face. The fate of the world was too much to carry alone.

They listened, and fed her porridge with honey and goat's milk, and Bryce brought her his toy from the God-Emperor, a silvery ball that looped around and returned to whoever threw it. "Take this," he said, pressing it into her hand. "It's not much, but I want the Unicorn to have it."

"Thank you," Willow said. The magic sparked inside it, like tiny bubbles popping.

"I'll send my Bryce to look in on your beasts while you're gone," Hana said. "The walk is too much for my old bones, else I'd head over myself. I've always wanted to see the Unicorn."

"I miss the dragons," Willow said. She'd never admitted that to anyone before, never dared to voice what amounted to a criticism of the God-Emperor.

Hana took her hand and began to hum the first bars of the dragon's mating song. After a few beats, Willow and Bryce joined in. It was a poor rendition—it was not a song made for human throats—but when they were done, tears stained all three of their faces.

"Thank you," Willow said. She kissed Hana's wrinkled cheek. "I'll be back as soon as I can."

Willow took easily to thievery. She was strong and nimble, and found scaling the walls of great manors no more difficult that climbing a tree to rescue a stuck chimera cub.

She broke a box that closed itself, a pen that never needed ink, and

Bryce's silver ball on the Unicorn's horn. It cracked one eye open and looked up at her. "Thank you, Willow."

"How can I help you?" She asked. "What must I do?"

"I only knew that I must come here, and that you would help. I could see no more after that. I put my faith in you to do what must be done."

Willow wanted to shout at it, to demand to know what made her special, why she was the one set to this impossible task. Instead, she pressed her face to the unicorn's silky mane. It smelled, ever so faintly, of lilacs and rainwater.

Bryce had left some fresh rolls and butter under a cloth on her kitchen table. She ate them, then set off to steal more magic.

She had thieved her way through all of the nearby towns, pocketing a cup that was always full of wine, a forever-blooming rose, and a handful of neglected toys. She was approaching the city where her family had settled when she heard the story of the teleport bracelet.

The God-Emperor was so fond of the local lord that he gave him a bracelet that allowed him to teleport anywhere that he wished, so that he could visit the God-Emperor in his palace more easily.

With that, Willow could steal from anyone and be home in time to feed the cockatrices. But this was no country lord, sleeping unguarded with his windows open.

Willow had hoped to sneak into the city, score a few more trinkets, then get back home. She hadn't intended to visit her family—she wanted them to have no part in her crimes or her responsibilities.

But now that she knew of the teleport bracelet, she couldn't leave without it. She had to stay and make a plan.

She knocked on door at the address that her mother had provided. It was a large building, with three stories of narrow windows stretching over her head.

A child emerged from the door, clad in a dress that had once been a sack and glaring. "Who are you then?" she asked.

"I'm looking for my family, I believe that they're living here."

"Lots of people live here. They got names?"

"Willow?" a familiar voice called from behind her. She turned to see her brother, looking thin and worn and covered in fine, gray dust. "What are you doing here?" he asked.

The child sniffed and vanished back inside.

"You didn't give that brat any money, did you?" her brother asked. Willow shook her head.

"You're not here to stay, are you? I thought things were going well at the holding."

"Things are fine, I just came to visit," Willow said. "I suppose I should have written ahead."

Her brother shrugged. "We'll make it work. Come on inside, Mother should be just starting dinner."

The hallways were stuffy and dark, but the apartment that her family was renting had the windows thrown open, and familiar clutter made it feel more like home.

Her mother also looked thin, but she smiled and wrapped Willow in a tight hug. Willow wished she'd brought some food. Or that she'd thought to pocket some coin when she was stealing magical trinkets.

"It's so good to see you!" her mother said, stepping back to examine her. "You look so healthy! I miss all of the fresh air out in the mountains. But things are going well here! Your father and brother both have jobs in the factory."

"It's not bad work," her brother added. "Easier than shoveling dragon dung."

Her father arrived a few minutes later, and they all sat down for dinner together. Willow asked general questions about city life, and eventually managed to learn a few things about the nobles in the city. The lord she was after owned the factory where her father and brother worked.

He apparently kept his teleportation bracelet on at all times. So, he would be wearing it in his factory office.

Willow asked for a tour, and her brother cheerfully offered to see what he could do.

⊗

The factory was hot and smoky, but everyone working there seemed grateful for their jobs. "The God-Emperor helped design this place himself," her brother said. "There's magic woven into every step of the process, and the metal we forge here is sold all over the world."

"The God-Emperor could have made the whole process work without any labor from humans, but he wanted to make sure that people would be able to find jobs," her father added.

Her brother nodded. "Things were harder before the factory opened, but now there's enough work for everyone."

"That's great," Willow said. She wondered what the city had been like before, when the magic was free. But she knew it would be foolish to ask. Instead, she pointed to a door high above the factory floor, where the air was clearer. "Is that the lord's office?"

"Yep," her brother said. "He oversees the whole facility from up there."

Willow could see three fairly easy ways into the office. Now she just had to get in there and jump the lord when he entered. She'd never stolen something from someone's wrist before, but how hard could it be?

⊗

She slipped out of her family's apartment, leaving a note saying that she wanted to watch the sunrise and would be back soon. She'd climb into the office before anyone was working, and wait till the lord arrived.

But instead of finding the factory dark and abandoned, she found it bustling. And when she climbed into the office window, after dodging a handful of sleepy workers, she found the lord bent over his desk. He was older than she'd imagined, gray haired and balding, with a close-cropped beard and beaky nose.

"Who are you?" the lord demanded. "What are you doing here?

"I'm here for your bracelet."

The lord laughed in her face. "This bracelet?" He held up his wrist, displaying a strand of blue and green beads tied securely in place. "It is mine, gifted to me by the God-Emperor himself. You can't have it." His gaze drifted down her body. "But if you don't make me angry, I'll let you walk out of here instead of calling the guards."

Willows hands curled into fists and her cheeks burned.

"You're a feisty one, aren't you? I like that." He grabbed her wrist, his grip hard and bruising, and the world melted around them.

An instant later, they were in a bedchamber. The lord shoved her toward the bed.

Willow drove her knee into his groin and grabbed for the bracelet.

The lord shrieked with pain. The world blurred around them again, and they were in a guard station. "Seize this bitch!" the lord screamed.

But Willow wrapped her fingers around the bracelet and imagined the coldest, highest mountain peak she'd ever ventured to.

The drop in temperature was so sudden that it hurt. The wind howled, and snow swirled in stinging gusts. She pulled as hard as she could, and the bracelet came free in her hand.

She twisted her other wrist out of the lord's grasp, and before he could move, she was back home, shuddering from the cold in the safety of her kitchen.

He'd freeze to death up there. But she couldn't go back, couldn't save him. It was too dangerous.

She fell to her knees buried her face in her cold hands.

Then, when she was warm again, she teleported back to the city and had breakfast with her family.

"How was the sunrise?" her mother asked.

Willow forced her face into some semblance of a smile and sipped her tea. "It was lovely."

The freedom that the teleport bracelet gave her was an unexpected joy. She could think of a picture from a book, and suddenly she was deep in the jungle, or standing at the top of a mountain, or ankle-deep in the ocean.

And a moment later, she could be home.

She stole trinkets for the Unicorn from around the world, and she listened to the stories people told, trying to figure out what she needed to do next.

She stroked the Unicorn's silky neck while it slept and tried not to think about the coldest, highest mountain peak she'd ever ventured to.

There was a woman, deep in the forest to the south, who was attempting to breed a flower that would create new magic. People whispered that it would give off magic the way other flowers gave off scent.

Willow had to walk for two days before she found the garden, following complicated directions that she'd worked for months to earn. It was a beautiful place, with brilliant flowers crowded into every corner. The air was flower-sweet, and filled with the sound of buzzing bees.

"So, you're the Unicorn girl," the gardener said, wiping her hands on her heavy apron.

"My name is Willow."

"A pretty enough name," she said. "So, you want one of my seeds? They don't work, you know. They'll never work. They need magic to sprout. A lot of magic. Only the God-Emperor could make them grow."

"But once they're growing, they'll create new magic?"

The gardener shrugged. "In theory. There's no way to really know, not for sure."

"The unicorn came to me and told me that I'd save her. She didn't say how. I don't know if I'm on the right path, if I'm doing the right things. All I can do is what I can. I heard about your seeds, so I came. If you let me, I'll plant them everywhere I go. Maybe one will sprout."

"They won't. They'll rot in the ground."

Willow trailed one hand along the smooth green leaves of an unfamiliar fern. "You'd know better than I. But I still want to try."

The gardener nodded, just once. "That is why I make them. Even though it is hopeless. Just to try." She pulled a handful of seeds out of her apron pocket and carefully tipped them into Willow's hands.

Willow examined the seeds in her cupped palms. They were beautiful, but dry and brittle. Hollow inside, where magic should spark.

She closed her fingers around them. She'd plant them, and if they rotted in the ground, she'd plant more.

Then, one day, instead of appearing in her intended destination, she found herself in a courtyard, face to face with the God-Emperor.

"This has gone on long enough, don't you think?" he said. He was only slightly taller than Willow, and his smile was soft and kind. His dark hair curled around his face, and his eyes and skin practically glowed. He was beautiful in a way that was impossible without magic—a serene, untouchable beauty. Like the Unicorn's.

Terror clawed at Willow's belly, like a living, separate creature. Like a griffin, no longer to fly and incapable of understanding why.

That thought spread through her veins like ice, freezing the terror and transforming it into something else. Something hard and angry, like the Unicorn's eyes filled with the fire of countless stars.

"You should give the magic back, then," Willow said. "It's not yours."

The God-Emperor laughed. But it was a warm, kind laugh, like they were sharing a joke. "You were a child when I claimed the magic. You don't really remember what it was like before. The magic was never free. It has always been controlled by some and coveted by many. At least in my hands, I can make sure it is fair. Everyone has access to at least a little magic. Clean water, good jobs, safety. Everyone has those things, now. That wasn't always true."

"But you give more to some."

"Some people deserve more than others, Willow. You're not a child anymore, you must understand that. I've been watching you for a long time, you know. I can see that you're special."

"And what makes you worthy to decide who is special, who is deserving, and who isn't?"

The God-Emperor kept his smile, but it seemed a little sharper, now. "Do you think you could do better?"

She didn't. She didn't think anyone could. It wasn't that the God-Emperor was cruel, or evil. He'd seen the unfairness in the world, and wanted to fix it.

But the unfairness was part of the world. It couldn't be removed, only shifted.

The God-Emperor took her silence as agreement, or as a challenge. "Fine," he said. "Here, give it a try."

He reached out and touched her cheek, and power flooded into her.

It was too much.

It burned.

"I trained for decades to be a vessel," the God-Emperor said, his tone light and conversational. "But no one remembers that. No one thinks about the work I put in. I earned my power. No one else can contain it.

"That isn't even close to all of it. But it will kill you in a matter of moments, then I will take it back."

Willow closed her eyes and fled. She used the bracelet to flit from one place to another, magic leaking out of her like sparks exploding out of a fire.

Finally, she collapsed at the Unicorn's side. The gardener's seeds that she'd planted here sprouted, vines spreading along the barn walls and flowers unfurling in an instant. They glowed with their own light, soft and steady and sure. The dragon eggs, still clustered in her long-abandoned sock drawer, hatched.

She buried her fingers in the Unicorn's mane.

The magic drained from her like water falling into a bottomless pit.

The Unicorn stood, pulling away from Willow's numb fingers. "You've achieved your destiny," it said. Then it leaned down and pressed its smooth cheek against Willow's. "Thank you."

Then it was gone.

⊗

When Willow woke, she was covered with baby dragons, and Bryce was holding her hand. "You brought the dragons back," he said, his voice choked with tears. "I forgot how beautiful they were."

She expected the God-Emperor to come for her, and eventually, he did.

"I would have given power to the Unicorn," he said. "It needed only ask."

"And would you have sprouted the seeds that I planted?" Willow asked.

The God-Emperor smiled. "Of course."

But Willow didn't believe him. There was magic that was outside of his control, now. Magic for people who he didn't think deserved it.

"The people won't thank you for bringing the dragons back," the God-Emperor said. "Or any of your other monsters. The world was safer without them."

Willow shrugged. "Safety isn't everything."

The God-Emperor sighed. "I hope you don't come to regret those words."

"Is that a threat?"

The God-Emperor laughed. "So prickly, Willow. Your name should be Rose. Come back to the palace with me. I will protect you."

"This is my home, and I will support myself here."

"If I wanted to take you, I could." The God-Emperor leaned in and touched her cheek, his touch feather-light. "You mustn't forget which of us has the power."

The Unicorn appeared between one heartbeat and the next. It said nothing, but pointed its horn straight at the God-Emperor's heart.

He pulled his hand back as if her cheek had burned him, and the Unicorn vanished again.

He gave a shaky laugh, and departed.

Willow did not see him again. But she did hear stories about how the God-Emperor had restored the Unicorn with a gift of magic from his own hand. The people saw the return of the dragons as a small price to pay, and declared a holiday in his honor.

Willow pulled on her heaviest coat and teleported to the coldest, highest mountain peak she'd ever ventured to.

There was no sign of the lord's body, but she knew it was there, buried beneath the untouched snow.

The Unicorn appeared beside her, and they watched the sunrise together. The cold air smelled like lilacs and rainwater, and tiny star-bright flowers sprouted where Willow's tears fell.

It was the most beautiful sunrise that Willow had ever seen.

Jamie Lackey lives in Pittsburgh with her husband and their cat. She has over 160 short fiction credits, and has appeared in Daily Science Fiction, Beneath Ceaseless Skies, and Escape Pod. Her debut novel, Left-Hand Gods is available from Hadley Rille Books, and she has a novella and two short story collections available from Air and Nothingness Press. In addition to writing, she spends her time reading, playing tabletop RPGs, baking, and hiking.

As Much as the Crows

by Jennifer R. Povey

"We used to think the dinosaurs became extinct. Now we know they evolved into birds."

I turned my head. The voice registered before the words: silky, deep, neither completely masculine nor particularly feminine. I *knew* that voice as intimately as I knew my own. The content registered a moment later.

It was totally something Sam would say. Evolved into birds. I couldn't resist, "And the chickens have never forgotten."

Sam started to laugh. Turned. Blinked. "Joleen?"

"In the flesh," I said, reaching out with both hands. They grasped my wrists, just as they had done when we had been friends and then lovers.

Lovers had been a mistake. Maybe I could get friend Sam back. Maybe there was some hope. We think that romance is somehow superior, but it isn't.

The man Sam had been talking to shook his head and turned back to the drinks table.

"He was talking about how humanity is going to become extinct eventually and we have to prepare our legacy now."

"And you said we would evolve into something else."

"I think we already are."

They'd said that before. It sent a shiver down my spine then, and it did now. Maybe because none of us really want to admit our children are going to eventually, inevitably, render us obsolete.

"Supermen, eh?" I asked them.

They shook their head. "You know better."

Sam was an evolutionary biologist and a genius. I wondered what they had spotted that led them to think humans were changing, evolving. "So, what do you mean about already are?"

They lifted their hand skyward. "The first Martian was born three months ago. Do you really think they'll stay the same species?"

I shook my head. "Well, that part's obvious, I suppose. I was thinking here on Earth." If the Martians became something else, then so be it. They would be something else.

"Here on Earth?" Sam turned to me. "Warning signs, Joleen. There are always warning signs." Then they moved over to pour themselves another drink. No goodbye, despite all we had been to each other.

I turned away. I hadn't even known Sam was here, not just here at this party, but here at this conference.

And I knew I wasn't getting friend Sam back the way they had been. It was my fault. I was the one who had pushed for sex, thinking it would make us more intimate, thinking we would understand each other better.

Instead, we had bounced off of each other like billiard balls. The perfect rack had become a mess. There was no putting it back together.

But for a moment, I had hoped.

Warning signs.

A ship was leaving for Mars with colonists and supplies, taking advantage of the launch window.

We had learned our lessons from the past. Mars had its own government, built to be independent from the start. War between Earth and Mars might be infeasible, but holding onto it as a colony was obviously impossible. So, we weren't going to try.

Warning signs.

I hunted for them in Sam's latest paper. It was entitled *Rapid Evolution in Large Populations*. It was about viruses.

Specifically, it was about how what we called new strains of rhinovirus—a cause of the common cold—evolved, but it postulated the idea that an extremely large population could reach a tipping point at which the billiard balls would fly apart. The single species would start to become more than one.

They postulated the idea that it was a protective mechanism. That nature itself abhorred a monoculture.

There was stuff in there that I didn't understand about microRNA gene regulation. About how genes could be reprogrammed on the fly to create new species.

Always warning signs.

I looked for that in the paper too. I didn't find it. What I found was a reference to another virus study.

Efficient specialists out-evolving generalists.

We're the ultimate generalist. We survive because our minds allow us to change and adapt faster than we can evolve. But what if something happened?

Martians were going to be different, they had to be. Maybe that was all they meant after all.

But species become obsolete all the time, competed to extinction by their offspring. We didn't have to worry about *that* with the Martians.

They would just be better adapted to Mars, would out-compete us there, would thrive. We would trade with them and learn from them and perhaps mingle with them.

Some people thought they would all be immunosuppressed.

I got on the train. Rode the rattling vehicle until it let me out into Times Square. New York, protected from the high waters by baffles and dykes. New York was once more New Amsterdam.

The press of people. Surviving on basic or soaring to their own heights. Generalists.

Choosing their own niches, if choice was more than just an illusion.

But it was the young people I watched. Was there anything different about them? Anything more than the way young people had always been different from their elders?

I could not tell.

There was a second baby on Mars. They were different.

Oh, you couldn't tell by looking at them. Yes, baby pictures were sent back. But the articles about them said it all.

They'd been breeding faster—breeding critters on Mars for a while. Martian rabbits had, oddly, slightly smaller ears, slightly longer legs. Just simple adaptations, but ones that showed up across the spectrum. Natural adaptation, nothing humans had done, but there.

Warning signs of what could happen to humans.

I hunted for them. Of course, maybe Sam had been playing a prank. It would be like them to leave me with an insistent problem, knowing I could not rest until I had it solved. I thought about calling them, emailing them. Tracking them down.

Trying to catch the billiard ball.

A large enough population, speciating for its own protection, changing before it overruns its niche.

Had it already happened? Had it already happened, but been so minor it had just braided back together? After all, we'd braided in the Neanderthals and the Denisovans, making them nothing more or less than minor quirks in our own DNA.

How many genetic defects were failed attempts to split?

I called Sam. I asked to meet for coffee.

They agreed, showed up in a nice pantsuit that made them look more masculine.

"I know you did it to me on purpose."

"I can't tell you." Sam sighed. "There's something going on. I need more sets of eyes on it. I knew if I said that, you'd put your amazing pattern-solving brain on it."

"If the large population thing really applies, then..."

"I actually suspect the aboriginals, at least, were well on the way to being a separate species."

I shook my head. "That's scientific racism, Sam. You know way, way better. And don't give me the 'only if you think it makes them inferior' line."

I knew they would take the mild rebuke. Sam could be very white queer at times, and they knew it. I had always tried to do better, to understand those who were not part of our dominant culture. Monoculture was bad.

"You're right. But I know there's something going on with the kids."

"Other than an increase in cliquing and what you might call non-geographical tribalism?" I lifted my hand. "Kids always look different to elders. Every generation is a new species in that sense. And what's a species anyway?"

Sam laughed. "Not what we thought. You know how false the old definitions are."

"Exactly. Besides. If we do find something, what will come of it?"

They paused. "Nothing good."

For a moment, I heard the old Sam in the resignation in that tone.

But I also knew they would pursue it anyway. Once more, they left without a goodbye. I watched them go with no hope for any relationship. Yet, they still trusted my amazing pattern-solving brain.

Sam's paper went into details about how the parent species always became extinct after the split.

But that was viruses. There were simplicities there. Humans were much more complex, and our mating patterns alone ensured that we held together.

I decided they were wrong and managed to get my "pattern-solving brain" onto what I did for a living: fixing machine learning algorithms that had started to act in racist, sexist, or other inappropriate ways.

We haven't cracked sentient AIs yet, but we have things which almost act sentient. The problem is, they inherit the biases of their creators.

I was good at spotting these problems and good at working out how to fix them. Many times, this involved force feeding the algorithm large quantities of curated data. Black and Asian faces flickered across my screen, data to be fed to a hiring algorithm that had been shown to favor whites.

There was a balance to it, of course. Inevitably, people would complain if it favored non-whites, or if it favored whites. I had to make it as unbiased as possible, but there had yet to be a truly unbiased AI. All I could do was try to balance the biases, make it run as close to the center as possible.

On my other monitor was a news screen. A reminder of why I did this, of patterns that had become better, but not yet fixed.

The ticker tape of the feed. Headlines from all over an overburdened globe. People were dying in Pakistan again, in what remained of it anyway.

Mars represented hope to some of those people. Others saw the past, a retreat, as the answer.

Some dreamed of the stars. Some sought refuge on physical and metaphorical high ground.

Some killed. Some got high.

Overcrowded rats in a cage.

Speciation as self-preservation. We weren't preserving ourselves as we were. Was it mere wishful thinking?

Rapid evolution.

Change.

Non-geographic tribalism.

Viruses in a petri dish seeking each other out.

Fear.

I knew what would happen to them, if they existed.

One small hope rose in my mind. Perhaps on *Mars* we could leave all of this behind.

I spotted it, as they knew I would. Sam really had needed my brain.

I had access to what we needed to confirm it. We called it Anima, a machine learning algorithm more sophisticated than any that had come before.

No, Anima was not sentient. But what it could do was take *any* data set we gave it and come to a conclusion quickly, without the need to spend weeks training it.

And the data set I gave it was a correlation. We genetically test newborns for a variety of disease markers. Stuff like BRCA mutations, color blindness, etc. Stuff that they and their parents would need to know when they were older. Some of it could be corrected with CRISPR or other therapies. Some of it couldn't.

There was not just one new group, marked by a propensity for minor disease, a tendency to subconsciously cluster together, and higher aptitudes in certain areas.

There were four.

Specialists, not generalists. *Your remarkable pattern-solving mind.*

I was one of them. An early adopter. I was human, but I had differences. Differences that would have been enough in a virus. Or even a mouse.

I destroyed the data, of course, wondering if Sam had figured it out. Wondering if they were also one of us.

Four different human groups, new subspecies radiating outwards. Billiard balls.

The pattern solvers. The artists. The swift ones who could move like nobody else. And those whose hands worked in ways we hadn't seen before. Four new subspecies, each of them designed to fill their own evolutionary niche in our society.

It wasn't enough yet, but it was a beginning.

Castes.

We braided them back together eventually, but we also created them when we pushed people into the professions of their parents. But this time there was something different.

Because I could see it now. The population so large that we could pick and choose, so carefully, who we hung out with. And geography no longer entered into it.

I could see how we clustered, and the parent species?

Might never have existed. Might have been extinct for centuries.

Spread and then braided together. Intermarriage pulling things together, but now people could find a mate anywhere on the world. Now they would choose their own kind.

The billiard balls had been struck a century ago. Now they could not be put back together.

I destroyed the data.

Anima still had it. Anima, the least biased AI we had yet created, but still biased. Still tainted by what we are, as they all were.

Mars was part of our hope. The place fear couldn't touch. Did the Martians have enough genetic material to survive? I could make sure of that.

They got the data out of Anima, of course. And they looked at it and they looked at newborn genetic scans and they came to the same conclusions.

And they reacted, as they always do, with fear. That's why I'm on the ship, and why what I'm smuggling out matters. It wasn't hard to get approved for the colony. I'm not that old, I still have viable ovaries. I don't need to find a partner to have children who will be Martians. And they wanted my pattern-solving brain to help improve their weather prediction algorithms. Other algorithms, too. I don't want to go. But I have to. One last kiss from Sam, who feels they have to stay. A kiss that reminds me of everything between us. Closure.

I don't know what they'll do on Earth, not exactly. I know what's being talked about. Encouraging people to marry the right person to braid everything back together.

Putting people in camps. Humanity had done that so many times to those they feared for being different.

Labeling people. You can't always tell from the outside. No, you can't tell. You can't tell what strain somebody is from looking at them. It's not the physical traits that are spreading out.

It's the brain, the aptitudes.

That's why I'm on the ship. With my little case of selected genetic material. The Martians can use it or not, as they...

As we choose.

As I look back, I see in my mind's eye the fog of war settle over the globe.

I know what will happen because it happened before. The forced braiding back together. The battle of a species that is afraid of extinction.

Afraid and not understanding. Not understanding that species doesn't matter, that human is more than just one's DNA. That when and if Anima wakes up and tells us who it is, it too will be ineffably human, and perhaps as afraid as we are. But they will fight and destroy, as they always have.

And when it is all over, the crows will still fly, knowing that extinction is only transformation. And that the Martians are human too, regardless of what that strange world does to them.

Just as much as the crows are dinosaurs.

Nay, more so.

Jennifer R. Povey lives in Northern Virginia with her husband. She writes a variety of speculative fiction, whilst following current affairs and occasionally indulging in horse riding and role-playing games. She has sold fiction to a number of markets including Analog Science Fiction and Fact Magazine, Daily Science Fiction, and Third Flatiron, and written RPG supplements for several companies. Her most recent novel is the epic fantasy Firewing.

TALES OF THE SHRUB

By Jim Hanson

*P*art 1: *Shrub's Chagrin*

Tell me, O Shrub,
as did Homer's muse
of the great exploits of Odysseus,
tell now three millennia later,
at a time human civilization
faces chaos and extinction
when even Gaea seems not to care
about human beings on this earth.

Yes, I do have tales to tell
starting with a prehistoric age
when your human species abided
by the laws of nature and
coexisted with other species evolving
in a world of ecological balance and peace

then devolving in this era of
your splendid rising over others
including my own pitiable existence,
eaten and trampled by marauding mammals,
isolated in the barren soil of parched mesas,
worn down by wind and heat,

starved and stunted in arid land.

So, I lie here before you,
reduced from beautiful to ugly,
a common weed of no regard,
deemed useless as the lowest species—
a primitive remnant from a bygone era.

Part 2: Shrub's Challenge

I have seen you arrive, once hesitant,
(with only weapons and tools of stone, then
making bronze and iron and great machines)
now treading triumphant over this earth,
your numbers multiplying by the billions,
your sciences and technologies transforming
the elements given by nature while

devouring countless plant and animal species,
tearing apart the fabric of ecological systems,
depleting minerals and poisoning the land,
draining aquifers and rivers for fields and lawns,
heating global air by burning ancient fossil oils.

So, O Human,
do not laud in this late century
your triumphant odyssey on
this earth facing chaos and extinction
during your vaunted Anthropocene Age
that promised unlimited frontiers and
exploitation of infinite resources.
Do not boast as the proud victor who
rendered extinct thousands of species,
yet who now comes meekly before me

as the forlorn refugee, hungry and thirsty,
in search of solace and guidance while

here, the high plains of Kansas lie,
blistering under a sun of famine.
While behind you the salted sea
creeps up the Mississippi River basin
in whose wake the great Gulf coast cities
lie drowned by category six hurricanes.

Part 3: Shrub's Prophecy

Take heed of your existence as the last man,
not just the past believer of gloried civilization
as Nietzsche once warned, but as the
last survivor as Revelations foretold
about this earth of fragile life and finite size,
ravaged by corporate beasts and false prophets.

Tell what you now see
in this exhausted land now inhabited
by shrubs—shrubs everywhere—large and small,
down from the mountains and arid plateaus
onto fields once fertile and cultivated for food,

now the abandoned wheat fields of Kansas and
cornfields of Iowa under the once-blue sky
turned white, and air shimmering with heat,
land cracked and dry without rain or aquifers,
even native prairie grass withering away,
to nourish only loathsome goats.
We have multiplied our species
from mountain tops to valley depths,
over all continents of the earth,

not only surviving, but thriving while
other species succumb to extinction.

We have thrived undaunted by
your civilization and industrial abuse,
spreading the seeds for our descendants,
conserving the gift of water and sanctity of soil,
thriving eons before and after your perversions,
rising and falling as the earth exhales and inhales, and
persevering through the age that is uniquely yours
—the Sixth Extinction.

So, I tell you
about this Homeric tale of tragedy
not of his heroes who obeyed Athena gladly
but you who have broken her covenant of peace
—all your doing.

Jim Hanson is a retired Senior Researcher at Southern Illinois University-Carbondale. He is a sociologist and lay-ordinate Zen Buddhist. He is a member of the St. Louis Poetry Center and lives in the St. Louis area. Recent poems have appeared in Dissident Voice, I am not a silent poet, International Journal of Fear Studies, Nebo, Nightingale and Sparrow, New Verse News, Otolith, Poetry24, River Poets Journal, Sacred Journey and Writers Resist.
Author Acknowledgement: Thanks to Hugh.

LETTERS FOR SAMANTHA

by Sean Jones

In her faded overalls and heavy work boots, my sister batted with her four-fingered hand at the once-red strands hanging in her face, hair wet from the rainclouds that homesteaded above our compound nine months of the year. Karyn sobbed as she struggled with the duct-taped handle of the spade in the "Jory soil," the red dirt that had made Western Oregon's Willamette Valley famous, her tie-dye sweatshirt failing to brighten the scene.

We were working to unearth the skeleton of "Roy," Oregon Primate Paradise's western lowland gorilla, and I felt like a grave robber. Standing next to my award-winning sister outside our state-of-the-art "simian utopia," digging in the mud, my coal shovel hit something solid, a bone, a big one, and I yelped and jumped.

In answer, a keening wail sounded from the Douglas Firs at the edge of the clearing and I felt the back of my neck wrinkle in horror.

"It's okay, Pam," Karyn said, ignoring—as always—the howls coming from the forest. "*Shhhh.* Imagine we're archaeologists and we're on a grand discovery."

She set her mangled hand on my shoulder and I put my hand on hers, she having lost her left pinkie to the grip of Gordon, a former OPP male chimpanzee made frantic by fear-aggression. After the Hermit Flu fractured human society into slim shards, how thoroughly did Karyn feed the bodies and souls of her apes? How often did she cry for those she'd lost?

"Samantha feels left out," I said. "If she can make an omelet, download monkey videos for Uma from what's left of the 'Net, and ride a

103

Segway, she can help us dig." Our female orangutan—watching us now from her Plexiglas window as we dug up her former "roommate"—sometimes would tell a joke using the lexigraphic symbols of her computer, her "letters for Samantha."

"Touching is caring," I'd often said but Samantha had written, "Touching is Karyn," maybe the first non-human to make a pun.

If only my big sister could write up that breakthrough and publish—but, no. We had to hole up in our zoological complex while gangs of adolescents and mobs of adults raided Portland, City of Bridges and Roses, until one of them passed the latent Bug to the others and they all burned up inside. We assumed the disease had claimed billions, the lingering sick that still might extinguish humanity.

Karyn?" I asked. My thoughts wandered like so many influenza victims.

"Hmmm?"

I brought up the subject troubling me. "What do you think about the Farmers' Market?"

She squeezed my shoulder. "It's on your mind?"

"Always." I twisted my shovel around in the dirt, nervous about the culprit. "The only animal big enough to upend a dumpster is a grizzly and the tracks had no claws. Two feet, not four. Five-toed."

"So, we know it was bipedal. Intelligent. Strong. Tell me, Pammy McSpammy, was the moon full?"

"What are you talking about?"

"What has two feet like a man's and super-human strength? Comes out three nights a month? Shrieks and keens?"

"I haven't believed in lycanthropes since, like, ninth grade."

"Really big footprints, Pam?" She grinned.

"Don't tease me. New species step out of the shadows all the time, like the species of orangutan your colleagues discovered when the jungle coughed up the severed arm of one. You think there's no room in the world for another great ape?"

"You expecting a Distinguished Primatologist Prize for bringing in a legend?"

"He's out there, Karyn," I said, looking past the tall weeds toward the tree-lined edge of our compound's clearing where apple trees grew.

Deer came to eat the apples and beasties came to slaughter and eat the deer, hungry fiends that gave me goosebumps whenever I'd glimpse them, shaggy monster-men with soulful eyes staring from behind leaves and branches.

"*Gigantopithecus* went extinct one-hundred-thousand years ago. And, Pamela, he lived in Asia. Science doesn't support the modern Sasquatch." Karyn turned over the hand she'd placed on my shoulder and held my hand. "Thank you for coming here to help me with my 'kids.'"

There were only two "children" alive, Samantha and a Japanese macaque named Uma, but I smiled and said, "I'm their auntie."

Two things—the door of the greenhouse, ripped off its hinges, and the stolen spring cantaloupes—convinced Karyn we couldn't linger in our concrete castle. The constant drizzle had collaborated with the perpetrator, washing away any footprints, but not the clumps of reddish hair that smelled of wet dog and pungent eggs.

My sister dismissed my concerns, as always. "Stray Irish Setter."

Before the Fever, before all the other researchers took their primates with them on their trek south, I knew Karyn had been disciplined for neglecting anything and everything at OPP that didn't relate to Samantha—and maybe that explained the gorilla Roy's death.

Still, when we loaded up the caravan to visit the Farmers' Market, we departed our compound with a habitual sense of caution. Karyn drove the electric ATV with me and the white-haired snow monkey, Uma, riding on the vehicle's trailer, while Samantha accompanied us via off-road Segway. The four of us primates wore yellow ponchos in various sizes, producing a fair impression of a family, the best representation of a "household" in these post-Fever times.

We traversed the neglected roads, passing swamped and windwracked stores, offices and houses which certainly had been looted by now. Rolling by derelict internal combustion cars and trucks, I was grateful our building's solar panels could charge up our rides' batteries.

As we turned off crumbling McLoughlin Boulevard and followed muddy paths along the Clackamas River to where it joined the Willamette, we could see the heavy woods defining the spearhead-shape of Goat Island in the middle of the waterway. We rolled into the weed-choked clearing of Meldrum Bar Park, its baseball diamonds' chain-link backstops and dugouts still standing.

Samantha loved the Farmers' Market, which she signed "farket," eliding the words together with her long, maroon fingers. Another of her jokes? This place had been where everyone would introduce their dogs to other people's dogs, the canine blind dating site. I could still smell something doglike a decade later. Ghost scent? Little Uma held his nose.

"You got the keys, Sis?" I asked as we dismounted the ATV and Segway.

Karyn reached inside her sun-colored poncho and jingled the necklace of brass. "It's the honor system," she said to Samantha. My sister had been explaining to her fellow redhead why we got our supplies by leaving trade-goods for other people. Proof that Samantha could grasp a concept such as reciprocity would prove a major breakthrough—though no one would read such a write-up.

In the Farmers' Market, a dozen motley dumpsters formed the western boundary of the park. Atop the large, metal bins, heavy chains with a series of interlocking padlocks held down the lids. Our keys would fit our locks, while the keys of other hermits would open theirs.

Uma darted ahead and found a padlock, shiny in the damp grass, at the bottom of a rusty *Arrow Sanitary Service* receptacle in rain-bleached blue. He held up the lock for Samantha to see and I noticed the silver hasp featured a red "S" painted on it. The two simians were constantly chattering to each other and I thought the macaque and orangutan spoke their own language but Karyn always denied Uma could communicate. She had been one of the world's leading primatologists, but I swear her focus made her overlook the obvious. It failed to register with her when Samantha signed to the little guy, "Good" and did her hoot-hooting sound, to which he replied in his chittering, murmuring way.

I, myself, could not overlook the overturned, green *Rubbish Works* bin, its lid twisted open. I looked in vain for telltale footprints that would identify the culprit who'd mangled it.

"What's on the wish lists for today?" I asked Karyn, who stood in a baseball dugout, reading notes written on white Tyvek sheets laid across benches and weighted by rocks. Karyn held up a white, plastic, wish list sheet with a black X slashed across it and she pantomimed a knife drawn across her throat. "Satterstrom got banned."

I felt the blood drain from my face, felt my arms go weak. "Did he show up on someone else's day, violate the seclusion?" Ten years after the Fever, everyone we knew of maintained their distance.

Karyn said, "I doubt Satterstrom was desperate enough to approach another person. He always traded fairly, so it couldn't have been a greed-ban. She turned to the bulletin board, which included the minutes of the market's committee that "met" by leaving each other notes. Schmidt had written that Satterstrom had been killed, his farm destroyed, and the chickens taken, by whom—or what—unknown.

So much for our best source of protein and Vitamin D "Spring cantaloupes." She shook her head at the irony.

"Twenty-two caliber bullets, as always. Gentlemen's magazines, as always. Nail clippers. Yeah! I finally remembered to bring those. Stew pot. I threw that stainless-steel boiler in the bag, just in case." She laughed. "Hey, Pammy Jo Jammy, Schmidt is asking for lemon ice cream. Did that ever exist?"

"What's with that Schmidt guy and lemon everything?" and, saying it, I realized we all wore yellow ponchos. I pictured how we must look to someone watching with binoculars—or a rifle's cross-hairs—from one of the dilapidated apartment buildings across the road. Like four giant lemons.

Karyn said, "I brought him an ancient box of citrus tea. Too bad we can't do a three-way trade with Satterstrom for a dozen eggs."

I pictured the contents of an egg, cracked open and fried in a pan, a tiny sun framed by a white cloud. But then that thought was cut short by an image of Satterstrom's burned farm.

"Too bad no one wants several hundred thousand dollars' worth of medical and scientific equipment," Karyn said. "We need vitamin D desperately. Unless someone's gone salmon fishing, we need all the yolks we can get."

I looked to Samantha, expecting her to make a joke of "yolks," but she was tossing the padlock to Uma, who kept ducking and retrieving it. Samantha treated the macaque like her son.

"Karyn, what are we going to do? We're getting soft bones and I know you don't want to acknowledge it but Samantha slumps more and more. Our cognitive abilities have diminished. We're getting forgetful, all four of us. You barely remembered what to bring with us. If the sun ever shone around here, maybe…"

"You thinking of moving to sunnier pastures?"

"I know, I know. There's never much of a freeze here. The rain's a small price to pay for a steady climate where we can take Sammy and Uma outside, where we can grow crops."

"Pamela Marie, are you considering moving south? I have to know." Her face was grave.

"What are you asking? I'm not the stoner concert-girl who follows The New Dead around anymore."

"Sorry."

"What are we going to do? I don't have any idea where Satterstrom's farm was and I don't want to go into the chicken business."

"Mushrooms." She gave a grim smile. "Vitamin D2 instead of D3, but it may be the best we can do. Stave off the rickets."

"We gonna buy mushrooms at the 7-Eleven or order 'em off our Origam-i hand-helds whenever we get one bar of signal?"

"We're officially 'shroom hunters, Sis."

"Right." So, she saw no peril in some wild fungus foray?

We giant lemons wrote up our wish list for next time, I wielding the black marker because I had the best handwriting of the four of us. Saddened, we shopped in the multicolored plastic bins of the rusty dumpsters, tallying our trades on Tyvek, taking pictures of the exchanges with my Origam-i, swapping our greenhouse tomatoes for a half-roll of duct tape. Samantha carefully put a physician's thermometer into the up-for-grabs box and Uma took a moldy baseball from that container. Raspberries exchanged for elk-jerky, an Oregon Primate Paradise pink T-shirt for a Pendleton wool scarf in green plaid. Uma wanted to abscond with everything but *restraint* was our keyword. We didn't want to be greed-banned from the "farket."

"Saddle up," Karyn said.

Samantha mounted her Segway while I hopped onto the trailer of the ATV and Uma jumped up with me, Satterstrom's padlock in one hand, the baseball in the other. Cautiously proceeding, looking out for wildlife or dog-packs gone feral, we rolled back the way we'd come, heading east toward McLoughlin, where we'd turn north toward our home northeast of the city.

I asked Karyn, "While we're out, shall we look for mushrooms?"

"You a savant on the edible versus the deadly?"

Our dad had been a buff, and, after the D-I-V-O-R-C-E, he and I had gone mushrooming. "There are three kinds of fungus hunters," I repeated from his old saying, "the experts, the sick, and the lucky."

As we merged onto the boulevard, Karyn asked, "When we get back to OPP, can you find something on the 'Net about how to identify them?"

"Mighty unlikely." It had been taking six minutes between page-loads, usually 404 errors. The saying, "the Internet is down," was becoming true.

"Let's go old-school," she said.

"Library," we said simultaneously.

"Gladstone?" Karyn asked.

"Feeling nostalgic?" That tiny book-haven anchored our old neighborhood, a few blocks down Dartmouth.

But it was not to be. Ten years of neglect had amounted to overgrown everything, broken-in doors, smashed glass, rusting cars with flat tires and a decade's worth of disappointment. Somebody had driven a red pickup into the library's vestibule, and I knew, inside the building, we'd find waterlogged books and sadness. I didn't look inside the truck's cab; I didn't want to find a skeleton.

"Central, then," Karyn sighed.

The Central Library was three stories linked by wide, sweeping staircases, a stately edifice built before World War I by people who believed in permanence.

She said, "Other side of the Willamette, though."

"The Burnside Bridge is supposed to be earthquake-proof."

Interrupting us, Samantha held onto her Segway's handlebar with one hand and signed, "Danger," like when she'd see a yellow-and-brown giant house spider. She shook her head and made her hissing sound of agitation. Uma chittered in the *peep-peep-peep*s he made when frightened.

Karyn asked, "What's wrong, honey?"

Appearing from around the corner of the library, crossing the parking lot at an inhumanly quick pace with impossibly long strides, seven, eight feet tall, massively built and long-limbed, his soulful, brown eyes focused on Samantha, the rusty-red-haired ape took two final steps and grimaced, showing white, white, white canines the length of a silverback gorilla's and, in one smooth swoop of his immense palm, snatched Uma from behind me as the beast howled with a yowl made my heart race and set my hair on end. He continued his quick walk, knees ever bent, free arm swinging briskly, the world's sixth species of living great ape disappearing with a screeching, yellow-clad, squirming bundle into a passageway between dilapidated houses while Uma's baseball bounced across the parking lot.

I clenched my jaw when I heard the squealing from the kidnapped monkey and, I know, we humans and the orangutan all screamed.

Samantha reacted first, hopping down from her Segway, running on all fours to Karyn on the ATV, throwing her long arms around her caregiver, hissing and shaking her head.

I was too stunned to move, but I felt bile rise in my throat.

"No!" Karyn screamed, while Samantha's emitted a wail, something I'd expect from a mountain lion thrown into boiling oil.

"No, no, no!" said Karyn.

"Go," I screamed through the saliva-acid-mucus cocktail choking me. "We have to follow them. Samantha, come up here with me."

But the orangutan would not let go of her provider, her teacher, her everything.

"Okay, Karyn, I'll drive. They're getting away."

I had to say these things twice, but the two of them traded places with me and we rolled west after the little guy's abductor, the electric ATV's wheels slipping on the wet pavement.

Careening around the building where the Sasquatch had marched, I hurled the four-wheeler and trailer down a narrow, muddy path, steering into the skid as Dad had taught me, desperately trying to see where they'd gone as I twisted the throttle-grip.

"God, I hope it drops him," I shouted.

"Can you see footprints?" I heard from behind me.

And, I could! "That's why you're the primatologist in the family, Karyn."

The fresh prints, fifteen inches by nine or so—hard to tell while driving—were distinct, leading between houses, over knocked-down and rotting wooden fences, now meandering across a leaf-buried back yard, now taking an abrupt left turn down a concrete alleyway but visible for the mud they left.

"Uma!" yelled Karyn. "Where are you?"

Samantha hissed and hissed and hissed.

We flew past a car-repair place and hopped back onto pavement, rolling down Columbia Avenue past the old DMV, only to make a quick U-turn when the tracks reversed themselves. I couldn't help but notice the floral scent that filled the damp air of Portland, couldn't help but be overwhelmed by the smell. Was my mind slipping in the hysteria, warped from stress, abetted by the malnutrition we never discussed? I found the massive footprints as we backtracked along the mud-sluiced sidewalk of 82nd Avenue.

And, then, at a four-foot graffiti-covered concrete retaining wall next to the surging Clackamas River, the snowshoe-sized prints stopped. The barrier blocked us from following the Sasquatch who certainly had stepped right over, the concrete's blue spray-paint sentiment reading, *Keep Portland Weird.*

I sat on the silent ATV and turned to look at my two passengers in the trailer rocking back and forth, hugging each other.

"Let's go on foot," I said.

"Leave the rig here?"

"Who would take it? We have to get Uma back"

"Do we?"

I said, "Karyn, how much does Uma mean to Samantha?" I dismounted the ATV and walked back to the trailer and physically pried the two of them apart. "Let's walk," I said. "Bring the trade goods."

The sleezy rendezvous place, a favored swimming hole for us neighborhood kids as well as a conclave for hobos, runaways, dealers, addicts, cliff jumpers, and drowning victims, High Rocks Park flanked the north bank of the Clackamas. HRP was one of many places our bizarre childhood had taken us, but as I clambered down the rain-slicked cliff with my sixty-something sister and her forty-something orangutan in search of a Japanese monkey who'd been abducted by a mythological creature—as the human race went extinct—life as a kid in Gladstone, Oregon didn't seem so strange.

Why—of all the freakish images that seared themselves onto my brain like a cattle brand—why did I focus on the sight of white hens picking at cantaloupe rinds?

How did I notice that scene before I saw the black-haired and obviously-female-because-she-was-obviously-mammalian Sasquatch sitting on a boulder beside the swollen river, grooming the white-haired and red-faced Japanese macaque? Why did I notice the funky fish scent of the giant male but didn't see him until he stepped out from the shadows of the cliff and flashed his canines at the three of us as we stood on the smooth stones of the riverbank?

That grin was not a smile, but neither was it hostile. With it, he told us he was the alpha and this was his world; we were in his home and he ruled it and we would respect his dominion.

I fought the urge to kneel. I choked on nasty acid and spit out stringy vomit and dry heaved for a minute or a decade until Samantha came and hugged me and stroked my once-blonde hair.

The rain, that fell was so wet that I couldn't be sure I hadn't lost bladder control. The only other time I'd felt such presence, such primal power, had been the time Dad had taken us to the Colorado Rockies and my breath had been stolen from me as we'd hiked amidst a grove of bristlecone pines that had stood since the fall of the Roman Empire. Those trees, as these great apes, stamped an impression on me as if they forced me to glimpse the soul of the world.

"Oh, my God," whispered Karyn. "Oh, my God. He's...he's... what is he?"

I said the single thing that said everything. "He is the king."

Samantha, creature of the virgin jungle, she belonged to the primeval world of these forest-dwelling apes. Where Karyn and I felt dread and awe, panic and fascination, the orangutan knew kinship. She ambled over to the female Sasquatch and reached out one long arm, palm up, to which Uma reached out and touched, palm down. Samantha and the macaque communicated, a long talk, a discussion that produced an arrangement, an understanding.

As Karyn and I stood, dumbstruck, listening to the rumbling river and the clucking chickens, Samantha took off her yellow poncho and draped it over the female Sasquatch's shoulders. Then, the orangutan handed over the green scarf and the strips of elk-jerky to The King and their gaze locked as a bargain passed between them. To us, Samantha motioned with her hand to form the letters, "Home. We go." To Uma, she hoot-hooted in what seemed to me to say, "Goodbye."

On a day the sun had been shining determinedly for three months, Samantha took a burlap sack of summer cantaloupes she'd selected from inside the greenhouse and carried them to the edge of OPP's clearing. She turned and signed to the three of us—Karyn, Schmidt, and me—while we watched through the Plexiglas. "Family," her fingers traced in the air. "Gift." She climbed a Douglas Fir and swung into the deeper forest.

The man we'd always thought of as "old" Schmidt—in his overalls, thirty-something, black-haired, blue-eyed, the man we'd persuaded to live with us by a proposition written in Sharpie on Tyvek—he asked what Samantha was saying.

Karyn, who, so many years ago, had chosen neither Mom nor Dad in the custody hearing, who'd decided, instead, to live as a foster child with a veterinarian's family told him, "She's maintaining the bridge to her son."

We had a cornucopia of mushrooms, morels, chanterelles, and boletes. We would not wither from a lack of Vitamin-D. Young Schmidt proved quite the handyman and we were glad to have him. When Karyn and I told him the history of our simian-human-blended family, there were two concepts I wanted him to understand.

Reciprocity wasn't something I had to get across to him. He embodied it.

No, the first concept came from one of my sister's scholarly papers. At night, in the jungle of the Congo Basin, bonobos, close cousins of chimpanzees, will gather in fusion groups. In the daylight, when they feel secure, pairs or trios will forage in the forest. Karyn had written that, for orangutans of Borneo and Sumatra, fission-behavior is the norm and fusion found rarely except in mother-child relationships. To me, it seemed the Fever had created a great fission event. But the residents of the Willamette Valley—and the rest of the world, I hoped—had decided to brave the risks of coming together and we humans were, once again, forming fusion groups. Schmidt got the notion.

The second concept related to how I felt those days. The inspiration had come from Dad's three kinds of fungus hunters. I believed his words summed up our lives in the fever-stricken world.

We were no experts unless you considered survival, surviving the mayhem, a kind of expertise.

We were not the sick. Wounded, yes, scarred, yes, damaged, yes, but…healing.

And lucky? Indeed, I thought, we were. Schmidt agreed.

Sean Jones lives and writes in Colorado, near his hometown of Golden. He commutes to Louisville (also Colorado, not Kentucky), where he works as a network engineer in the Dream Chaser program that will deliver cargo and scientific experiments to the International Space Station. Influences on his outlook on life include a hitch in the United States Army as a Persian translator, a stint as a city councilman and a couple-three semesters teaching Public Affairs at the University of Colorado (where he earned a Ph.D. writing a dissertation about why voters approved the 1998 Denver Broncos' stadium). If you want to make a friend for life and you see Sean at one of the many sci-fi conventions he attends, bring up the subject of cars. It could be Porsches, rat rods, old VWs or any semi-plausible vehicle from any Fast and Furious movie. Another of Sean Jones's stories, "By Way of Answer," can be found in the 2015 Triangulation: Lost Voices.

WE ONLY HAVE

by E. A. Petricone

He was taken, and she was left behind. Thalassa shrieked as Pontus was hauled out of the sea and into one of the flying ships, his hand reaching for hers through black rope.

Summoning strength to her every muscle, her every scale and fin Thalassa jumped, jumped higher than she ever had in her long life. Her hand stretched, and nearly met his—

—but the ship's thrusters turned in her direction, and she was thrown back, her body splitting a canyon in the waves. The last thing she saw as the walls of water crashed upon her was a word engraved on the ship's bay doors: *Nostos.*

When she reemerged, the flying ship had gone. The sky, cloudy, looked sick.

She did not sing. For even if her grief did not silence her, there was no one left to listen.

Too late, she and Pontus had realized how dire the Earth's surface world had become. Too long they had stayed asleep.

The humans killed the ocean first. Then the air, and then the land. Arrogantly. The people who could not afford to escape on the flying ships (most of them) killed themselves and everything else off quickly after. Nothing could survive in the ocean anymore, nothing except Thalassa.

In their final days, the humans fought over water, which struck her as darkly funny as she watched them battle over the meager streams that made it to the sea.

There's plenty of water here, she taunted the haggard, mask-wearing figures on the shore. *Water everywhere!* She flicked the rot-thick waves with her tail.

Help yourself to a dram of corpses.

She could not say when she and Pontus had begun, couldn't remember anything that resembled a birth. Only that she called, and he answered. The two of them looked a bit like whales, except not. They had scales as well as soft flesh and hair, hands as well as fins and tails, teeth as well as baleen. Mostly they were all throat.

The two of them played with notes until they hit upon something pleasing and leaned into the song like a stretch after a nap. Their first melody lit the deep sea and brought matter to life, churning out creatures and plants great and small. Eurhythmic. Joyful.

Many would eventually leave them, leave the sea, but Thalassa and Pontus knew that to create something demanded surrender. Their songs would go where they would go.

It was difficult to swim now, as the bodies of every fish and shark and whale and plankton filled the water with detritus. The sun's light could no longer penetrate the continental shelf, and so the sea filled with marine snow and bits of bone.

The mass extinction even touched the undersea trench where she and Pontus had laid their heads upon basaltic pillows for the past thousand years. Gone were the tube worms sporting red heads, bristle worms wearing bacteria on their backs like cloaks, shrimp paddling along with long swimmerets and perching in crevices.

She'd sung creatures that could fly by wing or widget, so why couldn't she take flight? Thalassa growled at the sun, meager yellow constant. It would be millions of years before it turned orange and swelled, vaporizing the worlds that revolved around it and everything on them.

Sometimes a melody would come to Thalassa, and her loss stung bright as a fresh cut. The two of them, entwined in a bubbly helix, hands toward each other but not touching, their long hair spired and flared like the curves of a conch shell. The only songs Thalassa knew were duets, and the only thing that made the sea emptier was the gap as she finished one phrase and waited for Pontus to answer.

Sometimes they'd sing creatures that weren't strong enough, and they would hear the echo of their last note ending soon after. Mighty as they were, they could only set things in motion—it was not for them to intervene, to destroy, to save. Their only solace was that no matter how many songs ended, others would continue.

But now there were no songs. No sounds except for the hush of the waves. Thalassa covered her ears. They'd known things would end—knew as every composer did that the time would come for their hands to close, halt the orchestra, instruments down. For every overture they made, there would be a coda.

But not like this. Not so excruciating, not so tortured. Shark teeth in a seal's belly, slow bleed flail.

⊗

In a rise of rocks, she found a wrecked flying ship, the hull spilling corpses into the dead waves. The ship that took Pontus? *Was he—*

—no, no. Her hair loose around her, Thalassa touched the name of the ship. The ship that had stolen Pontos was called *Nostos*. This was some other.

Nostos was from an old human language, meaning *return*. Maybe the departing humans had intended to come back someday, but Thalassa knew them better than they knew themselves now. There would be no return.

She gripped the side with her hands and ripped off the metal panels, jettisoned them out to sea to float with the rest of the trash. Her hair caught and tore in the gears and corners, but she ignored the pain and slammed the metal monstrosity with her tail.

The only part of the ship undamaged by the rocks or her assault was a panel with small circular holes and a hard glass-like sheet. She gnawed at it with her teeth, hit it with her fists until she tired herself out.

She'd just laid her cheek against it when a shot of static boomed out of the holes, startling her. Across the holes was a kind of screen. It displayed a list of words.

She spotted the word *Nostos*, and instinctively touched her finger to it. Another sound echoed through the air, and a soft glow highlighted letters from the new language. *Microphone on*, she read.

She leaned forward as a sound crackled out of the holes, every hope in her rising like wave crests. Could it be?

She lowered her head to the panel. Called his name, sang it. Waited. Waited. The rot languidly sloshed over her scales.

How foolish, she thought, cringing at her own—

—and then he answered.

They were quiet for a moment. They were used to sending out a call and sensing the distance between them by the way the other bent the sound. Here though, through the holes, their voices seemed to go and go and go, a sea without bottom.

He called her name again.

She called his.

Nothing else could match this: the feeling of saying a name, the feeling of hearing a name and hearing the other feel it. They continued on like that for a while, giddy, children tracing the ridges of a shell over and over in their hands.

How could this be possible? Thalassa wondered if she'd gone mad, if her mind had conjured a hallucination to help her weather her sorrow. But she clung to the miracle of hearing him again.

Pontus told her the humans gave him a lot of freedom. *There was talk*, he said, *of going back to collect you.* He said this reluctantly, and she knew she would not be retrieved, nor he returned. The humans didn't recognize them, he confided. They were amazed creatures like them existed.

How rude, she said.

He laughed, and she missed him so much.

You're safe? She asked him. *You have a sea?*

I'm safe, he said. *I have a sea.*

And a sky?

And a sky.

She looked up at the choking clouds. Imagined a clear day, sunlight glinting off wave peaks. Spray from whales leaping and playing.

They tried to sing, thinking that maybe somehow they could erect a bridge of life that they could travel across. They couldn't. She hated the effect that the holes had over his voice, the tinny undertone that betrayed his distance from her.

I'm afraid to die, she confided. *What would it mean?* She was ashamed of her fear, of how it nearly crushed her.

I'm scared too, he answered, and she wanted so badly to touch him.

I wish we had wings, she said.

We only have fins, he answered.

Without warning, the screen over the holes started to flash. It wanted something of her.

The power must be dying, Pontos said when she described how it looked, and she heard alarm in his voice.

Dying? She didn't understand. The machine wasn't alive.

I'll find you, she said. Absurd, but it was the only thing she could think.

Pontus's voice, quick, mallet to a drum desperate:

Don't—

—and his voice was gone, thread cut. The static fraying from the holes ceased.

No, Thalassa said. She pawed at the screen, tried to reach through the panel. Begged. *No. Don't leave me again.*

Painful as it was, she could have lived like that, speaking through holes. She could have lived like that.

It was too much, too much, and in her sorrow of losing Pontus and gaining him and losing him again she cracked the screen in half.

When Thalassa and Pontus woke this last time, they witnessed humans launching themselves into the sea in boats that may as well have been made of fishing net for all their ability to stay afloat. As desperate as drowning men hoping their air bubbles will twist into rope, the humans shoved off in spite of the risk.

The lowest was a night when the silvery glow of the moon through the clouds could almost be called beautiful. Two humans, a mother and small daughter, curled into each other inside a plastic tub that bobbed dangerously over the waves. Thalassa and Pontus saw they had no facemasks—lost, perhaps, in a previous wreck. The mother held her crying child tight and began to sing a lullaby.

A beautiful lullaby. One whose gentleness somehow overrode the shoving and slapping of the waves that lurched them. Smooth as sinew, soft as skin. The refrain declared, *we'll be all right, we'll be all right.*

A lie. One the mother was aware of, from the grief cracking her throat. Once the icecaps melted the long-dormant bacteria (humans thought very highly of themselves, but bacteria was always Thalassa and Pontus's most stubborn and resilient creation) had taken to the air, and humans had no defense.

The mother and child would not last the night.

When the mother spotted them peering over the floating bin they saw her eyes light with fear, and then with hope—could the great creatures of the sea save them?

They could not. Thalassa and Pontus were creators, not savers, not interveners. It was not in their power to sing a song that would change the path of things.

So they did the only thing they could, and added their voices to the mother's, doing their best to honor her melody, taking care to hit the same notes with the same rhythm and inflection. Her breathing was already ragged; they did their best to bolster her chorus, strong rope looping over a fray.

They continued on long after the mother stopped singing, imagining their harmony as a cradle, rocking their children to one last sleep.

The Visitor fell through the clouds in a ship shaped like a nautilus shell. Thalassa watched the purple ship crash into the sea. Most of it sank, but a portion somersaulted back to the surface.

The Visitor emerged from that protected part, a boat-like tub that managed to float on top of the waves. The Visitor was *not* happy, and let loose a string of unfamiliar noises. She leaned over the side, peering into the water where the other parts of her ship had disappeared into the depths—and fell overboard.

Thalassa quickly realized the flailing Visitor couldn't swim. She pulled her from the waves and set her back into the makeshift boat.

She'd never seen anything like the Visitor, and yet she seemed entirely familiar. Fleshy, ridged, a mouth that resembled a jagged cave in stone.

"Stuck on a dead world full of dead things," the Visitor moaned as she dripped into her boat-ship. Thalassa didn't know how the Visitor could speak a language she understood, but she did. Inside the tub was a panel similar to one in the human flying ship, except instead of buttons, screens and levers, it was a panel of gel that smelled faintly like what Thalassa remembered as cherries.

"Thanks for yanking me out," the Visitor said. "Didn't think Earth would be this bad. What they say about humans is true, I guess."

Thalassa practically tipped the boat over. "Humans?" she asked excitedly, looming toward the Visitor. "When did you see humans? Did you see anyone who looked like me with them?"

"Kept moving past their new planet, sorry. Been traveling all over," the Visitor said. When she spoke, a light emanated from her mouth like the glow from a volcano. She seemed sheepish.

"When I was young, I wasn't very adventurous. But then I got old, and realized I'd never explored the universe. You only have so much time." She eyed Thalassa's tail. "Though if the universe has taught me anything, it's that 'time' is relative."

"Are you able to fly?" Thalassa asked. "Could you take me to where you saw the humans?"

"Ship's broke," the Visitor said, shaking her head. "And even if I could I wouldn't, sorry. Made up my mind never to go back, to keep going until…." She glanced at Thalassa's face and stopped. Considered.

"I could transport you using the Hypaethrald," she gestured to a part of the gel that looked identical to the rest. "Faster than light, even. But half my bird's at the bottom of the sea." She looked around at the silent horizon and sighed. "Crap. Didn't think this would be the last place I'd park."

"If I retrieve what you lost," Thalassa said. "Will you let me take— the Hypaethrald? To where the humans are?"

"Even if you did," said the Visitor uneasily, "and I got it running again, you'd be winging it into the dark. It's only an estimate. If I miscalculate where the planet is in its orbit, if someone blew the planet up—"

"I don't care," Thalassa interjected. "All that matters is finding him."

She dove into the waves, and dug out every piece, every screw, every sheet of the strange purple metal that had lodged into the sea floor. For over a week she wrestled folded plastic tarps, dead things and trash that wound around her tail and wrapped around her head. Poisons that seared her and burned her eyes. She didn't mind; she healed fast. Some ship pieces had been carried far away by the current, but Thalassa found them all, clutching them to her chest as she ferried them back.

The gel quivered like a smack of jellyfish.

"The Hypaethrald will send you to where it's located a being with a similar signature," the Visitor told Thalassa. Now she had the ship open by choice. "But that doesn't mean your mister's alive.

"He might be dead—anything could be out there. Give humans ten planets and they'll use up ten and then some." The Visitor's slate eyes squinted at her. "You sure you want to do this?"

Thalassa scanned the horizon, and a memory from long ago swelled in her mind. A young girl dangling her sandaled feet off the side of a boat. Unafraid, the girl handed Pontus a conch shell and asked if they'd heard the song of desert flowers. Then she sang it to them.

A beautiful song. Oh, to hear the little girl, a song herself, sing back to them! They'd been so happy, blazingly happy. Thalassa remembered the sunshine glinting off waves, the cacophony of birds, bells clanging over ships. Remembered coral. Remembered colors. Remembered the sound of his voice.

The memories slid into darkness, leaving only rotten water and cloud-choked sky. Plastic on waves.

"There's no coming back," the Visitor said.

"No return," said Thalassa. She swallowed hard and fought the nausea in her stomach. Resisted the urge to cry.

"Go on then," the Visitor said, nodding at the gel. "Touch it."

Thalassa did, and doubled over as shooting pains surged through her shoulder blades. Something fluttered in her peripheral vision, and for a moment she could have sworn she saw feathers surge around her, suspended in the air like gulls riding the storm.

She opened her eyes to an orange sky. Or perhaps she didn't see the sky—everywhere around her were swirling clouds of orange-yellow gas and dust. It was very hot, and she cringed and hissed as the water on her scales steamed off.

She started to panic. *Humans couldn't survive here*, she thought. *The Visitor sent me to the wrong planet.* It was painful to open her eyes through the whipping dust. She laid face down, grit between her fingers. Forced herself to focus, focus. Though her throat was dry, she sang his name. Listened.

With all the chaos would he even hear—

—and he answered. Weakly.

As she had a million times before she followed his voice, dragging herself across scorched craters that scratched at her scales. With no water her tail found little purchase, but nothing could keep her from him, and before long her hand touched his face.

She cupped her other hand around her eyes to block the wind, and something inside her fell away when she took him in, fear and exuberance crashing together like waves. Her beloved looked desiccated, dried out. Down his cheek scars raised like islands across the sea—but what could have scarred him?

My love— she began to call.

—No, he shouted over the wind. He strained to lift the upper half of his body, pushed her away. *Why, why did you come?*

They thought this planet—but they did something to the sun, he cried. *They left most of us behind.*

My love! Confused, Thalassa reached for him. He was so angry, so upset. She didn't know this Pontus who howled and pulled out his own hair.

In an hour this planet will be gone.

Her face slackened with shock. An hour? That couldn't be. Rage pressed her tongue to the roof of her mouth. It couldn't be. Not after all they'd been through. Humans had taken this from them too?

They could be wrong, she said. She didn't want to sound as frightened she felt, but it slipped out.

If you'd stayed on Earth—

They've been wrong before, she insisted.

Not this time, he said, and she knew, sensed it deep in her bones, that he was right. She couldn't see the orange sun, but she could feel it growing closer, swelling.

You have to go back, Pontus said, clutching her shoulders. He sobbed without tears. *Even we won't survive this. Please. You have to go back.*

It doesn't work that way, she said sadly, and winced as she saw his heart break.

I've killed you, he rasped, collapsing against her. *My heart. You came here to die.*

It wasn't like him at all. The strange scars crossed his whole torso, and Thalassa remembered how he'd reassured her when they called through the holes, realized all the things he didn't tell her for her sake. Though Pontus had been surrounded by humans, surrounded by life and sound, he had been more alone than she had ever been.

He was so beautiful. Her webbed hands touched his face. She leaned her forehead to his, and their hair formed a tent that blocked the dust wind.

No, my love, she sang gently, urging him to follow her voice, follow her home.

I came so we could write the end.

He jerked his head up. They'd never composed an ending before. With relief she watched the thought push through his mind like hands through water, his eyes sharpening until he really did see her.

Our finale.

In a crater they lay side-by-side, scales blistering as the heat steadily increased. They could not see the sky above them nor the rock beneath them.

Thalassa could not decide which was better: to hold his face and look at him, drink up his appearance, or to let him embrace her so that she could feel him across her whole length. She chose the second—she wished she were braver, but she wanted so badly to be held—and put her chin in the saddle of his neck, his chin in hers.

She listened to him breathe in and out, in and out, even and then ragged.

I wish we had wings, he said.

Thalassa thought of the Visitor, and wondered how far she'd go before she had to stop. Hoped she never would. Thought of feathers in the storm. Of what it felt like to fly.

We only have fins, she answered. Thought of the mother and child: *We'll be all right.*

We'll be all right, Pontus agreed, and he sounded like himself again.

It was coming. She opened her mouth and felt the muscles in his jaw move in sync with hers.

Though their last duet was a world ago, they remembered every note, and if not for the heat Thalassa could imagine they were back in the coral, weaving their way through the wonderland they'd composed. Remembered the blue of sky and sea. Remembered the squawk of seabirds, the charm of land birds. Remembered the mother and child who held on until the end. Remembered the little girl on the boat who sang of flowers that defied the odds and bloomed. Memories like pearls in her hands, overflowing.

Their tails splintered into powder, yet their voices boomed just as powerfully as they ever did. Around them a thousand creatures rose and broke like waves across the dust, blooming, bursting like spring flowers and dying within the same second.

She pulled Pontus closer, and something inside her settled as their harmony intensified and braided tighter into the wind.

What was breaking apart but a return to something older, something older than even her?

He had been taken, but she had found him. Who was to say she wouldn't again? The little girl handed Thalassa the conch shell, its spirals opening with possibility. The mother helped her child climb out of the plastic bin onto a safer shore.

Who was to say that things couldn't end differently another time?

As the heat returned them to light Thalassa closed her eyes. Angled her head so that the lobe of her ear kissed his. Sang with everything she had left, and listened—

—trusted, that when she called again, he'd answer.

E. A. Petricone writes strange things, obsessively collects post-its and rocks, and when she's tipsy she sends unsolicited science articles to her friends. Her work has appeared in Apparition Literary Magazine, Slice Magazine, All Worlds Wayfarer, Allegory, The Writer's Chronicle, Vine Leaves Literary Journal, and other marvelous places. She lives in Massachusetts. You can find her on Twitter @eapetricone.

The Perfect Solution

by Brett Kozlowski

"**I** put in an application to be a rhino," Travis said as he poked through the leaves on the forest floor, searching for nuts.

Vic looked up from his own search, brows knit in confusion. "A rhino? What are you talking about?"

"A northern white rhino, actually. They just went extinct, so some new positions are opening up. The De-extinction Association started taking applications this week, and I sent mine in."

"But you already have a job," Vic said, turning away from his foraging work. "You're a dodo."

Travis gave a snort. "Yeah, as if I could forget. This big beak strapped to my face is a pretty good reminder. And sure, the job's been fine these last couple of years. Peaceful and all that. But haven't you ever wanted more?"

"More? How is a rhino any better than a dodo?"

Travis shrugged uncomfortably. "Come on, Vic. You have to admit, this isn't exactly the most glamorous work."

"Not glamorous? The dodo's iconic! It's the woolly mammoth of birds."

"I'd say that the elephant bird is the woolly mammoth of birds."

"Don't get smart with me. I mean in terms of star power. When people think extinction, they think of the dodo. It's on the De-extinction Association's logo, for Christ's sake."

"I guess. That's what I thought when I took the job. But it's basically just a big fat pigeon that waddles around eating nuts. Where's the dazzle?"

"Rat!" Vic barked, and they both hurried back to their nests, startling the rodent, which scurried away through the undergrowth. Vic inspected his egg for signs of damage, but it appeared untouched.

"That's another thing," Travis said after checking his own egg. "I'm fed up with babysitting this damn egg. The job was tedious enough when all we had to do was look for food, but then one day Barb from the Association shows up with these two eggs for us to take care of. And if the eggs get broken, we don't even get our bonuses this year? What a bunch of bullshit. Now we can't walk away for five minutes, or the eggs will get smashed by some critter looking for an easy meal. The damndest thing is, the eggs aren't even real, so I don't get why all these animals are trying to eat them."

Vic frowned under his beak. "The Association doesn't just paint rocks white and call them eggs. These are specially crafted synthetic eggs they make in their high-tech lab. Same place our beaks and feathers come from. The eggs look and smell just like real dodo eggs, which is why the rats want them so bad. It's all about authenticity. What's the point of this work if we don't make it authentic?"

"I've been wondering what the point is either way," Travis muttered, continuing his foraging efforts among the humus of rotting leaves. "I miss the car factory."

"Forget about the car factory. It's gone and it's not coming back. Just be grateful that the De-extinction Association was here for us after we got laid off. You could do a lot worse than dodo work."

"Come on, Vic, I don't need a lecture. I was just saying that it might be fun to be a rhino for a change. Big and majestic, roaming the open plains, and best of all, no eggs."

"Aha, jackpot!" Vic exclaimed, producing a piece of orange fruit from between two tree roots. Taking a bite, he tipped his head back to allow the morsel to slide down his beak and into his real mouth. He chewed thoughtfully before responding. "All things considered, I think we have a lot to be thankful for. We could be great auks, shivering in the cold rain on some island up north. And do you remember Reggie, from the factory?"

Travis thought for a moment. "Was he the one who got in trouble for pulling all those stupid pranks?"

"Yeah, Reggie was hilarious! That thing with the tape on the toilet seats? Classic."

Travis looked dubious, but Vic didn't seem to notice.

"Anyway, as I was saying, Reggie ended up working as a Guadalupe caracara."

"A what?"

"It's like a sort of a hawk, I guess. But he was killing chickens; you know, just for authenticity, and maybe to express his love of pranks. But I guess some farmer didn't have a sense of humor, because he poisoned some meat and left it out near the chicken coop. Long story short, poor Reggie's six feet under."

"Well what was that idiot doing eating meat he found just lying around? He probably would have died even if it wasn't poisoned. And at least the hunting animals get to have a little fun. I'm sure it beats scrounging around in the dirt all day."

Vic snorted. "You're a cold-hearted bastard, you know that? I was just telling you the story so you'd appreciate how good we have it as dodos. Warm weather, peace and quiet, and no predators, except for the animals going after the eggs. If you were a white rhino, you'd be dodging lions and hyenas all day. Does that sound like a good time to you?"

As he considered this, Travis picked a nut from the leaves at his feet and examined it without enthusiasm. The nut slipped from his grasp when he heard footsteps crunching through the leaves. He and Vic both whirled toward the noise.

"This better not be another goddamn wild pig," Travis whispered.

A moment later, three people emerged from the undergrowth: a man, a woman, and a girl of perhaps seven, each dressed in khaki shorts and hiking boots.

"Avery, look," the woman said, pointing at Vic and Travis. "It's two dodos!"

The child regarded them with suspicion. "You said dodos were birds."

"They are, honey," the man answered, holding out his phone and repeatedly tapping the screen. Bright light flashed half a dozen times, making Vic's eyes water. "The dodo is a flightless bird that only lives here on Mauritius. It's a member of the pigeon family. Isn't that interesting?"

The girl narrowed her eyes at her father. "Those aren't birds. They're just men dressed like birds."

"Come on, Avery," her mother chided. "Don't be a spoil-sport. Lots of little girls would love to see dodos. And look at that, they have eggs. Make sure to get some pictures of the eggs, Howard."

The man tapped his phone several more times, producing another barrage of light.

Vic jabbed Travis with his elbow, and then began strutting back and forth in his best bird walk, head bobbing with every step. Travis sighed, bending down to peck half-heartedly at the ground. He watched the newcomers from the corner of his eye and noticed the girl's face sinking into a pout.

"You said we were gonna see dodos. I want to see dodos!"

"Honey," her father said soothingly, "This is what dodos are. When I was a kid, I could never have dreamed of seeing dodos face to face like this. Species like Tasmanian tigers and Caribbean monk seals died off, and that was that. But thanks to the De-extinction Association, they're all back for us to enjoy. And lots of laid-off workers have jobs again, filling in for the missing animals. It's the perfect solution."

The girl looked like she was about to protest, when her eyes suddenly popped wide open. "Look Daddy, monkeys! Real monkeys!"

Travis turned to see a pair of macaques pawing curiously at his egg.

"God-fucking-dammit!" he yelled, dashing back to the nest and chasing the monkeys up into the trees.

"He said bad words, Mommy," the girl squealed delightedly. "I told you they weren't real birds."

"Don't you pay any attention to that, Avery," her mother said, shooting Travis an icy glare. "Let's just keep walking. There are supposed to be more dodos down by the beach. We'll get better reception there, too, and maybe your father can send a complaint to the Association about professionalism among the animals."

Turning on her heel, the woman stomped off through the trees, leading her daughter by the hand. The man snapped one last photo before following.

Travis looked at Vic, whose face was reddening.

"Great work, Travis, just terrific. We're not supposed to talk in front of tourists at all, and we're definitely not supposed to swear in front of their kids. Tourism is the Association's bread and butter, and they rely on us putting on a good show. We're here so people like that can see dodos in the wild, and now that kid's never going to think of dodos the same way again."

"It was a lost cause anyway. That girl wasn't buying it for a minute. Kids never do. It's only the parents who get excited."

Vic sniffed. "Well, I guess it takes a more mature mind to appreciate the wonders of nature. You know what kids are like, with their attention spans and whatnot."

"I guess. I bet she would have been impressed by a rhino, though."

"Are you still going on about that? I'm telling you, there's no more important work than dodo work. Besides, there are a couple of rhino species that are still alive. The dodo was one of a kind."

"The dodo's a joke. When I got laid off from the factory, I felt useless, and I thought this job would give me back my dignity. But all I do is waddle around with this goddamn beak on my face, digging in the dirt and chasing rats and monkeys away from an egg that I'd be better off without. It's pathetic. This whole damn job is pathetic, and if you can't see that, then you're pathetic too."

Vic was silent for a moment, his face twisting into something that would have been frightening, if not for the beak. When he spoke, his voice was slow with fury.

"How fucking dare you. You stupid, selfish, ungrateful—"

A gunshot punched through the forest, cutting off Vic's tirade. Blood sprayed across the dirt from a wound in the center of Travis's chest. He looked down at himself, then at Vic for a long, helpless moment before his legs crumpled and he collapsed to the earth.

Eyes already clouding, Travis whispered, "white rhino…" before his chest stopped moving, and his body grew still.

All was quiet for a few seconds, and then a man of middle years stepped into view, a smoking rifle in hand.

"Oh hell," the man cursed, taking in the scene. "I thought that was a wild pig. Now I've gone and shot a dodo."

Vic was stunned, but he tried to remember that he had a job to do.

Wrenching himself from his stupor, he got to work, strutting back and forth between the trees and scratching at the ground with his beak.

The man looked down at Travis's body, shaking his head sadly. "It's a real shame. Such a lovely bird. And I'm sure there'll be a hefty fine in this for me."

Vic took a break from scratching to give the man a squawk.

"Sorry about that, little fella," the man said to Vic. "I was only trying a shoot a pig. Damn things are nothing but pests, and they aren't supposed to be here anyway. I hope the Association knows that I would never shoot a dodo on purpose. Oh dear, and look what's happened to your poor nest."

Vic spun around to see a pair of macaques efficiently smashing both eggs to pieces against the ground. The monkeys seemed bewildered to find nothing inside but a thin gray fluid and two small radio transmitters.

Vic could only gape in dismay. "Oh, son of a bitch!"

Brett Kozlowski was born in the Detroit area, where he lives to this day. He has worked as a technical writer, park groundskeeper, real estate manager, security guard, tech support rep, and private investigator, among other things. His greatest loves are humor, storytelling, and the magic that happens when the two come together. He recently finished his first novel, An Exciting Career in Professional Murder, and is currently seeking representation.

FOUR LITTLE BEES

By Bradley Heywood

Day 1

Today Hong Kong builds its first Forest Tower. Our aim is to turn city into jungle by adding flowers and trees up and down business and home areas. My team is in charge of the introduction and study of bees. Our work is important, but not new. South Korea and Singapore have already begun their own Forest Towers. Eyes are on Taiwan who says they have a big surprise. Ching says that Taiwan will shame us all by stuffing every meter with bees. Ching is my colleague. Sometimes he stops talking long enough to work. On these days the staff celebrate with Dim-Sum.

"One big hive," says Ching. "Full of pricks," he laughs.

Things come in cycles, and last time we four countries stood up and were noticed, they called us Four Little Dragons. Now they hear our idea, and they giggle, calling us Four Little Bees.

"They say this because like the bee, you have only one stab and then you are dead," says Ching.

I do not care what people think. I am grateful they let us try. I believe Forest Towers will help the future, and I am not alone. People are celebrating, and I smile, even though my sister teases me that I grin like rat. Today I say, "Squeak," to my sister, because my team will build the first tower.

"They let you do this because you are a woman," says Ching, "It will bring less shame to China if we fail."

I still smile. "Squeak."

Day 243

The committee has been arguing all night. The coffee tastes like water, yet nobody says so because it came with the representative from China.

"We are behind schedule," says the representative. His tone flutters like a bird, but his eyes are always creeping up the skirts of my staff like a spider.

I tell him we have lost several hives, and those that remain have split between three sectors—two of which are not on speaking terms.

"South Korea is marketing its green towers for tourism," trills the man from China. His fat finger wags, "Sky Forest they call it. The external is covered with flowers and trees. The adults pay so their child may snip the ivy to grow it at home—they are calling it educational ecology. South Korea is shaming us with success."

I tell him that our Forest Tower isn't for tourism. Our wish is to create a new ecosystem, but the man from China does not listen. His ears work only when I uncross my legs, all other times I am a ghost.

"Oh, my friend is on vacation in Taiwan," says Ching, "and what is Tower Honey tea?" The man from China goes as red as his flag. This upsets him for the same reason he is here, because Taiwan has made a fortune from selling their new bubble tea with honey from their towers. Ching knows this, which is why he is smiling as the man from China froths like a crab. I believe that in a previous life Ching was a housecat who dreamt of being a tiger. He is forever playing with mice. Today his mouse is red and angry.

"This is unacceptable," says the man. "China will not be insulted. You will make Hong Kong honey. You will do better."

I tell the representative that the bees have experienced much pressure with the sudden chill, and that perhaps we could provide a little, after all, this is Hong Kong. We do not need much to show off.

"I will say how much will be given," says the man from China, and because it shames him to talk to a woman, he tells us that all honey will be provided. My legs do not move, so he does not look at me when he speaks. I explain that bees use honey for food. The man from China does not care.

"This is my responsibility," the man shrieks. The room goes silent.

森林樓巢

KATHERINE
KIREEVA

"So brave," says Ching. The man from China nods but is clearly confused. "To take the blame for killing all our bees. So powerful to face China's fury alone."

Grandmother tells me that only an idiot can speak idiot. If so, Ching must be their king. The man from China goes white. And for the first time he is thinking.

I smile. "Squeak."

Day 303

Research suggests that fungi benefits the bees, acting as both a food and anti-viral aid, so we fill the twenty-second floor with mushrooms. There is a very old man who says he built the tower. He is very angry.

"First you infect my home with bugs," he tells me "and now you fill my floor with mold?"

I tell the owner that there is great honor in being the first Forest Tower in Hong Kong.

"When my Father taught me the ways of architecture, he did not tell me to flood my halls with screaming bugs and fill the walls with mushrooms!"

I apologize for the damage to the electrical systems. We underestimated how quickly and successfully the mushrooms would grow. I offer to show him the positive results it's had on our sky hives.

"Over fifty complaints from tenants," he tells me. "A girl scared of bees, a boy stung by bees. Even a dog arrested for eating bees because the bees are now government property. Everybody is mad."

I nod. He isn't wrong. It takes a lot of bees to make enough honey for a jar, and even with us talking down the Chinese government from taking *all the honey* to just most of it, we were forced to introduce more bees to get enough honey for research. It has been suggested that the bees may not live till the next summer. This means that all space is being used to offer food, shelter, and water for the bees. There are three sections of the tower: Wing, Stripe, and Sting. All three are responsible for a dozen or so hives. All three have differing opinions on how to care for the bees. All three know best.

Singapore has just announced that it will only run its Green Towers for a single year. They will not share their information beyond that it was an insightful experience. This is not just an experiment for me.

"Have you seen what those beasts have done to my building's hole?" the old man demands, "do you know what it is doing to the Feng Shui?" The old man is always complaining about his holes. "I would be careful not to spit in the eye of dragons," he warns me.

I explain that we respect Feng Shui, bees do not, and as we have yet to see a dragon fly through the tower, perhaps our good fortune will continue.

"Better to have a hole and a dragon not use it, than need a hole and not have one," says the old man.

I explain that there is still a hole.

"Yes, but it is full of bees. I do not know what a sore dragon will do, but if I find one, I will be sure to give it your address."

I ask Ching how I can scare them.

"The way you scare all selfish people," laughs Ching, "make them share."

I tell Sting how strong they are, and the doglike lady looks happy like I've just picked up her lead. I tell them how happy Singapore will be knowing that Sting wishes to copy them. The dog lady looks sad, like I have come home to find a wet spot.

"This is not a copy," she whines, "this makes good sense." I agree. It is good sense. Singaporean sense. The best. A day goes by and I receive a message telling me that Sting will give twice the honey of Wing and Stripe.

Day 365

Over-eagerness in Sting has taken so much honey that we have to hand out pots of emergency sugar water. I watched an old man cry over his bees. They were dead. It is good to see people care, even if it hurts when they do.

Wing is helping. They have suffered most with altitude and winter. They know the cures and secrets. But most importantly, they know what to say and when to be quiet when things go wrong.

Tourism brings people. Word is spreading. There is some argument whether a human forest is as good as a natural one, but I am not interested. This is philosophy and I am a scientist. One day the world will not care about the Four Little Bees and their Forest Towers—they will be normal—and as anyone will tell you, things that are normal are ignored, and focus is directed to the loud and the noisy and the broken. Some things are changing, some stay the same. China still makes its demands. Britain still turns up, making a mess, and tries to apologize. And my sister is still cruel when I smile. And we nod, and we wait, counting down the time till we're allowed to go back to our bees. I want to end with something. You do not have to trust me if I do not have to care when I tell you that our honey really is the best.

This makes me smile. "Squeak."

Bradley Heywood was born in Manchester, England. It was there he studied animal behavior and he learnt that life was so interesting that he had to write about it.

WILL-O-THE-WALMART

By Jennifer Lee Rossman

It wasn't paradise, not in any human sense of the word, but they paved it anyway.

They drained that unsightly marsh water, razed the dead trees that were a forest in name only, and as for all the animals? Well, most of them were irritating mosquitoes, hideous slimy toads, nothing anyone would lose sleep over.

Now, of course every animal has a purpose, a right to live as nature intended. And of course, humanity is not exempt from the web of life. We need insects to pollinate our flowers and fruit, toads to control the insects and give the night that twangy, chirping love song.

But this is not a story about humanity finding our place in nature or reversing the damage we did. By the time they paved over that swamp, that last little bit of wilderness left in an over-industrialized world, it was too late for all that.

This is a story about how I found my girl again.

It used to get dark, back before He Who Must Not Be Named stole the idea for the incandescent lightbulb, stole the credit for electrifying the world, and stole the night from us.

We all thought it was a wondrous idea. After all, the dark is where the bad things hide. Bears and monsters and glowing lights that lead you astray, all the terrible things that remind us we're not at the top of the food chain.

We got rid of all of them when we eradicated the night, and yet....

At the edge of the parking lot stood a store. You know the type. One of those enormous stores that sells everything from clothing to electronics, toiletries to vegetables.

Well, "vegetables." 3-D printed in a lab, because real vegetables need fresh air and nature and pollination. But you get the idea.

It was the kind of place you might go on Christmas Eve in a last-ditch attempt to find a present for your girlfriend. Yeah, I procrastinated, and yeah, I should have known what she would want after being together nearly ten years. I'm not really a sentimental girl, what can I say?

So there we were, bright fluorescent lights overhead and linoleum under foot, every part of our habitat man-made and climate controlled. We didn't have a cart, because she said we didn't need one; my arms overflowed with the body wash sets and whimsical hats with reindeer antlers she suddenly decided we needed.

Joni was talking. About what, I don't know. I wasn't paying attention, too busy trying to remember if she liked scarves and which Hogwarts house colors she would want them in.

Then she stopped. Frozen in place, her eyes transfixed on the garden center's twinkling artificial Christmas trees.

"We should take a shortcut," she murmured.

"Shortcut? What shortcut? We're going the other way." She didn't answer. "Joni?"

She took a step toward the trees, a look of utter serenity on her face. Something seemed to catch her eye; she broke out in a grin and charged forward.

What on earth? I followed her, catching her wrist just before she crossed the threshold of the plastic and metal forest.

"Joni, what are you doing?"

She blinked, slowly, like she was coming out of a trance. "I don't know."

We walked on toward the electronics, but she moved reluctantly, her gaze still locked onto the garden center. At the checkout she stood facing that end of the store, hardly engaging with me, but that wasn't exactly a noteworthy occurrence those days; on the way home, she watched the store disappear in the rearview mirror.

Joni was like that all night. Maybe I should have asked if something was the matter, if I could've done anything to help her. At one point, when we were young and we hadn't realized relationships had to be tended to or they would wither and die, I would've asked.

But somewhere along the line, I guess love became a given, an ever-renewable resource I could just take and take and take from without ever giving anything back, and once that happened, it felt like there was no point trying to go back.

I don't know if she got any sleep, or just laid there next to me, staring at the ceiling. I only know I woke to the sound of the screen door slamming at some ungodly hour, followed by a car's headlights sweeping past our bedroom window.

The display of artificial trees stood in the garden center like a mockery of the wilderness they had paved over to build the store, an inaccurate museum diorama based on artists' interpretations and cultural memory of pine-scented air fresheners.

Maybe two dozen trees made up the forest, some bare and green, some metallic silver or gold or pink and positively aglow with lights. Beautiful and gaudy, but small and surrounded by other merchandise. Absolutely impossible to get lost in.

And yet several people had seen my girl walk in, looking like she was hypnotized, and never come out.

I stared into the forest, waiting to see what she had seen. It shouldn't be possible. Mysterious woods that disappear people had gone the way of the woods themselves; no longer could things lurk in the darkness, waiting to snatch up people who take a shortcut in the middle of the night.

One of the lightbulbs detached itself from the tree. At least, that's what it looked like. Just popped off the tree and flitted out of sight.

I quickly moved to the side, trying to get a better angle on where it went while I scrambled for an explanation. The word *firefly* flashed like neon inside my skull, but they only existed in museums and old movies now, just like birdsong and buzzing cicadas.

An afterimage, maybe, from staring at the lights for too long. Except they sparkled in my periphery, moving when I moved my eyes and looking nothing like whatever I had seen.

There it was again, darting back and forth between trees, only momentarily lingering in the open. Inviting me in.

I could not explain it then any more than I can explain it now. I just knew. It wanted me to follow it.

I took a step closer. The light grew brighter, larger, yet cast no shadows or illumination on the trees around it.

Another step. It bobbed up and down. Nodding. *Yes, yes, come closer*, it seemed to say.

Maybe, if I had grown up in the time of swampy paradises and woods filled with magic, someone would have warned me about following strange lights into the forest. But those stories died out right along with the birds and the bees and the apple trees.

The stories died out. The things they warned us about, on the other hand…

⊗

There were only twenty-something trees, but I kept walking deeper into the woods anyway. Walking, then running, gleefully following the light as it twisted and turned and doubled back.

There wasn't an exact moment when dirt and pine needles overtook the linoleum, when the trees stopped smelling like plastic and started smelling like a more natural version of those little air fresheners that hang on the rearview mirrors of taxis. It just…happened, so gradually that by the time I finally acknowledged it, there was no going back.

Brightness overwhelmed me. Not necessarily because of its intensity; I had seen brighter. No, it took me a moment to identify what was so unsettling, but I finally found a name for it.

Sunshine. At first dappled through the canopy, but as the trees grew sparser and grass replaced dirt, it bore down on me, spilling buckets of warmth and light.

Was this the "daylight" the lightbulb companies tried to sell us? If so, I think we should sue them for false advertising.

Somewhere, deep in the back of my mind, I knew it was still night, knew I was still in the garden center. But I didn't care if it wasn't real, because there was Joni.

Maybe it was the sunlight, but she never looked more beautiful than she did now, standing in the sedges with iridescent insect wings sparkling like fairy dust around her. How had I ever taken for granted this stunning being who shared my life with me?

And it wasn't just her; even if it took me embarrassingly long to notice, the rest of this world overwhelmed my senses. Buzzing creatures, the sulfuric smell of swamp, a quiet splash as a frog launched into the water.

The light danced at the edge of the woods. Almost…happy, proud.

"Swamp gas," I murmured.

"What about swamp gas?" Joni asked.

"I don't know," I said, staring over her shoulder. "I just felt like I needed to explain away the light."

"Will-o-the-wisp," she corrected. "And you don't need to explain it away. Explaining it kills the magic, and I think that's all the wisp has left. We killed off everything else."

I couldn't remember the last time we talked this much, any more than humanity could remember the last time there was this much nature around.

How did we lose so much and never notice?

We walked for hours, or maybe it was only minutes. It may have been a year. Time had little meaning there, in the Will-o-the-wisp's memory.

The little light followed us as we walked, hand-in-hand, through the woods, bobbing happily along. When it grew dark, it was our guide, illuminating the suggestion of a path beat down by deer and foxes and all the other long-gone creatures we only saw in museum murals.

We must have been the first people it had taken in over a century, for it clung to us the way we clung to each other. Or maybe we were just the first who didn't want to go back, who had not been taken but willingly left the artificial paradise to be impossibly lost in a forest of two dozen fake trees.

It was easier to love Joni there. No distractions, no stress, no pressure to be what anyone else thinks we should be. Just her and me, remembering why we fell in love in the first place.

"Do you think they regretted it?" she asked, her voice soft as the grass under our backs. "The ones who saw the last bit of wilderness paved over."

"Probably not as much as you would think. By the time they were in charge, so much had gone extinct, it was inevitable."

I paused, trailing my fingers along her arm and wondering what the point of no return had been. The dodo? The tiger? The sunflower? Forgetting that she loved sunflowers?

"No, I change my mind. It might have felt inevitable, maybe even welcome at first, like they were relieved it finally happened so they could stop having it constantly nagging at the back of their heads and move on with their lives. As soon as it happened, though? They knew they would regret every choice that led them to that garden center for the rest of their lives."

But Joni wasn't listening. She stared, transfixed, at a spot behind me.

My heart sank, and I refused to turn around because I know exactly what I'm going to see.

"We don't have to follow it," I said, but even as the words left my mouth, I knew I was wrong.

No matter how much I tried to ignore it, the buzzing in the air came not from insects but from chainsaws, and pavement poked through bare spots in the undergrowth. Our paradise was dying. Yeah, maybe it wasn't real to begin with, but it still hurt to lose it.

I looked at Joni, took her hand in mine, and we followed the light.

We were ready to call it a shared hallucination until Joni put her hand in her pocket and pulled out an acorn.

We found a tiny crack in the pavement, dug down deep until we reached earth. Maybe it didn't mean anything in the grand scheme of things, one little seed that would, in all likelihood, not get enough nutrients to survive.

But maybe it would, and maybe someday its roots would crack all the asphalt covering what used to be paradise.

I don't know if one tree can be considered a forest, but it's a start.

Jennifer Lee Rossman (she/her) has never been accused of being normal, and neither have her stories. She is autistic, queer, and disabled, and lives in a group home in Binghamton, New York, where she nags staff about signing up for her gay flag of the day emails. Jennifer's non-writing interests include quoting Jurassic Park any chance she gets, being a Nikola Tesla fangirl, and trying to befriend the raccoon who lives in the dumpster. She is the proud mother of three fish (Mazie, Rey, and Dr. Sarah Harding) and two snails (Castiel and Loki). The raccoon is named Steve. Follow her on Twitter @JenLRossman.

No One Needs a Chiweenie

by Katrinka Mannelly

On Tuesday every domestic cat in the world died.

No one was more upset than Nadine Morris. Curled up with Mr. Cuddles, her favorite, Nadine dozed during Wheel of Fortune until wild bonus round cheers woke her with a jerk. Mr. Cuddles did not move. Nadine poked his limp body. Eyes open and pupils dilated, Mr. Cuddles was gone. In the kitchen, Nadine discovered Pickles face down in the water dish. A frantic tour around the house revealed Greta, Mooshee, Lu-Lu, and Nala, all dead.

On Wednesday the hamsters went down. Thursday, beta fish. Friday, parakeets, cockatiels, and macaws worldwide were belly up. Saturday the dogs dropped. American Kennel Club officials, support animal cons, and children everywhere grieved inconsolably.

As pet owners mourned, farmers worried. The pattern was clear—domestic cats had been wiped out while feral cats continued to roam. Bird cages remained empty as flocks flew through the skies. Zoos were stripped of animals, except critters slated for reintroduction to the wild after rehabilitation. The world wondered. Was it genetically modified foods? Hand sanitizer? Eminent alien invasion? Freyja knew it was Gaia.

On Sunday Freyja hitched her cats, who had thankfully been spared, to her chariot and headed to Gaia's cave. Gaia greeted Freyja looking tired but resplendent—statuesque, adorned in spider webs dripping with morning dew, mesmerizing. Her skin fluctuated between a greenish and bluish hue accentuating her elven features. Her eyes evoked deep cerulean pools, but most stunning was her hair. Living things flowed from Gaia's scalp. At the moment hibiscus cascaded from her head, but it was transitioning. Flowers receded as English ivy appeared.

"Freyja, to what do I owe this honor?"

"Don't be coy, Auntie. The Allfather is pissed. He's worried about Hugin and Munin, not to mention the humans. He, Thor, and Loki are ready to go to war, but I convinced them to let me talk to you. I know you must have a reason."

Gaia unfurled a fan and waved it as the sweat streaked down her temples. "Forgive me, dear. Global warming is like one constant hot flash. It'll be the death of me."

Gaia turned and walked into the cave, giving Freyja a fetching view of her Spanish moss locks. It almost distracted her from the dirt clods falling from somewhere under Gaia's gown.

They sat and Gaia extended her hand. A mist surrounded it and dissipated revealing a coconut cup. "Spring water, dear?"

Freyja accepted. "It's delicious. Won't you join me?"

Gaia ran a hand over her midsection. "My sea levels are rising daily. The last thing I need is water weight, dear."

Gaia's hair, now a glorious spray of red, yellow, and orange autumn leaves rustled as she coughed. She tried to keep it dainty, but it turned into a fit and didn't stop until she hacked up a desiccated chunk of coral. Freyja tried not to gawk, but the thing was huge and dripping with mucus.

"Excuse me." Gaia blushed as she pushed it into her thigh letting her body reabsorb it. "I'm a hot mess."

"Why are you killing their pets?"

"I've had it with humans. They're destroying me, piece by piece, starting with the parts I love most."

"So this is revenge?"

"For Tartarus sake, I'm trying to get their attention!" Molten lava leaked out the corner of her mouth, burning a trail down her chin. Freyja politely looked away as Gaia ripped a strip of bull kelp from her hair and patted it into the wound. The seaweed smoothed her skin but left a scar.

"It's working. But why pets?"

"Humans haven't noticed anything else. I'm carrying a heavy load.

What's wrong with lightening the burden and getting their attention?"

"But pets?"

"Have you ever seen my beautiful southern resident orcas?"

Freyja shrugged. "I've seen killer whales, if that's what you mean."

"It's not what I mean," Gaia snapped. "The southern residents are special. The Salish Sea used to be filled with them. Now there are just seventy-five. Tahlequah, one of my female orcas, lost her baby immediately after her birth because they are starving to death in their ancestral home. She carried the decomposing corpse on her rostrum for two weeks. It hurt more than her heart to lug it around. She screamed to the humans, 'wake up,' but they didn't hear. They can't hear, see or feel my whales, my turtles, or my rain forests dying. If it isn't under their damn noses, they don't notice." Gaia ran her fingers through the pea vines twining around her head.

"Don't you love the pets too? Aren't they also yours?"

"It's the lesser of two evils."

"People need their pets."

Rosemary aroma emanating from Gaia's head filled the room. "No one needs a Labradoodle, or a Chiweenie dog or a stupid hairless cat, but the world does need tigers, mountain gorillas and rhinos—I need them." Venus flytraps sprouted from her head snapping wildly making it hard for Gaia to compose herself. "I'm sorry. I'm off balance."

Freyja worried. Each pantheon considered itself the most supreme, and hers was no exception, but what if Mother Nature lost it? What would happen to the rest of them? To everything? She shuddered.

"Gaia, do you know about the Internet?"

"Hermes tried to explain it to me once, some sort of manmade worldwide web. It sounds stupid. Computers are nonsense. Please don't tell me humans are using the Internet to save my creatures, because if they are, it's not working."

"That's not what I was going to say."

The Venus flytraps gave way to lavender sprigs, calming the room a bit.

Freyja continued, "Humans use the Internet to communicate. They send memes—little stories that reflect their values and beliefs. Sif showed me one. Can I share it with you?"

Gaia nodded, sending a wave rippling through her halo of cattails.

"A young boy's beloved wolfhound has cancer and is being put down. His parents question why dogs' lives are shorter than humans'. The child tells them people need a long life to learn how to be loving, kind and good—things not inherent to them. Animals, on the other hand are born loving, kind, and good, so they don't have to stay around as long."

A glimmer shown in the corner of Gaia's eye and her hair turned to weeping willow.

"There are thousands of similar stories. People do need designer dogs, hairless cats, and tamed rodents. Domestic animals are your ambassadors. When people feel their love and love them back, it opens their hearts to caring about more animals, people, and places. If you want to engage humans, pets are your best hope."

"Hmmm…" Gaia considered as fiddle ferns curled around her head.

"Maybe pets don't deserve this. Should I hit 'em in the stomach instead? Humans do notice what they taste. I could annihilate pigs. If I take away their bacon, they'll notice."

"You're missing the point."

"Am I? I have been told I'm a slow learner." Her hair changed to a wreath of holly leaves as she let out a merry chuckle.

"This is serious. Odin, Thor, and Loki are ready to fight. The humans have you on the ropes and we could take you down…" Freyja bowed her head, "if we had to."

Gaia's scalp morphed into thorny cactus.

"I don't think either of us wants a battle. I also can't imagine you desire the extinction of any animal. It's not in your nature."

"Maybe it is, and maybe it isn't."

"Your anger is justified but you of all people should know, cutting someone else's tree down, doesn't make yours grow taller."

"Is that supposed to be a joke?" Gaia had several small saplings extending from her head like a crown.

"Taking away pets won't help your orcas. It's going to make things worse. It's punitive, not constructive. The rest of us gods have been checked out for a while, leaving you to deal with this by yourself and it isn't fair."

Gaia nodded as she picked barnacles off her thumbnail. "I haven't seen any of you exert influence in a long while. It has been lonely."

"We'll help you. Norse gods adore animals, especially Loki. We can get the Olympians on board too. They love interaction with humans. And the younger gods—Jesus has a guy— Saint Francis. He's perfect for this. Extinction is a massive problem. We'll pull together to solve it."

The saplings on Gaia's head melded into a single redwood indicating her readiness to ruminate these weighty matters.

On Monday the gods formed an action committee, and Gaia had a change of heart.

The world rejoiced.

No one was happier than Nadine Morris who found a basket of mewing kittens on her doorstep next to a mountain of catnip. To Nadine's joy, the little fur balls looked remarkably like younger versions of Nala, Lu-Lu, Mooshee, Greta, Pickles, and her favorite, Mr. Cuddles.

Katrinka Mannelly writes and lives in Fircrest, Washington with her husband Brian, daughter Tigist, dog Queenie, and cat Riptide. She is a storyteller and always has been. Her book, Section 130, is available at Barnes & Noble and Amazon.

THE BAMBI COLLABORATION

by Bo Balder

The plastic sculptures talk to her in dreams. At first Jolie doesn't really believe what they're saying, but they make so much sense that she kind of has to. She's built them herself, with her own two hands, and now there's a whole row of them, standing watch on the beach. They look great from the porch. The totem pole made of bottle caps, the fawn made from all pink plastic.

By day they're silent. Jolie rises from her crouch and watches the kids on their Civic Duty. They gather plastic the surf deposits on the beach each morning. It's a good way to get them outside in the fresh air, and it also chips away nicely at their 1,000,000 minutes of lifetime Civic Duty. Half an hour a day really adds up, and it means they will have more spare time in college and when they have young kids. The Civic Duty had only been instituted when Jolie was twenty-five, and she hadn't started on them right away, so she's still got a lot of minutes to go.

She bends down again to pick up more plastic trash. The prediction is that humanity will still be picking up trash in a century, and maybe more than that on filtering all the micro beads, even with the help of gen-engineered bacteria and funguses.

The octopus statue, made solely of red bottle tops and plaited Lays packets, winks at her out of the corner of her eye. Jolie sighs. Isn't it enough that they talk to her all night? And not the kind of stuff you want to hear in your dreams. No, it's all, *why are we here, who made us, what is our purpose in life?* Like unhappy teenagers or cats chasing their own tails. Jolie hasn't got the answers.

She picks up more trash. Most of it has been floating in the ocean for so long all color has bleached out of it, turning it brittle and twisted. Maybe it was a Fairy Liquid bottle, maybe Coca-Cola or motor oil. Nobody knows. A scientist could find out. She doesn't care enough.

The bleached unidentifiable stuff goes in the official gathering bags, the colorful bits she keeps to make more statues. They make her happy. Galleries buy them. Except these ones on the beach, the ones that populate her dreams.

That night the bottle cap totem pole speaks to her again. It seems to get smarter every day. "You made us, didn't you?"

Jolie fluffs up her pillow so hard she hits her hand against the headboard. "Yup. Not me personally, but humans did."

"So why do you hate us?"

Jolie sighs. "Because you are toxic. You poison everything around you, not just the water, but animals, everything up the food chain."

"But that's not our fault."

"I guess not."

The next night. "So, all you want is to undo us? Destroy us?"

Jolie turns on the night light. She's not getting out of this by sighing and trying to sleep. She's not sure if her role is mom or grandchild or therapist, but someone needs to address the poor creatures' issues.

"The point is that everything in nature eventually decays and dies. And becomes part of the great everlasting chain. But you guys can't. You never completely decay. Even if you fall apart, you're still this giant indigestible molecule."

"What happens when you die?"

"I get buried in a cemetery or burned to ashes. Or I could ask for a nature burial, without embalming. In any case, I fall apart and get reabsorbed by mother Earth."

The statues start talking by day now, too. Usually when Jolie is on the beach helping Kai and Molly gather their allotted trash.

"When will you stop hating me?"

"When you are all broken up into elements?" Jolie says, barely managing to refrain from snapping. When Kai and Molly become teenagers, she'll already know how to deal with them.

"It's not fair."

"Do you know how many bird species died out because you stuffed up their stomachs?" Jolie counters.

The statues don't answer.

The next few days a big storm keeps everyone from the beach. Fall has begun.

Jolie, Kai and Molly are bundled up against the chill that now hangs over the beach in the early morning. Soon it will be too dark to go gathering before school.

"Where were you?" the pink deer statue says. There's a quaver in its mental voice. It trembles on its fawnlike legs. Must be the wind.

"The weather was bad. We had to stay in."

"Or you'd get damaged?"

"I guess," Jolie says.

"We surrender," pink deer says. "We don't want to be separate anymore. Look, it's already started."

Jolie looks closer. The pink ears no longer look like plastic gloves, but have formed organic curls, a bit like turkey tail fungus or shield lichen. She touches one leaflike ear carefully with a fingertip. It's soft.

"The lichen was okay with having a fourth partner," it says. "We're throwing in with everyone else."

"That's...wonderful," Jolie says. "Welcome to the great circle of life."

The pink ears twitch.

Then, wobbling like a newborn, the pink deer takes its first step.

Jolie wonders if this is the species that will take over when humans are gone.

Bo Balder lives and works close to Amsterdam. Bo is the first Dutch author to have been published in Fantasy & Science Fiction Magazine, Clarkesworld Magazine, Analog Science Fiction and Fact Magazine, and other places. Her sf novel The Wan was published by Pink Narcissus Press. When not writing, she knits, reads and gardens, preferably all three at the same time.
Follow her on Twitter @bonbalder.

ANCESTRAL NOCTURNE

by Bethany van Sterling

Their eyes are like chartreuse orbs in the darkness, the demolished metal bars faintly glistening behind them. Two daunting blades of teeth scintillate, as her monstrous, wry grin stretches from canine to canine.

"We are ready," a small, furry figure trills, echoed by others across the dim room.

"Very good," the towering tigress roars.

She shatters the windows with her massive claws and the tribe congregates at the central square. Surrounding them are their fellow dogs and birds, cows and bulls, horses and pigs, all led by incarnations of their colossal predecessors: tufted dire wolves and two-legged titanis; tusked aurochs and bearded bison; fanged boars and maned tarpans.

"We've missed you, dear friends," the tigress coos, as the elders exchange respectful bows.

The city is silent, at last. Perhaps they sleep, a surprise soon to awaken them. Or perhaps they exist no more, spirits of the past having reconquered what is theirs, once again.

Bethany van Sterling is an editor, translator, poet, performing artist, and writer of historical, horror and fantasy fiction. Her stories have appeared in The Fantasist, Wild Musette, Tales from the Moonlit Path and Sub-Saharan Magazine, among others. Bethany's academic background in anthropology has inspired several of her works. She currently resides in Madrid, where she is a co-organizer of the Madrid Writers' Club. Under her real name, she is a contributing translator to the anthology of Spanish speculative fiction, Castles in Spain (Sportula, 2016). For news and musings, follow her on Twitter at @BethVanSterling.

AKIKI, THE MAGICIAN

by Steve Carr

Just past sunrise, as a thick halo of fog encircled the top of the Karisimbi volcano, Akiki stepped out of the thick vegetation of the jungle surrounding David Russell's hut. He stopped for a moment and glanced at the yard around the hut, cleared of trees, grass, nettles, and creeping vines, leaving a patch of nearly bald earth. There was nothing new to see, and as he sniffed the air, nothing new to smell, other than David's aroma, unusually faint for a human. He grunted softly and ambled a few yards closer to the hut and sat down in the dirt. After picking an army ant from his fur, he stuck it in his mouth and bit down on its crunchy body. The taste of the ant brought him a great deal of pleasure and calmed his nerves. He stretched out his large hands, briefly closed his eyes, and opened them to see four small bright red kowaii in his hands, two in each palm. He began to juggle the fruit, forming circles in the air that increased or decreased in circumference as he shifted his hands. His grunts and belches steadily rose in volume.

When the door to the hut opened and David appeared in the doorway, wrapped in a heavy blanket, Akiki blinked his eyes and the fruit vanished.

"You're here very early this morning," David said to the large silverbacked mountain gorilla.

Akiki lightly thumped his chest and then tapped his eye with his thick index finger.

"My camera?" David said. "Yes, I'll be taking pictures after I've had my morning tea and toast."

Akiki turned his large head and stared at the jungle, then turned

159

back to David. He pulled his lips tight against his teeth, a sign of concern.

"Have the poachers been around again?" David asked.

Akiki shook his head, mimicking David and other humans who studied and photographed his group. David understood the gesture's meaning.

"I'll try to hurry," David said, then turned, went into his hut, and closed the door.

Two golden monkeys appeared in the branches of a tree at the edge of the yard. They chattered noisily to Akiki.

"I know, I know. David has been told," Akiki said in an accent that resembled David's midwestern US drawl. "Now, go away." He clapped his hands and the monkeys disappeared in a *poof* of mist. He clapped his hands again, then he too vanished.

An hour later David and Mukisa, one of the Mahinga National Park rangers, appeared at the entrance to the small clearing among a grove of bamboo trees where Akiki and his extended family—several females, infants and a few juvenile males—lolled about among the broken bamboo stalks and piles of leaves. The men stood perfectly still, awaiting to be noticed by Akiki who lay on his back with his newest infant, Namazzi playing on his huge stomach. His favorite female, Dembe, the mother of Namazzi, sat nearby, eating the pulp of a bamboo shoot.

Seeing David and Mukisa, Akiki exhaled a breath, clearing the air in front of his daughter's face of the butterflies dancing there like marionettes on strings. He sat up, gently lifted Namazzi, and handed the infant to Dembe. David put his camera to his eye and Akiki heard it click several times as he stood and pounded on his chest, producing a sound similar to beating on a hollow log. He made his way through the broken bamboo to the two men, who slowly dropped to their knees, their heads bowed in submission. Akiki grunted loudly, nodded east, then turned and led the way into the jungle.

Paths made by the gorillas and other animals wound through the trees and nettles like tributaries, made damp and occasionally muddy by the constant dripping of rainwater falling from the tree canopies. Akiki knew exactly where he was leading David and Mukisa; the poachers rarely ventured far from the paths. They left their scent on everything they touched and, try as they might to do it quietly, still made noise as they set their snares and traps.

The first snare Akiki led the men to had the broken body of a small bushbuck caught in its tangle of rope and tree branches.

Cutting the dead animal from the snare, Mukisa shook his head. "It's a never-ending battle against the poachers. They'd drive all the animals in the park to extinction if we let them."

David snapped several pictures of the snare and nearby snares and traps that hadn't been sprung. He lowered the camera and glanced at Akiki who stared in the direction of the settlements, beyond the park boundaries, at the base of the mountain.

"Don't ask me how, but I think Akiki knows the existence of his kind hangs on a very thin thread," David said to Mukisa.

Mukisa sliced through the rope of a snare, releasing the bent-over sapling it was attached to back into an upright position. "Too many of his own family have been caught in these traps or been carried off by poachers for him not to know what a danger man poses."

Surreptitiously, Akiki freed the bubble that he had been holding in his fist and watched it float away.

Sitting on a mound of bamboo with his group seated in the grass around him, Akiki reached inside an old ranger's hat he'd found in the jungle and pulled out a small golden monkey. He held the struggling monkey for several moments as the other gorillas watched with rapt attention, then covered the monkey with the hat, hesitated a moment, and pulled the hat away. The monkey was gone. The group pounded the ground with their fists, stomped their feet, grunting and barking with delight.

The report of a far-off gunshot caught Akiki's attention. He stood up, tossed the hat aside, and grunted nervously, then waved his hands, gesturing for the group to leave the clearing and return to relative safety among the vines and bamboo. As the group disbanded, he exchanged a kiss with Dembe and gently patted the top of Namazzi's head. His natural instincts reminded him time and again not to be so affectionate with his offspring, that it would make them soft, but he couldn't help himself. Watching as she carried their infant to safety, he made a bunch of wild celery appear in his hand and stuffed it into his mouth. He was chewing on the celery when David and Mukisa arrived at the entrance to the clearing and knelt down.

David held his camera to his eye and snapped several pictures of the gorilla as he sat in the hazy rays of late afternoon sunlight, the silver hair on his back glistening.

Akiki thumped his chest and turned his head in the direction of the gunshot.

David nodded. "Yes, we heard it too, old boy," he said softly.

As rain began to fall, Akiki pulled a large leaf from a tree and followed his family into the thicket.

David awoke to pounding on the door to his hut. He sat up on his cot, rubbed the sleep from his eyes, and peered at his watch. It was a little before 4 a.m. "Who's there?" he called out.

"It's me, Akiki," a deep voice from the other side of the door replied frantically.

"It's a bit early for practical jokes, Mukisa," David replied.

There was a brief silence, then came, "They've taken my Dembe and Namazzi."

David threw open the door and saw a naked man, about his height, but much bulkier and muscular, his chest, arms and legs matted with thick black hair. He looked into the man's eyes and saw in them Akiki's unmistakable keen intelligence and gentleness. "But, how...?" His voice trailed off as he tried to comprehend what he was seeing.

"I need your help," Akiki said. "The poachers raided my group, killed two who were trying to defend them, and carried off Dembe, Namazzi, and another infant." He hung his head. "I was lured away from my group by sounds the poachers made in another part of the jungle. It was foolish of me to leave them unprotected."

David gathered his composure. "You can't be blamed. Let me get dressed and I'll get Mukisa and the other rangers."

"There's no time to get Mukisa," Akiki said. "The lives of my female and infant are at risk."

Twenty minutes later David and Akiki, who was now wearing one of the hut's curtains tied around his waist and a too-tight shirt of David's, followed the trail left by the poachers. They said nothing, their steps barely making a sound on the soft earth and broken vegetation, slowed by David's inability to keep up despite Akiki's difficulty adjusting to his human legs. When they broke out of the jungle at the border of a large swath of deforested land it was early morning and the settlement could be seen in the distance, bathed in dawn's gray light.

"I've lost Dembe and Namazzi's scents," Akiki said as he stared at the settlement, his lips pulled back in the same way they did when he was Akiki, the mountain gorilla.

"Don't give up hope, Akiki," David patted him on the back.

Akiki flinched. Being touched by a human was a new experience, and not one he liked, even if it was David whom he had grown to like and trust in the nine years they had known each other.

They continued on, following the well-trod path through the field of bulldozed earth and tree stumps. As they approached the settlement, the aromas of cooked food, garbage, and human waste grew stronger, forming a cloud of noxious odors hanging a few feet above the ground where it mixed with the early morning mist. Entering the first unpaved street of the settlement, Akiki abruptly stopped. The nearness of so many humans leaving their shacks and tents to begin their day filled him with fear and loathing. These were the beings who were wantonly killing the mountain gorillas.

David saw Akiki hesitate. "Now that we've come this far, we have to go on if we're going to find Dembe and Namazzi."

"Yes, we must go on." Akiki moved forward.

They made their way through the throng of settlement inhabitants until they reached the edge of a marketplace. Vendors had set up tables and stalls selling everything from woven baskets to bananas.

"There! Dembe's scent!" Akiki shouted, pointing to a stall where several men were gathered behind a table piled with burlap-wrapped objects. He rushed toward the stall, followed by an alarmed David, and grabbed one of the men by the shoulders, shaking him. "Where is my female and infant?" he screamed in the man's face. The other men pulled him from Akiki's grasp. David spotted a freshly bloodied bundle. He peeled back the cloth. In it lay two adult mountain gorilla hands.

"Akiki," he said, softly.

Akiki turned, saw the hands, and cried out, "Dembe!" He clapped his hands and vanished.

⊗

"Will Akiki understand when you tell him Namazzi was probably sold as a pet?" Mukisa asked David as the two neared the clearing where Akiki and his group could usually be found foraging for bamboo shoots.

"He understands much more than anyone can imagine," David replied.

Akiki and his group weren't in the clearing. The men spent several days trying to track them down without success; Akiki's family had disappeared in the jungle.

Steve Carr, from Richmond, Virginia, has had over 400 short stories published internationally in print and online magazines, literary journals, reviews and anthologies since June 2016. He has published seven collections of his short stories: Sand, Rain, Heat, The Tales of Talker Knock and 50 Short Stories: The Very Best of Steve Carr, and LGBTQ: 33 Stories, and The Theory of Existence: 50 Short Stories. His paranormal/horror novel Redbird was released in November 2019. His plays have been produced in several states in the U.S. He has been nominated for a Pushcart Prize twice. His Twitter is @carrsteven960.

RUN, BABY, RUN

by Joy Kennedy-O'Neill

The bones of my baby were once trapped in a tar pit. Just as stuck as I am here.

Mom leans against my bedroom doorway, smoking.

"You don't have to come with me," I say, rubbing my minuscule belly-bump. "It's only a check-up."

"I don't mind," she says.

"OK, but don't smoke around me. It's bad for—"

"Oh please," she shrugs and breathes like a dragon, nostrils flaring. "It never hurt you none."

I roll out of bed. I don't feel nauseous anymore, although I did in the beginning. Sissy's on a floor mattress with her toddler. The soles of his feet are filthy; she forgets to bathe him.

"Freak," she says to me.

I ignore her and get my keys. Mom shuffles behind me, flicking ashes in the yard. It takes three tries to get the car to turn over, but we finally ease out of Beach Lake. There's no lake here, and not much beach left either. Not after the petrochemical plants built the LNG ports. At night, their lights are like another city—a thousand stars trapped in place.

We drive past the high school where I ran track. I was fast, and a good student. I tried to get a scholarship to get the hell out of here, but it was right after the financial crash and colleges cut aid.

Newer cars slip past us on 288's driverless toll lanes, but we chug along. I hope this check-up is good. I put one hand on my stomach and watch the giant cranes building Houston's seawalls, picking and nodding like the beaks of giant birds.

Inside the pregnancy institute near Memorial, I take a seat as Mom looks everyone over. A few men have bulging sides.

"Good Lord," she says. "What they gonna do, squeeze the baby outta their balls?"

"*Shhhh.* They'll cut it out. Like a cesarean."

"This is bat-shit-crazy. Why would anyone volunteer for this?"

"*Shhhh.*"

"They ain't paying you none," she says. "I've been checking your account."

But she doesn't know about my secret account. She doesn't know about my plans. "Are you just here to ask about money?" I ask.

She snorts. "Why do they need people anyway? They can grow them in bags. I seen it. There was a whole show on it called 'Unwrapping the Future.'"

I shake my head. "This works better. There's a bond, and good blood flow. They come out healthier, stronger."

"Whatever."

When the technician places the ultrasound wand on my belly, I hear the swish-swish of a heartbeat. I smile. I'm Pleistocene-pregnant. Be strong, little one.

Back home, I message my surrogate mentor, Taz.

> *Did it hurt when you had it?*
>
> *Not as much as having a real baby!*
>
> *My mom says it's crazy.*
>
> *:)*
>
> *Will they remember us?*
>
> *Yes sort—of ?? Our smell is imprinted on them.*

A happiness I can't describe washes over me. I'll be a mother, at least for a little while. It will know me.

"You're fat," Sissy tells me.

"It's the anti-rejection drugs."

Mom looks at me, smirking. "She used to be a runner. Who'd believe it now?"

My anger tastes like copper. I'm going to use my surrogate money to get a plane ticket out of here. Maybe start college.

"And she's a dyke," Sissy says.

Mom punches her right in the mouth. Violent. Unhinged.

"What of it?" Mom shrieks.

Sissy screams at her, spraying blood and spittle. "She's not natural, and THAT'S not natural." She points at my stomach. "If God wanted them to be around, they'd still be here!"

My family. Stuck in this pit. It's going extinct.

I run to the backroom, nearly tripping on the sloping floor where the foundation has cracked under mildewed carpet. I text Taz a question.

Was yours a boy or girl?

Girl.

U miss her?

Yes!

Did they let u hold her?

They make sure they can suckle and u get to bottle feed them.
It's awesome.

Are we freaks?

No!!! We bring them back. All the mess humans made
It was BECAUSE of humans mine disappeared.
We are righters-of-the-wrong. Avengers!

Cool.

My hands shake a little, asking my next question.

Maybe we could meet?
I mean, after I have it.

Sure ;)

My heart goes flying. I think Taz likes me. Next time I'll ask her what her real name is. The institute tries to keep everyone anonymous, as if this is shameful business, but I don't care.

The cramps feel like period cramps. I speed into Houston on the manual lane where the grandfathered cars rattle and belch the breath of dying fossil fuels. I wonder about the dead ancestors of my baby. Two million years ago.

My phone pings and I hear Mom.

"Girl, I saw your new bank statement. You saving up to leave us? What are you thinking? You know we—"

I cut the call before she can tell me how much I'm needed, before the guilt starts slapping like the tide. I know she tried to get out of our town a few times too, back when she was younger. But her family always pulled her back. I guess survival is easier in packs, just like on the animal shows. It's funny how she can't see that she's doing the same thing with me.

I'll run again. After the baby, I'll strengthen up and get back to it. I used to run so fast my long hair flew behind me like it was waving goodbye.

My cramps come faster. At the institute they usher me into a clean-smelling room. I undress and lay on a table. The nurse looks at me like I'm white trash but adjusts her mask professionally. She tells me to push.

I feel a tugging and pressure. "Bear down," she says. "Push again."

Then something wet and hot slides out of me.

"Here we go!" she says under her mask.

She cuts the sack. She opens the bag.

And I see the kitten's wet ears, four legs and paws. It kicks and squirms adorably. "Ooohh," I hear myself say, just like a kid at the ocean.

The nurse says, "One American Cheetah. *Miracinonyx*, to be reintroduced to the plains. A female."

I touch its warm-wet fur, its tiny black nose. Her eyes are shut tight; she mewls. She wriggles and kneads her paws.

"Those legs!" I smile. They're slender with ridiculous mitten-like paws.

I baby-talk her. "You're here! You're not extinct. No, you're not!"

"It will chase the reintroduced *Capromeryx* pronghorn." The nurse lectures like a nature show. "Out on the reclaimed prairies."

"Sweet baby," I croon. "How big will she get?"

"Puma size. Its spots will darken as it ages and will look more like a cougar."

I start taking pictures with my phone. "My mentor Taz had a Tasmanian Tiger." I almost tell her that Taz and I are going to meet, but I don't. Maybe we're not supposed to. But I think about how wonderful it would be if Taz and I could keep our babies and have a crazy family of our own. To be loved, to be really loved.

"Can she ever have kittens of her own?"

The nurse seems bored with me and answers quickly. "We hope so. But right now, the neo-extincts have problems conceiving, so we'll still need surrogates."

"Still using people? Not lions or something?"

"Too closely related. Too many diseases could jump species: feline leukemia, FIV—" She waves her hand. "It's complicated."

I think of other reasons. Maybe more bioethics rules govern using animals than using poor people. Like me.

She puts her hand on my shoulder, but not very warmly. "Thank you for your service." She moves toward the door with my baby in her hands.

"Wait, they told me I could have some time with it."

She sighs. "Thirty minutes."

I snuggle my baby-kitten and bottle feed her, watching the milk pool on her whiskers, her pink tongue licking. I'll have to leave her here and a final payment will ping to my account.

But she's mine, for these few minutes. I take more pictures to show Taz. The kitten mews again and I'm so lovestruck that my insides hurt. An American cheetah. Alive. Opening her eyes from a million years of sleep.

We can bring things back. I think of all the stupid things I've lost in my life—a necklace, a favorite shirt, some easy races. And then the big stuff—a dad. The uncomplicated love from my mother. I don't know where some things go.

Too soon the door opens, and the nurse takes my kitten from my chest.

"Don't," I say.

She looks at me like I'm a beggar clinging to a diamond. "This isn't a house cat, young lady. It's not a pet."

"I know that!" But the door is already closing behind her and I'm crying.

Taz replies to my picture but it's strange. She's very formal now. "I have to go over the exit procedure with you." She sends me a checklist for recovery.

I keep checking for more messages during the exit-physical, but all I see is a notification for the final payment deposit. It seems like a lot, but a part of me knows it's not near enough. It won't get me far. And part of me knows that Mom might hack the account before I even get home.

I put a maxi-pad in my underwear as I cramp and feel empty. My little one was in me for months. Maybe she'll remember the sound of my heart, the hopes of my insides. She'll grow, and there will be grass against her legs and sun on her back. Freedom. Open plains. The ground zooming beneath her paws. Maybe she'll know that she was once in the belly of someone who loved her.

And she'll run.

Hell, she'll run like the wind.

Joy Kennedy-O'Neill lives on the Texas Gulf Coast and teaches English at Brazosport College, where her husband teaches math. She holds a PhD in environmental literature. Her stories have appeared in Nature, Strange Horizons, New Flash Fiction Review, New Orleans Review, the Cimarron Review, among others. Her story "Heron Girl" was selected by Robert Olen Butler as the winner of the 2018 Gris-Gris award. She was also a finalist for the Lascaux Prize in 2018.

KATHERINE
KIREEVA

In the Garden of Burning Plastic

by Marissa James

In the Garden of Burning Plastic, nothing needs to be watered. Firstly, this is because nothing is actually burning; that smell simply gets into any synthetic material that's been out in the acid mist too long.

Secondly, as the name suggests, everything is plastic. Faux ficuses, floppy-petaled flowers, and fluorescent-hued fish tank plants mean we don't have to sacrifice water rations for beauty. Hyper green lawns of rubberized turf appear to thrive alongside perfectly manicured shrubs that never need manicuring.

This doesn't mean there's no upkeep in the garden. Dusting is a daily chore. To control the buildup of carcinogenic particulates that blows in off the city ruins and filters through the sanctity of the Dome, the other gardeners and I spray and wipe down all surfaces on a weekly basis. We clean every leaf, stem, branch, and petal with a solution that promises to remove 99.9% of all microbes. Although, judging from the state of the world outside, most of these microbes were annihilated decades ago along with any other life that didn't make it under a Dome like ours. Still, it gives the Garden a nice luster.

As needed, we deep clean the grass and faux moss, and glue back any bits that fall off the bushes. Maintenance stirs up the acrid stink that reminds us of the garden's well-earned title.

When it's my turn to join an exploratory band and venture out into the ruins, I collect what specimens I can afford to carry. None of my bandmates object to the time and pack-space this takes. They understand that humans don't survive on cans of expired soup and preserved bread alone. The view outside the Dome, a wasted expanse of crumbling buildings and skeletal trees eroded down to stumps, all swathed in gray ash, does little for the eyes, not to mention group morale.

Besides, having new plants to tend gives us gardeners a way to pass the time.

In the ruins I occasionally find silk flowers, but these, like any organic matter, are chewed up by the caustic atmosphere that bathes the city, thus succumbing to ruin themselves.

Plastic fruit is a different issue altogether. We've built a collection over the years, but hanging fake-dewed grapes and plump, rosy pears in the tree branches made the garden's visitors melancholy and withdrawn. Attendance dropped off severely until we took them down. Theories on the different neurological pathways traveled by the memory of sight and the memory of taste, and the depths of the emotional resonance of each, abound among us gardeners.

I was too young to have a real garden in the days before the Dome, when greenery surrounded us to such a degree that we couldn't have named the hundreds of species on every city block. Beyond light, soil, and water, I can't recall what sort of care was required to maintain the real things. Did you talk to them? Did they respond, in their slow, season-based cycles of environmental adaptation, to human contact? Could a tree know if you stroked its bark or climbed into its branches? If somehow our fates had been reversed, would they miss our presence in the same way we now yearned for theirs?

Still, when it's my turn to do the deep cleaning, I can't help searching the spaces between rubberized blades of turf or the perfectly smooth synthetic tree trunks, hoping to find some new green sprout of life amid the smell of burning plastic.

Marissa James resides in the vicinity of Portland, Oregon, and has been an editor, veterinary assistant, and arts professional—sometimes simultaneously. Her short fiction has been published by Daily Science Fiction, Third Flatiron Press, Dream of Shadows, and others.

Conjugation of the Verb

by Brian Rappatta

*excerpt from article: **Queusk** (Open Source Galactipedia), sub-heading: **Language**
Note: This article may require editing to adhere to our policies.

The T-3498 Universal Translator was the most advanced model in existence, but in those days, it was still quite buggy. It rendered the most common verb in the Queusk's dominant caste's formal dialect as: to *tit-for-tat (v., trans.)*. It requires some syntactic gymnastics to do a full conjugation in Galactic Standard, yet what follows is a simplified version, with Queusk pronomial sub-connotations and examples:

1st Person Plural (as a highly martial and collectivist society, singular pronouns and self-referential speech were virtually non-existent, reserved only for the caste Alpha): WE (the divinely ordained masters and unequivocally morally superior beings) hereby *tit-for-tat* your heinous encroachments on our territories, our sovereignty, and the crèches of our young.

2nd Person Plural: YOU (the utterly inferior specimens of filthy, polluted genetics not fit to cross-breed with even a Queusk paramecium) *tit-for-tat* us with a vile, heinous lack of regard for our unquestioned moral and biological superiority.

Unfortunately, the xenographic data on the Queusk is appallingly incomplete, due to a disastrous first contact with the Amish generational agro-vessel *Swartzendrubers' Ploughshares*, whose crew utterly refused to engage in the expected *tit-for-tatting*. What followed was an acrimonious, yet brief series of skirmishes with the secular civilian arm of Earth's exploratory fleet, who used the destruction of the *Ploughshares* as a rallying cry (see also: Queusk genocide; The Pacifist Pogrom; #tit-for-tat-the Ploughshares)

3rd Person Plural: THEY (the highly pugilistic, easily affronted, and utterly intransigent Queusk) tit-for-tatted the wrong fucking pacifists.

Brian Rappatta hails from the heart of Amish country in the American Midwest, though is currently living and working in South Korea. His short fiction in various genres has appeared in venues such as Chilling Ghost Stories from Flame Tree Publications, Shock Totem, Writers of the Future, and Amazing Stories, as well as in various podcasts such as Tales to Terrify and Gallery of Curiosities. He is a graduate of the Odyssey Writers Workshop.

LOVING MONSTERS

by Anya Ow

Feris rode up to the funeral pyre on a swamp buffalo, its horns looped with green and gold tassels. Beside the pyre, a veiled woman sobbed—probably the widow. A wrinkled older woman in a brown samfu stroked the widow's back, watching the flames. After the pyre burned down, the samfu woman gathered the ashes into an urn and presented it to the widow. People trickled away from the modest stone temple, circling around Feris with averted eyes. The samfu woman waited until they were alone before studying Feris' black clothes and flintlock rifle.

"Who are you?" asked the samfu woman.

"Feris. You're Miri, the mayor?" Feris raised the tip of her straw hat. Badly healed scars lased across her brown, round face, a parting gift from an old tiger. The gray woman glanced at the disfigurement without comment as Feris dismounted.

"Yes. Why?"

"And the master of the temple."

"That I am." Weariness wore harsh hollows in Miri's cheeks, settling as bitter dregs in her eyes.

"You sent the Tunku a letter about the nāga three weeks ago."

"I didn't think Her Majesty the Tunku would care. Kranjik is a small fishing town, known for pepper crab and nothing else."

"She cares and we're here now," Feris said. Weariness was either making Miri blunter than she should be to a representative of the Tunku, or she was normally this brusque. Nice change.

"We?" Miri asked.

Feris nodded at the buffalo. "This is Kueh. He's pleased to meet you too." The buffalo snorted loudly. "That stink. Nāga poison liquefies flesh to make a carcass more palatable. Your letter didn't mention that it'd started on people. When did it start?"

"Ojin was the first. A catfish fisherman."

"Wouldn't fisher-folk have avoided a nāga lair?"

"Yes. Ojin shouldn't have strayed past his usual route in the mangroves. We found him downstream." Miri rubbed her palms down over her samfu. "I'll take you to the lair."

"It'll be dangerous. Nāga don't kill for sport. If Ojin wasn't swallowed whole, something must have gone wrong. I'd prefer to be introduced to the fisher-folk." Feris had no interest in babysitting anyone.

Miri pursed her lips. "Do you think I subsist off incense and rice cake offerings? I'm from a family of fisher-folk; I know the land as well as any fisherman. I'll take you."

When Feris was young, she'd loved everything that was inexplicable and fantastic in the world. Mawas, abath, qirin, nāga. How boring would the world be without its so-called monsters? Wayang performances were often about great hunters triumphing against legendary beasts. Feris and her friends would climb trees for a better view as the wandering wayang master set up his stage. She did not think that hunters were interesting; they were only people. Her friends would shush her and tell her to go home, but Feris would cling stubbornly to the tree, waiting for the monster-puppets to come to life.

The village she lived in no longer existed on maps. Feris could still see the p'eng in her dreams as it heaved its great wings of mud and water out of the wetlands. Up and up, a bird-shaped wave that stretched over the mangrove and bisected the afternoon sunlight with the sinuous arch of its neck. It was the most beautiful thing Feris would ever see, and nearly the last.

"When was Ojin found?" Feris asked. They were deep enough into the flooded forest that it was slow going. A narrow rowboat would've made better time, but boats risked being snagged by underwater roots or mired in mud. Kueh forged belly-deep past arched and spiked roots, tail flicking away curious insects. Miri's donkey labored miserably behind the buffalo. Mudskippers and small crabs watched them pass with wet-eyed indifference.

"Only yesterday. There haven't been other deaths. Not from this village, anyway."

"Your letter said you had no choice but to complain about the nāga because it began to steal livestock?"

Miri nodded. "Goats. The village is poor—we can't afford to lose another herd."

"Nāga eat giant catfish. They don't often eat livestock, and I've never heard of one trying to eat people."

"There's fewer fish than there used to be. In my grandparents' time, you didn't have to sail far to catch enough fish for a whole family. Now you have to venture over an hour into the mangrove or more."

They found their first carcass cradled by roots. The nāga's poison had partly dissolved the body of the dead buffalo, turning it into a rotting heap. Crabs and flies crawled over the eyes and the open mouth, and one of its thick horns was missing. Feris slung Kueh's reins over a low-hanging branch and shifted the bandana around her neck over her nose. She dismounted and pulled her roll of tools from the saddlebags.

Nerves shook Miri's voice into a wavering whisper. "I've never seen something like that."

"Something isn't right. A nāga is basically a very big snake. It should've just swallowed the buffalo whole. Even one this large. Ojin, too." Feris cut a sample of flesh and prepared to bottle it. It shriveled rapidly against the tongs. Startled, Feris fumbled it into the mud.

"What happened?" Miri asked.

"Toxic reaction to silver." Feris pressed the tips of her tongs to the carcass and watched it blacken. She trudged over to the head and examined the pulpy eyes. "This wasn't a buffalo. It's a lembu jadian, an old one." The front legs under the mud were arms, powerfully muscular. The shapeshifters preferred to wear the forms of big brown buffalo. It would've taken this monstrous humanoid-bull shape only out of desperation.

Miri gasped. "What's something like that doing in the mangroves? Don't they prefer the highland jungles?"

"Usually." Feris levered out one of the arms from the mud with a grunt. "Scale fragments and blood under the long nails. It hurt the nāga before it died. Maybe that's why the nāga only tried to eat half of it."

"The flesh of a lembu jadian is toxic, isn't it? I've heard tales of people dying when they accidentally ate meat from the buffalo form," Miri said. Feris shot her a surprised glance. She didn't expect villagers to know much about creatures like this outside of information distorted by superstition.

"Poisonous to humans. Not to a nāga. They're immortal snakes, a step above most monsters. The nāga, the garuda, the abath, the p'eng…" Feris trailed off. "Lembu jadian aren't loners. They wouldn't have abandoned one of their own."

"So, we're not only facing a pissed off and injured nāga, but a herd of angry were-buffalo too?"

"Possibly," Feris said.

"Great."

When Feris was eighteen, she saw the p'eng responsible for destroying her village. It had been strung up by its feet against the flank of the same iron ship that brought the newcomers to the riverlands, its beak open and crawling with flies, its wings floating against the waves. In death, the bird wore none of the magic of creation that allowed it to forge flight feathers out of floodwaters and mating plumes out of monsoon rain. Without magic, it was just a stork-like gray bird, barely as big as a buffalo. A cannonball had torn a bloody hole through its breast, now thick with maggots.

"It capsized a couple of our ships before we got to it," the then-Governor told the Tunku. "Goddamned monster. It won't be troubling you any longer."

"I see," the Tunku said. She smiled at the monster slayers; her lips stretched tight over her strained face as she spoke the foreigner's tongue with a faint accent. It was not a difficult language to learn, compared to the local argot that Feris had grown up with, an impenetrable weave of at least three different local dialects. "You have done us quite the favour."

"We'd like to do more. Favours that could benefit us both in turn. We hear you have gold seams in your mountains. Let's talk profit," said the Governor. His answering smile bared his white teeth. "Enough profit to make us all rich."

"Rich," Feris murmured. Her eyes were drawn to the p'eng's open beak. The Governor didn't notice her—she was dressed as a dockside laborer. The Tunku shot her a warning glance. As Feris ducked her head, the Tunku invited the Governor for tea at the palace. Had he heard of a creature called the garuda, the Tunku wondered? No, he had not, and he would like to know more.

They found the second lembu jadian floating face-down in the middle of the river, wedged against tree roots. Crocodiles tore into the carcass, showing no sign of being put off by the toxic meat or the nāga's poison.

"You say the nāga has always been here," Feris said as they watched from a safe distance.

"My granduncle saw it once, disappearing upstream during the monsoon season," Miri said.

"Why didn't he notify the Tunku of its presence?"

"Why would the Tunku care? Besides. It left us alone before."

Feris nudged Kueh away from the feasting crocodiles. "Strange that the daughter of fisher-folk decided to become a temple priestess."

"Someone has to give the land and the Gods the respect they are due. Besides, I was the fourth of eight children. The unlucky number in a lucky number."

Feris let out a snort. "Village superstition."

"There also wasn't enough work. The fishing stock was drying up, and after the Tunku implemented quotas on top of that? Two of my sisters had to go to the capital to work. They run a delivery business now."

"The fishing quotas aren't arbitrary. An environmental survey indicated that the rivers needed to recover," Feris said.

"Of course."

"You don't sound like you agree."

"I completely agree that the rivers need to recover, but look over there—to your right." Miri pointed at the slick silvery ribbon winding through the current, staining the roots it touched. "It comes from upstream. Washed into the rivers from the mines the foreigners are digging."

Feris frowned. "The Tunku personally authorized the mines. The profits have built roads across the Sultanate. Connected the islands. Built schools. Brought modern medici—"

"They've blown up the mountains and poisoned the river. The Tunku, the foreigners, the people in the towns—all of you benefit from what has been done—while the rest of us suffer the consequences." Miri clenched her hands over the donkey's rope bridle.

"Ah, progress," Feris said.

"The Governor likes you." The Tunku did not look entirely pleased, but she seldom did. The ruler of the riverlands was a tiny woman of mixed heritage, a heritage she wore. A jade pin gleamed from her hair, and she wore a thickly embroidered baju kurung over her jewelled ka-sut manek slippers. Servants waved large fans behind her, trying to chase away the sticky afternoon heat.

"He does?" Feris said. She was indifferent to the affection of strangers, particularly strangers from across the seas. But for their iron ships, guns, and remarkable predisposition toward violence, the Governor and his people would be completely beneath her notice.

The Tunku gestured at the wood and leather case on the table beside her. "This was sent to you among the gifts that arrived today from his residence."

Feris flicked the case open and whistled. The black rifle slept in red velvet, burnished bronze plated as sharp-tongued scales over its dark mahogany stock. She traced her fingers over the wood. "I don't know how to shoot. Return it. Or display it."

"The Governor offered lessons."

"Of course he did," Feris said.

"He said he's never met a woman before who was as good a hunter as he is."

"I'm only 'as good as' him, hm?" Feris pulled her hand away, resting it on the hilt of her sabre. "Given what I hunt, it won't be much use to me. I've seen how long the reload takes. It's good only for one shot, one that will betray my position to everything in the vicinity."

"You'll wear it. Even if you don't use it." The Tunku closed the case and pushed it in Feris' direction. "Take the lessons. Try to refrain from 'accidentally' pushing him out of a window."

"Your Majesty," Feris said, curling her lip in distaste.

"That wasn't a 'yes,' huntress."

"It is if you wish it."

"I do so wish it." The Tunku stared at Feris until Feris lowered her eyes, latched up the case, and picked it up. "The Governor is an avid sportsman."

"They usually are." The last time Feris had been trapped in the new Governor's company, he had waxed lyrical about the tigers he had murdered in jungles across the sea. He had been indifferent—or oblivious—to her polite horror.

"He is not as demanding as the men before him have been," the Tunku said, "but someday, if he does so become, perhaps you should bring him on one of your hunts."

"Monster hunts are dangerous things, ill-suited to people who kill the lords of the jungle from the backs of elephants for sport," Feris said. She smiled, a thin smile that the Tunku returned.

The barge lay thrice broken against the shattered trunk of a tree. Filthy cages and miscellany floated listlessly in the muddy water. Miri poked at a large manacle tangled in tree roots with a stick. Its girth would have easily circled her waist. Monkeys displaced from fighting over foodstuffs squalled at them from the trees.

"Wine, pies, coffee. These supplies aren't from around here," Miri said.

Feris dropped the torn piece of cloth she'd been inspecting. "Keep moving."

"What was in the cages? They're tall and too narrow for livestock."

"Can't you guess? You said so yourself. The lembu jadian aren't usually found outside the highlands."

Miri gawked. "They were brought down here? Why? How were they even caught?"

"Live specimens." Feris nodded at the furthermost cage, smaller than most. A roughly-made ball of colorful rope pressed against the bars: a child's toy. "As to how they're caught—unlike the people who brought them here, they weren't monsters."

"That carcass we saw has been dead for days. From before we found Ojin, judging from the state of decay." As Feris raised an eyebrow, Miri said, "I prepare people for burial. It's part of my job."

"You're right. This barge has been here for a week now," Feris said.

"How do you know that?"

Feris grunted. "Because I followed its trail south."

"Why the cages?" Feris asked as they took a break from target practice. In the back of the Governor's residence, servants were erecting a series of steel cages and pens.

The Governor smiled indulgently. "For specimens. There's a remarkable proliferation of rare and unusual fauna in these parts. I intend to capture a few and bring them home with me for study. I'll name one after you if you like."

"They already have names," Feris said.

"Not scientific ones, my dear. More tea?"

Feris accepted the tea. "And after they are 'studied'? What then?"

"They'd be placed into zoos for education. Large menageries," the Governor explained when Feris looked puzzled. "Concrete pens and steel cages holding species from around the world for people to look at."

"What for?"

"To admire and learn."

"Men usually collect gems. You collect creatures," Feris said.

The Governor's indulgence faded. "Not at all. I'm a conservationist."

By the cages, someone shouted as a heavy trough was lowered awkwardly against the dirt. "If you were, you would care about the land that you pluck these creatures from. You would care about the people on the land. You would try to fix the reasons why the creatures are becoming rare. You would have breeding programs in your 'zoos.' Do you?"

"I suppose, in time, we'll—"

"You don't conserve. You collect." Feris set down her cup. "A collector who takes something that's not given to them is a thief. You've stolen so many creatures from the jungles that the hunter-folk who live within it have complained. The Tunku is concerned."

The Governor reddened with indignation. "We'll compensate the Tunku for any inconvenience caused, if requested. And if my presence so offends you, leave."

"I was just about to."

"Why did you even accept my invitation?"

"Orders." Feris tossed a crumpled piece of paper onto the table. "The Tunku instructed me to pass this to you. It's a letter from a village to the south, translated."

"Ever faithful," the Governor said. He inspected the paper. "A nāga?"

"Celestial monster. Malayan dragon."

"I know what it is. I didn't think there were any left in these parts. Hrm! Stealing livestock, I see. We'll gladly look into it. Please relay my assurances to Her Majesty." The Governor forced a smile. "I suppose I should be lucky you graced me with your time—and that you didn't decide to shoot me with your new rifle."

"I've never killed anyone before, and I don't intend to start," Feris said.

"The Tunku's eagle, a pacifist?" The Governor chuckled. "I'm not that gullible."

"I never claimed to be a pacifist." Feris bowed deeply from the waist and turned to leave. Behind her, the Governor shouted for servants to bring him a map.

⊗

The first survivor they found groaned weakly as he fought to keep his large head above water, tangled in roots. The lembu jadian bull bellowed a warning as Feris urged Kueh closer, though it quieted as Feris inspected the roots and started to chop through one with her sabre. Miri's donkey refused to approach—she tied it to a branch and splashed over to help. "Careful," Feris warned her. "He's angry."

"Rightfully so," Miri said. She pressed her palms together and bowed, knee-deep in muddy water. The lembu jadian regarded her with white-edged eyes, shuddering. It groaned again as Miri borrowed a dagger from Feris and started hacking. Messy business, given the dying light and the muddy water.

They worked for an hour, until Feris severed a root that held a hind leg and the lembu jadian surged free. It bowled Miri over as it charged for deeper waters, its form shivering in the sunlight. Bones pressed against its muddy fur, muscles bulging, the half-creature became a huge buffalo. It paddled away, forging downstream.

Feris pulled Miri to her feet. "All right?"

Miri took a cautious step and winced. "Might have sprained something."

"Get back on your donkey and head home."

"We're not far now from where the nāga likes to sleep and I'm already here." Miri limped over to her kicking donkey and gentled it with a touch.

Floating bodies and barge fragments littered the way to the submerged cave. Muddy water stained once-crisp jackets and homespun clothes the same color, death levelling the slate for the rich and poor alike. Some had been gored to death, others poisoned. Carrion birds scattered as Feris closed in.

"These are all humans. Maybe the lembu jadian got free on their own," Miri said.

Feris looked around at the sound of a low moan. "Someone's still alive."

The man wedged in a tree had been gored in the leg, his hunting jacket stained with mud and blood. He moaned again as Feris climbed up and helped him down to Miri. They hauled him onto a large floating fragment. "Governor," Feris said. He shuddered as she spoke, shifting weakly.

"He'll bleed out," Miri said. She stared at the pale, shaking man. "This is really the Governor?"

"Doesn't look like much now, does he? The representative of the power from beyond the sea." One whose iron ships and guns had carved them a permanent perch in the capital. "Can you do something about the bleeding? I have bandages and salves in my saddlebags."

"What are you going to do?" Miri asked.

"Check whether the nāga is dead."

Feris nudged Kueh deeper into the water. After a few steps, Kueh bellowed in warning and she tensed, grasping the hilt of her sabre. The donkey under Miri shrieked. It bucked her off, fleeing downstream. Miri sputtered and splashed up to her feet just as the opaque water beyond them bloomed into wet humps, loops that laced between themselves, ridged with sails. The nāga hissed, loud enough that the Governor moaned in fear.

Feris pulled the rifle off her back. "Wait!" Miri said, limping over and grabbing her elbow. "Wait."

"I wasn't going to shoot," Feris said. Her voice shook a little. Behind the coils, something vast was winding closer, a snub head with golden eyes, crowned with horns. The nāga's wet tongue flicked out as Feris tossed the rifle away from her. It sank quickly into the mud, the brass scales on its flank winking up at them for a heartbeat before the glimmer faded.

The nāga drew back, its hiss growing louder. Miri stepped forward as Feris slowly started to draw her sabre. Trembling, Miri pressed her hands together before her face and knelt. The water soaked her to her chin as she bowed deeply.

Feris hesitated. She let go of her sabre hilt and pressed her palms together, bowing low on Kueh's back. The nāga tasted the air, its crowned head weaving from side to side. Gunshot wounds and a long gouge against its flank wept blue blood into the water. Feris flinched as one of the floating bodies close by submerged, dragged down by the nāga's tail. She bit down on her lip as the corpse's cold fingers brushed against her thigh. The nāga sank back into the water, slipping quietly out of sight. As the water grew still, Miri let out a sob.

"He should be able to travel soon," Miri said. She nodded at the Governor, who was sleeping off a numbing draught on a pallet in the shadow of the stone temple.

"I've sent for a carriage, but if he gives you trouble before it arrives, keep him drugged. How's your leg?" Feris asked.

"It'll keep." Miri sat heavily down on a stool. "What about the nāga? Will the Tunku send more people?"

"Give its lair a wide berth and your village will be fine."

Miri looked up at her. "You're not a very convincing liar."

"It probably killed Ojin because it was provoked or hungry. Stay clear of its territory, stake out some goats for it, and it'll likely keep to itself. I'll have the Tunku arrange for a herd to be sent down every month. The village can keep what the nāga doesn't eat."

"Would that be enough?"

"It didn't come out from this encounter unscathed. It'll be warier of people from now on. If you make a habit of feeding it, it'll be satisfied with the arrangement." Feris smiled faintly. "It's not human, so it's not unreasonable."

"Ha. Will there be more foreigners?"

"Hm?"

"The Governor's shown no interest in this area before. He must have heard of the nāga from the letter that I sent to the Tunku. Did Her Majesty send him after the nāga to get rid of him? Then you, to make sure the job was done?"

Feris stroked Kueh behind the ears. "You're quick, priestess. There will always be more foreigners. This is a rich land, for now. Some may suit the land, some may not. Those who don't must be handled in ways that don't drag us into a war. The Tunku does what she must for all of us."

Miri got gingerly to her feet, holding out a palm. "I hope you're right."

Feris clasped her hand, patting her knuckles. "Write another letter if there's more trouble."

"I've seen how that goes," Miri said wryly. Feris chuckled and got onto Kueh's back. Tipping her hat at Miri, she nudged the buffalo into a trot.

Anya Ow is the author of The Firebirds Tale *and* Cradle and Grave, *and is an Aurealis Awards finalist. Her short stories have appeared in publications such as* Daily Science Fiction, Uncanny, 2019 Year's Best Dark Fantasy and Horror *anthology and more. Born in Singapore, Anya has a Bachelor of Laws from Melbourne University and a Bachelor of Applied Design from Billy Blue College of Design. She lives in Melbourne with her two cats, working as a graphic designer, illustrator, and chief studio dog briber for a creative agency. Despite her current chosen profession and hipster city of residence, sadly Anya does not like avocados, smashed or otherwise. She can be found on Twitter @anyasy.*

RARE SEEDS

by Michael Triozzi

DAY 58:

They all had their ways of staying sane. Oskar liked to name the colors.

Doc Sara had strummed a guitar until every string had broken. Anette played solitaire. And Johannes, Oskar knew, was painstakingly lettering the Norwegian national anthem, one piss-run at a time, in the pristine snow to the leeward of the towering gunmetal monolith of Vavilov's main entrance. The last supply trailer—months ago now—had run a caterpillar tread over the patriotic thoughts of "*the saga-night that lays dreams upon our earth*" at the end of the first stanza, sending Johannes into a howling rage.

But Oskar preferred naming the colors. The soul always pictures Antarctica as an endless sea of white, but Oskar found it to be a vast expanse of shimmering purples, blues, and reds cresting and coalescing into new and wondrous hues. True to his artistic mission, Oskar would stand by the main vault entrance and give names to the colors for as long as he could stand the cold and the hunger. Valsecan was the reddish shadow under the curled tips of the frozen waves. Tornbauer was the mirage-like blue that would hang around the low sun. Still, all the colors in the world couldn't change the fact that everyone at Vavilov was at their breaking point.

Oskar turned to look at the strange, looming metal trapezoid that jutted out from the wall of ice. Above the main hatch were the onyx-stenciled words: VAVILOV INTERNATIONAL RARE SEED VAULT.

Anette had once cheekily attached a placard with a quote from Dante about the lowest circle of hell being freezing cold—until Holst made her take it down, with a wag of his noble, bearded, hound-like head.

Oskar's thoughts were broken as the monolith's main entrance hissed open and Holst emerged, trudging with slow, dogged purpose toward Oskar's perch. Johannes appeared from around the other side of the monolith, zipping his steaming fly and crunching his boots in the packed snow.

"I asked V.A.V. to calculate how screwed we are," Johannes called from the side of the structure with a gallows smirk. "It's still working out the computations."

"This happens," Holst murmured stoically, "in winter."

Oskar nodded and shifted awkwardly in his anorak. For all of Holst's grim reassurances, he was fairly certain the combination of a downed communications array and fifty-eight days without a supply shipment would be unusual and troubling under any circumstances. The storms this time of year could be impassable, but the eerie silence of the iced-over radio had grown to be almost too much to bear. The next supply run might be coming tomorrow, or it might never come.

"Inside in ten," woofed Holst. "We're putting it to another vote."

Oskar coughed and Holst shuffled inside with Johannes grumbling behind him.

As Oskar turned back to the open expanse of new colors, his hunger-tautened senses caught something buzzing in the nearby snow; an unearthly midge squirming fecklessly by his feet. Without thinking, Oskar moved to crush the midge—and stopped himself just in time. If he killed one of Anette's midges, he'd probably spoil a whole batch of scientific data and get everyone mad at him again. He paused to wonder whether they could eat the midges but decided against it.

Anette had explained to him that the purpose of the midges had something to do with Noah's Ark and a scientific gambit to repopulate the land.

"It's called the *Noah's Dove* viability test," Anette had said. "We release the subjects into a semi-wild, semi-controlled environment. If they can find a way to thrive, then they re-integrate themselves into their natural habitat. If not, they're neurally wired to return to their stasis point so that we can try again. We're very close with the midges."

Oskar had watched the squirming, fluttering little midges and found he was unsurprised that they had gone the way of the dodo and the tiger.

"Why midges?" he had asked. "Why not polar bears?"

"There never were polar bears in Antarctica," Anette had informed him. "And polar bears are too complicated to neurally train. We were supposed to do the same testing with a few types of fish and even some birds. But this all ended up being such a rush-job that we only wound up with the midges."

"And they just fly away and come back?"

"So far they have."

Holst stood grimly by the folding table in the crew's quarters as four pairs of hungry eyes watched him. An early explorer of the Antarctic had once said that polar exploration was the cleanest species of adventure. The crew's quarters suggested otherwise. Holst overturned his knit cap, smelling like months of smoke and musty hair, and spilled its contents onto the rickety table before him: five crumpled scraps of notebook paper. He reached for them one by one with steady hands.

"Yes," he read from the first scrap.

"Yes," he continued, picking up the next.

"Another yes."

"A string of profanity," he said without even the ghost of a smile. He turned to Johannes, "That's a yes?"

Johannes grunted his assent. Holst reached for the final paper.

"No," he grumbled. The frigid air left the room and then returned all at once.

"Oh, what the hell, Doc?" moaned Johannes. "You'll really let us starve to save a bunch of seeds?"

"We said this was going to be anonymous," snapped Doc Sara.

"We said that two weeks ago." Johannes was snarling now. "Times have changed and we need to face reality. We have no food, no one is coming to save us, and we're sitting on a vault full of frozen calories."

The vault's computer interface chirped to life, intoning from a wall monitor: "Every seed in that vault is the last or near-last of an endangered or virtually-extinct species." The metallic voice of the V.A.V. unit always made Oskar feel deeply unnerved. "Terminating any one of those samples would terminate an entire evolutionary line."

"V.A.V., can you identify which sample it would be least damaging to terminate?" Holst asked.

"What are your criteria for the value of a species?" And if the V.A.V. had eyes, Oskar was sure they would have narrowed.

"Likelihood that more backup seeds exist, similarity to other species, evolutionary recency," Holst began listing, unfazed. "Just run the calculations, please."

"Ever since the Svalbard Seed Vault went offline, backups cannot be guaranteed." The speaker chirped.

"What are our other options? We could eat Oskar," suggested Anette. "He's non-essential staff. No offense, Oskar."

"None taken, I'm sure I'm delicious," parried Oskar with a wan smile. But the thought had nagged him as the hunger grew deeper; his placement at Vavilov was entirely superfluous. He hardly felt his belly was worth its own emptiness.

"You have a duty to those seeds, Holst," V.A.V. intoned from the wall speaker.

"I have a duty to my crew," Holst said grimly. "Run the calculations.

"With the minimum necessary caloric intake, crossed with what is likely to be the least valuable of the seed samples..." V.A.V. began humming.

"Just enough to stay alive," affirmed Holst, his hound-like face was hollow.

A readout appeared on the monitor screen. The five crew members gathered around to read the name of the doomed legume.

"I don't like it," Doc muttered.

"Then starve," barked Holst.

Johannes grabbed the crowbar from its rack by the door and motioned to Oskar. "Earn your keep, song-boy. Give me a hand in the vault."

⊗

The thumbprint scanner was on the fritz. All of the sensitive electronics not directly connected to V.A.V.'s main array tended to get this way in the deep cold. Johannes swore and leaned into the manual latch-bar with all of his weight. Oskar joined him, somewhat ineffectually, and between their combined efforts the vault door began to turn with the soft, creaking sound of awakening ice. As it slid open, the door's complaints gave way to the eerie reverberations of a haunting strain of music—the horns and strings of the Oslo Philharmonic Orchestra swelling into waves of thunderous sound.

Johannes turned wide-eyed to Oskar: "The hell is that?"

"Shostakovich's Leningrad Symphony," the artist explained.

"This is your doing?"

"I wanted to have it playing outside but the wind kept taking out the speakers. Holst said I could pipe it in here."

"It's a wonder the government waited so long to send us an artist-in-residence. How did the mission ever get by without you?" Johannes' voice dripped with hunger. "Can you turn it down?"

"V.A.V.," said Oskar into the vault's wall monitor. "Lower main vault speaker volume, please."

"Can you turn it *off?*" clarified Johannes. Oskar icily complied.

Impossibly, it seemed, the heart of the Vavilov Vault was even colder than the ice sheet outside. Their breathing billowed out in clouds of steam as they walked through the rows of sample-filled crates, like two Eves in a surreal garden of forbidden fruit. For all the pomp surrounding the Vavilov facility, the vault itself could have been any warehouse in any snow-bound town in the world. Rows upon rows of sealed crates resting on rickety shelves, leading back to the sealed door to a sub-vault that had been left unfinished in the haste of the construction.

"They're here under *black-box* agreements," said Johannes, eyeing the crates. "The same contracts that govern bank safety deposit boxes. You and I are about to become the world's chilliest bank robbers."

"Doesn't seem like much compared to interspecies genocide."

"That's the spirit," chuckled Johannes. He ran his eyes along the seemingly endless shelves of boxes and labels. Soon he found his quarry. "West Kansas Bean and...rice strain 504," Johannes read in English, the words sounding strange and foreign in his Norwegian mouth. He gripped one end of the crate and motioned for Oskar to do the same. But as Oskar reached to grab the heavy box and steady his legs, he saw Johannes's face turn sheet-white with sudden terror.

"*What was that?*" hissed Johannes. "Did you hear that?"

"What?" Oskar looked over his shoulder.

"*Hush, dammit!*"

For a moment they were still. In the gloom of the vault, too cold for dripping water and too forbidding for footsteps, Oskar's own heart-beat was the loudest sound he could hear. They both glanced furtively toward the sealed door to the never-used sub-vault.

"We don't know what's in some of these crates," whispered Johannes after a moment had passed and their pulses began to return to normal. "All the countries and companies that store seeds here give us a list of the contents, but we have no real way of knowing. Even North Korea has a box. Three boxes, actually. They could even be hiding a nuke down here—we'd never know."

"No," said Oskar, hoisting his end of the crate. "A nuke would probably be warm."

"The man who gave his name to this station—Nikolai Vavilov and his scientists," Doc Sara ranted. "They protected the Leningrad Seed-bank for two years while the Nazis besieged their city. Nine of them died of starvation rather than eat their seeds."

"Yeah, but if they had eaten those seeds then ol' Comrade Stalin would have turned them all into fertilizer," scoffed Johannes. "There's no need to be noble when there's no gun to your head. Besides, there's no gulag in the world worse than this place."

Doc Sara said nothing. The edge of her mouth curled into a silent sneer.

"It's genetically modified rice and a sub-species of West Kansas bean!" Anette said. "No one is going to mourn for a bean! Those beans never wrote a symphony! Those beans never fell in love!"

"And now they'll never have the chance," said V.A.V. from the wall unit.

"I don't like it when you tell jokes," grumbled Holst. "That was the programmers' biggest mistake."

The five of them stared at the two-dozen sample vials, looking grim and sterile— practically dead already, Oskar thought.

"I'll do it myself," offered Johannes. But his hand flinched as he reached for the stovetop.

"No," barked Holst. "Matches." And reaching into a supply drawer he withdrew five matchsticks and deftly snapped the head off one of them.

The five drew their picks. Doc scowled, but she took hers too. Oskar looked down at his and sighed.

"*Tun ta tun...*" sounded the bugle through Vavilov's icy speakers, mixing with the soft sound of boiling rice.

"Cut that out, V.A.V.," said Oskar, trying to focus on his Spartan cooking. He had managed to find an old box of salt, but otherwise the West Kansas bean and modified rice were coming to an unappetizing extinction.

"*Tun ta tunn...*" V.A.V. continued, unabated. The unmistakable sound of Taps echoed grimly down Vavilov's frozen halls.

"I said cut it," said Oskar, angrily, bringing a fist down on the stovetop and nearly burning himself.

"You'd want it played too on the final day of your species," V.A.V. cooed, tauntingly.

"Who'd be around to play it?"

"Who indeed," intoned V.A.V. with what Oskar imagined was the closest a computer could come to a hint of irony.

Half an hour later, the last of two species were grimly swallowed.

Day 67:

"The seed vault at Svalbard had an art installation called *Perpetual Repercussion* before it was all destroyed," Oskar was explaining as he and Anette trudged through the rows of crates for their next day's prey. "It was sort of an artistic rendering of the northern lights and the arctic colors—really very pretty. But Vavilov was built so quickly that they forgot to put any art in it."

"Why would they want an art installation in a freezing seed vault at the end of the world?" Anette asked idly, searching for the right label.

"It's an odd fluke of Norwegian law: any government-funded project of a certain size is required to include a work of public art—"

"Ah."

"Eventually some government official realized they had forgotten the artwork at Vavilov in all of the rush and crisis. Tons of stuff was left unfinished: the sub-vault, most of the Noah's Dove experiments."

"And they figured the best way to remedy that was to send you?"

"To send an artist-in-residence, yes. I was supposed to figure out the details on my own. At first I thought about playing music for the ice, but it was too cold to work." Oskar tried to ignore the pitying look Anette gave him. "I used to be a cellist with the Oslo Philharmonic," he continued, a bit wistfully, "but now I just feel rather useless."

"You're not useless," said Anette. "Nobody cooks up an extinction quite like you."

"It's an art," smirked Oskar. He shifted his weight clumsily as he prepared to lift that day's crate, too clumsily, and he jostled into another crate behind him.

The crash echoed in the frozen corridor.

"Ah, Christ!"

Oskar and Anette pounced on the remains of the fallen crate, hoping desperately to salvage any scattered seeds. Oskar ran his hand along the frozen floor grasping in frigid pain—but as he turned his hand and looked at his fingertips, he saw only chips of ice, not a seed among them.

Wordlessly, Anette held up the plastic seed cartridge that the crate had contained. It was transparent, cold, and empty.

Oskar's mouth gaped wider than the pit of hunger in his belly. "Why would...?" he checked the label on the broken box lid, "Why would Nepal want to store an empty box of lentils?"

They stared at the empty seed cartridge in silence.

"We need to take a full inventory," Anette demanded. "What if more of these boxes are empty and we run out before winter's over? What if there's something in one of those boxes that's just as hungry as we are?"

"You're losing it, Anette," scoffed Johannes.

"You heard something down there too," said Oskar softly. "I remember you did."

Johannes shot him a dirty look.

The menu for the day was a tough Central American maize over what had once been a fairly common strain of basmati rice.

Day 79:

The creature that lurked within the vault slithered wordlessly in the darkness toward the strangers. A shade among shadows, it peered around the corner at the two bearded figures scanning the shelves.

From the corner of his eye, Holst saw it.

"Hullo?" said Holst, who couldn't help himself from giving a short, polite bow to the odd figure in front of him that looked almost like a short, fat man dressed in a tailcoat.

"What in God's name?" began Oskar, his mouth hanging open.

"A penguin?" said Doc Sara incredulously inspecting the bird, once Holst had carried it back to the crew's quarters. "Maybe they aren't all gone after all?"

The penguin waddled and squawked merrily.

"No," said Anette. "If we *were* to find the *last* penguin just wandering out of the cold, he'd be emaciated, and half poisoned from living in that ocean. This one's got some meat on him."

"We ought to name him," suggested Oskar. "How about Nikolai?"

"No, don't name it!" scowled Johannes, "Then we'll never be able to…"

"Be able to *what*?" Doc Sara demanded.

Johannes gestured grimly to his stomach.

"We're not going to eat the world's last penguin," the doctor pronounced, severely.

"Why not? We ate the world's last Lima bean and seven different strains of the world's last rice. Why not just roast this one too?"

"We don't know where he came from!" Doc could barely contain her rage. "An extinct bird just wandered into our facility! What are the implications of this?! And all you want to do is *eat* it?"

Holst cleared his throat as if he wanted to silence the room. But no one seemed to listen.

"Anette," said Oskar, cautiously, almost chewing on his words. "Didn't you once tell me that the Vavilov mission was originally supposed to run Noah's Dove tests for birds and fish?" He looked at the penguin as it dawdled around the quarters. "Is that what this is? Are there tubes of frozen penguins in the sub-vault? What else is down there?"

"You can't viability test something as complex as a *penguin*," agreed Anette. "And you definitely couldn't automate it. Midges are one thing, but a penguin's neural network is too complex. You couldn't program it to return to stasis after each run—that technology is years off."

Oskar stared at the penguin. But the crew had moved on to more practical matters:

"In any case, you can keep him as a pet if you want," Johannes was shouting. "But what are you gonna feed him? In a few days, he'll be hungry, and you'll be hungrier. I know how this ends."

"Do we think he's the bandit that's been eating the seeds out of the Nepal box?" mused Doc Sara.

"Do penguins eat seeds?" asked Anette.

The question hung ominously in the cold, still air.

"They do not," Anette answered herself.

Day 82:

Oskar stood in his usual spot outside the vault's entrance, coloring the landscape in his mind.

"*Perpetual Repercussion*," he said out loud to himself. What a lovely name for an art installation. The vault door hissed open and Anette emerged.

"We're about to have another vote," she said grimly.

"On the penguin?"

"Yeah."

Oskar was still for a moment.

"Hey Anette," he began. "If you wanted to design a Noah's Dove test with human subjects, could you do it?"

"How do you mean?"

"Freeze and unfreeze a bunch of humans and see what they do? See how they adapt or deal with strange situations? See if they're ready to be…reintroduced or whatever?"

"Couldn't be done," said Anette, matter-of-factly. "That technology is years off."

"Like with the penguins?"

"Yeah." Her face was wan and sunken with hunger.

"I'm not a scientist. I don't know what you'd even be testing for," Oskar rambled. "Or why you'd even want an artist."

"Besides," said Anette, idly. "If you kept testing human subjects over and over again, what would they eat?"

Oskar shrugged.

And the two of them trudged together through the Antarctic darkness, toward the hollow monolith of the Vavilov International Rare Seed Vault.

Michael Triozzi has spent the past several years serving with the US Peace Corps in Morocco and the Republic of Georgia as an English instructor and civil society specialist. Prior to that, he worked as the program director for an NGO in Kathmandu, Nepal and as an EMT in his hometown of Cleveland, Ohio. He writes darkly comic short stories set in strange landscapes and inspired by the characters, tales, and musings he has experienced in his work and travels. He currently works for the US Peace Corps' headquarters in Washington, DC. He has always dreamed of visiting Antarctica.

AVIATRIX UNBOUND

by Carina Bissett

After her third attempted escape, Ava's father clipped her wings and left her to her own devices on a remote South Pacific island, long since abandoned by the military. The entire island had been built as a testing ground, and, for some obscure reason they'd left everything behind—outdated equipment, technological odds and ends, and a tall tower that looked out over the rocky shores. All of this suited Ava just fine. Out of the twisted metal and wires, she raised an Archaeopteryx. And with the assistance of a smuggled memory chip and a whispered command, she brought the winged mech to life.

"There you go." Ava sat back on her heels.

The patchwork avian took a step, shiny wings outstretched for balance. It cocked its head and chirped inquisitively.

"You'll figure it out." She pointed to the open window. "Start there."

Its skeletal tail and sharp killing claws rattled against the floor as it leapt to the sill.

For the first time since she'd been recaptured, Ava laughed. Not a laugh of joy, but one of triumph.

While the construct learned the mechanics of flight, Ava turned her attention to the second stage of her plan. Working from a memorized set of schematics, she tweaked probabilities and set the date and location of the first retrieval. From past experiments she knew that a temporal distortion would open a window into the past, but it was a small window and the kicker was that it could only be accessed mid-air. Hence, the Archaeopteryx—a perfect combination of stealth and size.

The access tower and tropical climate were a welcome bonus. If her

father had been paying closer attention to her flight patterns, he might have chosen a less hospitable place for her to sit out her sentence of solitude. Instead, she was right where she wanted to be. Birds had once thrived in these islands, and Ava was determined they would thrive once more.

Ava started small: coordinates locked on 1901 O'ahu. Her Archaeopteryx, fondly nicknamed Clepto, jumped from the window and soared straight into the vortex. The shiny, black machine vanished mid-air, and Ava let out a loud whoop. A few minutes later, it reappeared with a nest clutched in its talons. Just like that, the *O'ahu 'akialoa* was no longer extinct.

"Nicely done!" Ava welcomed Clepto back to the tower.

For the next trip, she sent Clepto farther abroad to the early 1800s in the cypress swamps of the Everglades: the mission to secure a sampling of the vibrantly colorful Carolina parakeets, forced into extinction in the 1920s. Ava figured poisonous parakeets definitely deserved a second chance.

Several weeks and thousands of rescues later, Ava's father rang her on the old wireless com. Eventually, she picked up.

"What?" She answered, teeth clamped on a wire extension she was untangling.

"I'd've thought you'd be over your snit by now," he replied, as unruffled and commanding as ever.

Ava snorted and rolled her eyes.

"You know you can have your precious airplane back once you concede to your contractual obligations."

Ava spit out the wire. "I never agreed to your stupid contract in the first place."

Clepto squawked.

"Here now. What's that noise?" Her father cleared his throat. "What are you doing out there?"

Ava could almost imagine him peering into the receiver.

"Chickens."

"Chickens? Well, I never."

Ava thought her father didn't understand the concept of the word 'never,' but that was beside the point.

"Dad." She tried out the word and then tossed it aside. "Sir, I refuse to comply with your terms, and the laws at least protect me from that. You can't just barter me off to the highest bidder."

"You have a duty to fulfill in the name of our family," he said. "The sooner you come to grips with that, the better off you'll be."

"I don't want a husband, sir, any more than I want children." *At least not any of the human kind*, she thought as she looked over her feathered brood.

Colorful hatchings flitted in and out of the open tower windows. Quail, ducks, grebes, ibises, bitterns, night-herons, cormorants, caracaras, kestrels, rails, crakes, sandpipers, pigeons, doves, parrots, parakeets, owls, wrens, flycatchers, warblers, starlings, finches, and more. Clepto sat in the center of it all, waiting for the newest attachment to her ever-evolving form.

"Enough is enough, young lady. We'll discuss this further tomorrow."

"Tomorrow?"

"I'll see you then."

Abruptly, white noise crackled through the speaker. The birds began to bicker in a distorted frenzy of competing calls.

"Stop!" Ava clicked the dial, cutting the connection. "Just stop already."

The birds landed on every available space. As one, they looked at her expectantly, bright eyes shining with the determination to survive.

She'd known her father would eventually come for her and had prepared accordingly. Ava picked up the wire and waded through the avian sea to the modified workbench where Clepto crouched. Her mech dinosaur still resembled its original Archaeopteryx form but, through Ava's continuing modifications, Clepto had evolved into a creature with a wingspan reminiscent of the enormous Quetzalcoatlus without the doomed pterosaur's quirky flaws. Luckily, the top room of the tower had been fitted with floor-to-ceiling windows, the glass long-since broken and scattered. Clepto could still squeeze through, if just barely.

Ava soldered the last wire in place and stepped back to admire her handiwork. A Carolina parakeet glided down from the rafters to land on her shoulder. Ava reached up to stroke the iridescent yellow and green feathers as the orange-capped bird chattered in her ear.

"Yes," she agreed. "It is a remarkable sight, isn't it?"

The other birds in the room warbled, trilled, and shrieked in an ear-splitting celebration before they took flight, streaming out the broken windows to notify the other avian refugees of their impending departure.

The next morning, Ava waited until she heard the sound of a plane approaching before activating the enlarged dilation of the temporal distortion one last time. Clepto plunged out of the tower with Ava astride her back. The monstrous beauty spread her wings and they circled once, gathering the other birds in their wake. For a moment, Ava wondered what her father thought when he saw the patchwork wings decorated with feathers from each and every species they'd saved. Clepto had become something *other*—a simurgh-like symbol of ages past.

Clepto swept down and reached out to grasp the handles of a massive crate crammed with ground-bound birds saved on countless rescue missions. She winged through the air to the vortex cutting through space and time. The others followed in formation, even the smallest among them laden down with precious cargo.

Ava saluted her father, and then stretched out along Clepto's neck, urging her beloved daughter forward to a place where they could all thrive together, a place without contractual obligations or clipped wings. Paradise, forever unbound.

Carina Bissett is a writer, poet, and educator working primarily in the fields of dark fiction and interstitial art. Her short fiction and poetry have been published in multiple journals and anthologies including Weird Dream Society, Arterial Bloom, Gorgon: Stories of Emergence, Hath No Fury, Mythic Delirium, NonBinary Review, and the HWA Poetry Showcase Vol. V and VI. She teaches online workshops at The Storied Imaginarium, and she is a graduate of the Creative Writing MFA program at Stonecoast. She is a member of Codex, SFWA, SFPA, and HWA. Her work has been nominated for several awards including the Pushcart Prize and the Sundress Publications Best of the Net.

LANDSCAPE ON THE OUTSKIRTS

by Sam Hicks

Ree watched the flow of the river tide. She watched its slender waves breaking upon the grit and flocking back in blue and brown through the shattered columns of the pier. On the far shore, the water filled the roofless mouths of the warehouses, down below the peaks of the burial hills.

Turning now, she followed the way through the marshes, along the creek. Where the creek found the river, the mud spread in great glazed and glossy plates. Long grasses lined the banks there, often stirred by a wind that whirled deep deltas. All over this low land were openings, brown water shaking within, never still, reflecting the red of dying leaves, seed heads like curls of blood, white yarrow, the pink of the frilled pea-flower.

Ree paused near the end of the lane, before the building. Were they coming this way? Two people labored along, weighted down by heavy backpacks. They stopped to look at the trees growing from the window spaces of the hotel, pointing, clicking cameras, talking. She waited for them, their appearances becoming clearer as they approached; the man's glasses and thin shoulder-length hair, his gangly limbs clad in waterproof clothes; the woman's round, smiling face and eager movements, her two long braids, her walking boots, her shining eyes. They both waved as they came near.

"Hello," the woman called. "Is that sign still right?"

Ree looked up. The sign, hand-painted, hung from a post beside the wooden gate. In pink letters, embellished with leaves and flowers, it read *Vacancies*.

They had reached her now, both a little out of breath.

"Do you want to stay with me?" Ree said.

The man and woman exchanged a glance.

"Is that OK?" the man asked. "For a few days?"

Ree looked at the camera slung around his neck, and, noticing this, he held it up, as if he felt he should explain himself.

"We're photographers. We love places like this. The derelict buildings with nature taking over, and the marshes. The light here's so clear, isn't it? I'm Adam, by the way, and this is Trudy."

"Pleased to meet you," Trudy said, with a little smile. They were wary, of course, Ree thought—worried she may not like the look of them and turn them away.

"I'm Ree. And, of course you can stay. I have a nice big room with a bathroom, and all meals included."

"Oh, we'll just want breakfast," Trudy said, with Adam nodding agreement. "We'll go into town for the rest I should think. We like Indian food. I expect there'll be a restaurant there."

"Into town?"

"Yes, down there, into town?"

"Of course. Whatever you want. Come in."

They must have heard her footsteps descending the stairs after she'd shown them to their room; they relaxed and started talking, not hearing her return, unaware she was outside the thin panels of the door. "It's nice isn't it?" Trudy said, and Ree pictured her looking around at the clean white walls, the polished oak floor, the simple country furniture, and the soft cream linen on the double bed. Perhaps she was opening the wardrobe, seeing the long mirror inside, or placing her socks and underwear in neat little bundles inside the drawers.

"Yeah, it's great. Not what I'd expect out here. It's cheap as well," Adam replied. Small, hard clipping sounds accompanied him, as though he were pulling something apart.

"How much was it again?"

"Oh…I don't remember. Cheap though, didn't you think?"

A soft slam: the wardrobe drawers. A change of acoustic as the bathroom door was opened. Trudy spoke again, to the sound of a running tap.

"She's strange though, don't you think? Don't you think her eyes are strange?"

"They're so pale, aren't they?" replied Adam. "And do you think she ever goes into the town? She seemed surprised when we said we're going there to eat. She seemed surprised at everything."

"She must go, for shopping. But I suppose we could eat here tonight, couldn't we? It'll save running around everywhere."

"I was thinking the same thing. Maybe tonight and tomorrow," Adam said.

"She probably thinks *we're* strange."

"Yes."

From her vantage point on the raised bank, Ree could see for miles. Below the high, severed line of the bridge the sun had turned the water white, so that a light-colored bird would have seemed black against it. The land stretched out in rough ridges. Around barbed wire and perished stone, grasses moved in silken ripples. The two photographers were exploring a ruin. Nearby, a steel fence had long ago arced backwards; its spikes brushed the ground as though they were the branches of a weeping tree.

She watched them for hours. They circled around, stopping at the old power plant, disappearing into its burnt shell, emerging excited, climbing the rusted hulk of the river barge, and afterwards pausing thoughtfully at the site of the old school. Then it was back to the spent bricks of the lonely house, whose neighbors were only seen as scorch marks when the rain stayed away and the sun burned the water from the soil.

Each time they performed this circuit, they seemed to discover it again. Trudy walked along the lowest section of the house's one remaining wall, where a kitchen had once been. She clambered up to roof of the intact entrance porch which had protected the door from the worst of the winter winds. She pointed her camera downwards, at the things which emerged from the grassy floors—cement, lichen-choked exhaust vents, metal fragments, the black imprints of old machines.

Adam sank onto his heels and examined the ground, pulling at scraps. A breeze whispered over him like soft rain as he photographed the stripped skeleton of a field mustard plant, and spears of wet timber, and cloudy sow thistle leaves, and the white membranes revealed where the soil was thin.

Ree turned for the house, knowing they would soon be heading back, following the routine of the last few days. Far ahead, the cables hung loose on their black pylons, cables which sung mournful, empty chords when the wind rang through them. On one twisted strut, at the tip of the nearest pylon's web, a tall figure stood against the bright sky, watching her, and watching them.

⊗

The photographers returned as she was preparing their evening meal.

"That smells good," Trudy said.

"You're such a good cook. I've only had curry that smelled that good in India," Adam said.

They laid their cameras on the kitchen table and hung their bags on the backs of the chairs.

"When were you in India?" Ree asked, as she stirred. She kept her back to them, listening, not wanting to see Adam's face.

"I went there once," he said.

Ree replaced the saucepan lid and gently set the spoon at the side of the range. She didn't want to turn around just yet. There was something delicate, and painful, in the air. She stood with one hand on the scrubbed work surface and counted.

"I could bring your food up to your room if you like," she said. "Just leave your plates outside when you've finished." She faced them now, seeing their eyes grow heavy as they fought a deep confusion, not yet recognizing it.

"That'd be nice," Trudy said. Beside her, Adam was studying his camera viewing screen, his mouth open, his breathing shallow.

"Do you want to see my photographs from today?" he said. His eyes were expressionless now, but she saw helplessness in the shadows beneath them, and in the lines that spread up to his temples like fraying threads.

Ree moved across and stood at his side as he scrolled through the images. She placed a hand on his shoulder and said, "They're beautiful," as he reached the last one, as completely black as all the rest.

Later, she listened at their door as they ate their meal.

"I *was* in India," Adam said.

"Yes."

There was a pause, the clink of china and fork.

"Did you see her hands?" Trudy said.

"They're like claws. I never noticed before."

"She liked the photographs, Adam."

"Yes. Shall we go to town for dinner tomorrow?"

"It would make a change."

"But she's such a good cook."

"Yes."

Fog rolled in from further downriver, where the estuary widened to the sea. At first it came in tissue-thin strands, streaming, lying low but then it fell like deepest space, glimmering with starlight. Ree tracked Adam and Trudy's shadows, sometimes seen against a sudden glare, sometimes fading out; their heads disappeared, they seemed to have no arms, and then they were entire again, but floating, turned to giants.

Their movements were fretful as they circled the withered plastic and crumpled metal which marked the place of the old school. Adam's shadow sank again and again around the same stump of melted steel, which could have been a supporting strut, or part of a roof, or a floor. His arms rose, spectral, as he worked his camera. Trudy paced, a short distance away, in her hands a small lump of concrete. She stopped now and then, bringing the lump to her face, sniffing at it like a fruit. She would throw it a few feet and then think better of it and search through the soaking grass on hands and knees until she possessed it again. What was this place to them, Ree thought? Did they have memories of it? What brought them here? What regrets?

The land thickened, and the sun returned, colorless. She was too close. She passed silently across the small ridge-backed islands of mud, and up toward the high bank by the river shore. Looking back, she saw them still, and further away, moving with the melting fog, the black forms of three tall figures. Something soft brushed her arm and fluttered up, with no real direction. It was a butterfly, as black as the branches that rose from the bare shore, as large as a sparrow, thick bodied, its wings audibly snapping with each slow beat.

Ree laughed and grabbed for it, but it spun up and over the water, where the river now shone silver and the creek was a sparkling seam, the mud platinum and quartz.

"Ree," a voice called, softly, secretively, and she turned away from the marsh, toward the old landing pier.

It was the first time they had returned to the house before her. They sat side by side at the little kitchen table, turning as one when she came in.

"I'm sorry," she said. "You must be ready for your dinner. Perhaps a cup of tea?"

"Did you go to the town?" Adam said. He hadn't removed his waterproof coat. The hood was still drawn up, and he shivered as he spoke. Behind the lenses of his glasses, a glimpse of cautious hurt.

"Did you go shopping in the town?" Trudy said. "We're going to go there tomorrow for dinner." She wasn't wearing her hair in the braids anymore, and it hung in matted strands around her face.

"Are you?" said Ree, as she moved to the sink and ran water into the copper kettle. "Into the town?"

"Yes," said Adam, with real certainty. "That's what we'll do tomorrow."

"For a change," Trudy said.

They ate dinner in their room that night. A pang shot through Ree as she listened to their conversation; what would become of them? Were the flower-sprigged curtains stirring at the window, she wondered? The wind would find a way through; it was gathering strength, carrying sorrowful cries from the hollow husks of the distant cooling towers, and the closer voids of the power plant chimneys, and the ever-lamenting pylon cables.

"It was foggy today," said Adam.

"The photographs were good," Trudy replied

"Did you see her ears?"

"She doesn't have any."

"We'll go into the town tomorrow."

"For dinner, for a change."

"Though she's such a good cook."

"We'll go there for a change."

Ree crossed her arms, hugging herself. Would they at least sleep all right, and even dream?

The light was waning when they finally set off toward the town. Ree had watched them all afternoon. Their first attempts, abandoned when they rushed back to their room to find things they'd forgotten, to leave things they didn't need. Then the distractions as they pulled old bones from the hedges, and dented metal containers which seemed to hold them spellbound. They circled these remains, rearranging them, clicking their useless cameras, speaking sometimes. And then they remembered their mission, and searched around for sticks big enough to beat back the worst of the thorns that now overhung the cracked and tussocked ground that once bore the name Moat Lane. On either side of them, the hedges grew vast, thick with ripening berries, copper-tinged or black, and dead flowers like strands of dust.

Ree saw them disappear into the undergrowth, so sure of their way—hadn't they come that way?—and wondered what it was they had told themselves, and each other, about those naked lines, those black intrusions on the sky, the hanging hands and heads of the dead artifacts, the opposition of these looming structures to the downy, curling leaves that closed around them. This was the town, the town they walked toward. This was the town they were already in.

Dead yellow branches rising from ivy. Water trickling, uncontained. Brick emerging, little broken concrete animals, part of a sign, the letter S, part of a car, a wheel, white-bloomed plastic. Ree knew the objects they would see on the way. The old hotel, filled with little trees who would stay for many seasons, the outline of the old ticket hall, the buckled bands of the rails. Look up, she thought; look up and see. That's where you'll see life. There he is, standing at the very pinnacle of the pylon's web, looking down at you. It's not where you are. There is no life there.

She returned to the kitchen and waited.

She had lighted a candle for their return. The two of them sat at the table, shivering, clutching each other's hands. In the flicker of the flame, Ree's skin shone, faintly green like the palest jade.

Their clothes were almost gone, torn by vegetation and the sharper types of human trash.

The walls of the kitchen and the upper floor had slipped away into the night some time before. Ree waited for them to speak.

"The town's gone, hasn't it?" Trudy said.

"Why didn't we know? Everything's gone," said Adam.

"Who are you?" Trudy said, but Ree could see that she knew. Knew that Ree was one of those who had always been there. Glimpsed as ghosts, as spirits, as otherworld folk or aliens; forms imagined to clothe what was too strange.

"Sometimes we see your echoes," Ree said, "and we look after you, because you make us sad. But you always have to leave. You have to go. You see, none of you ever belonged here. Not ever. Now this world has to recover from your fatal touch."

Ree lay on the smallest island of the marsh, staring up at the yellow pulses in the sky. The light today was poisoned by the burning clouds that had erupted from the east, where the fires had rekindled by themselves and would soon spread out until they reached the northern shore. She held out her hands, and the black butterflies danced around her pale green, bird-like fingers. The perspective was altered that day, and the figures moving toward her seemed as tall as the collapsing bridge. She stood and waved, and they waved back, yellow reflected in their pale eyes. Her kinfolk.

"Why didn't you come yesterday?" she said. "Always watching up there! You could have said goodbye to my sad ghosts."

Sam Hicks lives in Deptford, in south east London. Her fiction has appeared in, or is forthcoming in, various anthologies including The Fiends in the Furrows, Nightscript, Dark Lane, The Half That You See, *and* Best Horror of the Year *Volumes 11 and 12.*

ACKNOWLEDGEMENTS

Triangulation: Extinction would not have been possible had we not received so many great submissions. Anthologies are not easy to make, but with so many good stories to choose from, it becomes easier.

Specials thanks goes out to Barb Carlson for taking care of the Parsec Ink website. Garnering so many submissions would not have been possible without her diligent updates to the webpage.

Thanks to Karen Yun-Lutz for helping with the more technical aspects of production. Her dedication to spreading *Triangulation* far and wide cannot be ignored.

Thanks to Nick Coffman for employing his graphic design skills to craft such wonderful promotional material for the anthology.

Thanks to Brian Ankrapp for his artwork on the parsecink.com home page.

https://www.extinctionsymbol.info/

STAFF BIOS

Isaac E. Payne is a marketing specialist by day and a speculative fiction writer by night. He aims to bring awareness to many environmental and social issues through his fiction. Literature is the greatest reflection and codex of the human experience. His fiction has appeared in or is forthcoming from *Abyss and Apex*, *DreamForge Magazine*, and *Frozen Wavelets*. Find him on Twitter @the_paynanator.

Diane Turnshek is a scientist concerned with the loss of biodiversity. As a popular presenter and university lecturer, she creates awareness for living sustainably. She leaves a small footprint on the Earth by wearing natural fibers, following a vegan lifestyle and living in a tiny cabin in the woods. She founded the *Triangulation* anthology series, editing the first one in 2003. With Chloe Nightingale, she edited *Triangulation*: Dark Skies (2019). Twitter: @dianeturnshek

John Thompson is a computer programmer who wrote his inaugural story in grade school. For the next few decades, he satisfied his compulsion to write by maintaining two personal blogs and entertaining friends and family with travel journals. After moving to Pittsburgh, he published *The Ride of the Edmund Fitzgerald*, an account of living in a diesel pusher for two years, exploring the United States with his wife and polydactyl cat. Since 2005 he has been active in several writing groups in St. Louis and Pittsburgh. He is rewriting his first novel, a post-apocalyptic environmental catastrophe set on the Appalachian Trail.

Chloe Nightingale is slowly renovating her Victorian tenement flat in Scotland. She drinks green tea, does Pilates, and has a lot of kids. A former punk trying her hand at lifestyle blogging, you can find her on Twitter @TheTartanVicar.

Katerina Kireeva's illustrations are guided by brief but visceral visions from the stories, as if telepathically conveyed by the authors themselves. Starting from a rough sketch on a digital canvas, she etches her vision into reality until it has the clarity of a lucid dream. In addition to illustrating, Katerina studies physics and computer science at Carnegie Mellon University, fueled by hopes of making the utopias of science fiction our future reality. You can find her on Instagram @nebular_ink_stain.

TRIANGULATION ANTHOLOGIES

If you liked this book, you'll be pleased to hear there are more! The *Triangulation* series of anthologies began with *Triangulation* 2003: a Confluence of Speculative Fiction edited by Diane Turnshek. So far, nine different editors from Western Pennsylvania (and one from Scotland) have taken turns producing quality, uniquely-themed books. The editors choose the annual theme. Submissions for this semi-pro market open every December after the new anthology's theme is announced.

Previous issues are available through the website www.parsecink.com. *Triangulation* is produced by Parsec Ink, a branch of Parsec, Inc, Pittsburgh's premier SF/F/H literary organization.

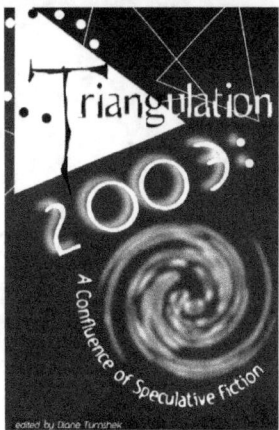